PALM TREES AND POISON

THE CLARISSA BELL MYSTERIES

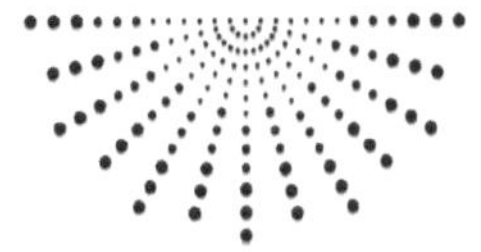

TRACY HIGLEY

STONEWATER BOOKS LLC

CHAPTER ONE

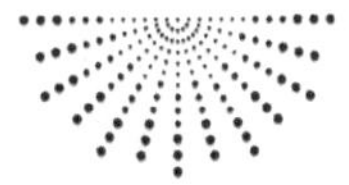

December in Egypt. Where holiday cheer meets heatstroke.

I swiped at my forehead and leaned forward from my place in the back of the motorcar, to catch a glimpse of the approaching Luxor estate. Hopefully I didn't look too damp, arriving mid-morning with the sun already doing its best to cook everything in its path.

Lady Blackwood's estate rose from the desert like an apparition of British colonialism-meets-Egyptian-revivalism—all soaring pillars and dramatic arches grafted improbably onto what had once been a more modest colonial mansion.

"Good heavens," I murmured to Annie, taking in the sphinx statues flanking the entrance with expressions that seemed less enigmatic and more dyspeptic. "I believe someone's been reading too many penny dreadfuls about the exotic East."

The estate had come into Lady Blackwood's possession through her late husband, Lord Charles Blackwood, a minor aristocrat who'd managed to purchase several acres of prime Luxor real estate through a combination of charm, questionable paperwork, and the British Empire's general attitude that anything worth having was worth claiming.

The front gardens featured an attempt at recreating an

ancient Egyptian pleasure garden, complete with reflecting pools that were currently reflecting a dispiriting amount of algae. I noted with professional interest that the landscape designer had managed to include several historically accurate plant species—though I doubted the ancient Egyptians had arranged them quite so enthusiastically around a croquet court.

Annie stepped down from our hired car, eyes wide as she took in every detail, no doubt for future correspondence with her sister back in New York. This would fill at least three letters, possibly four if she included a full description of the rather alarming hieroglyphic frieze someone had added to the portico—which, unless I was mistaken, currently proclaimed the virtues of "sacred cat bathroom."

She fluttered a hand in front of her face. "I declare, this heat is absolutely wilting."

I bit back a smile at the proper "lady's companion" act, and the gleam in her eye. Nearly a year as my hired assistant had done little to tame Annie's appetite for adventure—thank heavens.

A large wooden door swung open to invite us, with a young man—not Egyptian, clearly imported—bowing and smiling us into the front room and then the Salon, where lotus columns stretched up to a ceiling painted midnight blue and enthusiastically peppered with gold stars bearing only a passing resemblance to actual constellations.

And someone had made a valiant effort to merge Christmas traditions with the Egyptian aesthetic. Branches of Mediterranean Cyprus and olive leaves wrapped around the lotus columns, and a massive cut palm tree dominated one corner, hung with an eclectic mix of glass ornaments and tiny gilt sculptures of Egyptian gods. Amusingly, the usual cinnamon holiday scent was mingled with the distinct aroma of Egyptian frankincense.

"Dr. Bell! Oh, how absolutely perfect you're here!"

Lady Blackwood burst into the room like a whirlwind in purple silk, her elaborate coiffure listing slightly to port.

Behind her loomed a man who had clearly ironed not just his suit, but possibly himself as well.

Lady Blackwood clutched my arms. "I am so glad you agreed to join us for the Winter Solstice Event!"

I'd known the woman all of a week, but she had clearly painted me with the pathetic loneliness of a single female scholar, alone in Egypt for the Christmas holiday.

She beamed at Annie. "And Miss Evanwood too! You dear girls must be exhausted."

"This is so kind of you, Lady Blackwood."

"Winters, do see to their luggage," Lady Blackwood directed the impressively starched man. "Miss Evanwood, perhaps you'd like to oversee the unpacking?"

After six months of my mother's suffocating New York society events, Lady Blackwood's scattered warmth felt like a breath of fresh air.

As Annie followed Winters with a perfect curtsy that certainly concealed an eyeroll, a familiar figure appeared in the doorway opposite.

Nigel Montague.

I couldn't help myself—my habitual mental filing system kicked into gear.

Specimen: Nigel Montague (Academic, Spring 1923 vs Present), Notable Changes: Physical Aging Indicators.

More gray peppered his temples now, deeper lines etched around his eyes.

Yet that familiar kindly professor demeanor remained unchanged from our last encounter at the Graeco-Roman Museum in Alexandria.

"Dr. Bell!" His face creased into a genuine smile. "I'd heard rumors you might grace us with your presence."

"Professor Montague." The tension I hadn't realized I was carrying eased slightly. Despite his apparent comfort with the devious Rosamund Fairchild last spring, he had been helpful when Quinn and I met him at the museum, searching for connections to the British conspiracy we now knew as "Operation Indigo."

"I trust you're still pursuing your research on pigment authentication?" he asked, eyes twinkling. "Lady Blackwood's collection might interest you."

"Oh yes!" Lady Blackwood clutched my arm again. "You simply must see the Astral Sphere. The pigments alone... though of course we must wait for Professor Thorne's demonstration. He'll tell you all about his most revolutionary theory about its astronomical alignments."

Montague's smile tightened almost imperceptibly. "Yes, Thorne's... *theories* are certainly revolutionary."

The word choice made Lady Blackwood's enthusiasm falter slightly. "Now Nigel, you know how passionate my Charles was about—" She caught herself, color rising to her throat. "Well. We must keep open minds about new interpretations of the evidence."

To be frank, I wasn't too excited about Jasper Thorne's "theories" either. But when my digsite director had introduced me to Lady Blackwood in Giza last week, her mention of the blue-pigmented Astral Sphere snagged my interest, and her subsequent invitation to attend her Winter Solstice Event and stay through Christmas seemed a good chance to investigate.

Besides, I'd been back in Egypt more than a week, and had yet to lay eyes on Benedict Quinn. So, any hopes for Christmas... camaraderie... could be left at the door.

In fact, eight months of corresponding with Quinn about Operation Indigo had yielded frustratingly little progress. His letters maintained a studiedly professional tone, though occasional flourishes of wit made me smile despite myself. His last note had claimed he was "perfectly useless" without my "superior powers of observation," but I'd dismissed it as mere flirtation.

Still, the possibility of a new lead had been impossible to resist. I'd left word for Quinn at Shepheard's Hotel yesterday before departing Giza, though I told myself it was purely professional courtesy.

Annie had insisted on accompanying me, of course. "Someone has to make sure you don't spend the holidays buried in dusty tombs," she'd said, expertly packing my evening clothes. A knowing twinkle in her eye suggested she had other motives, but I'd pretended not to notice.

Lady Blackwood was still chattering enthusiastically about the solstice celebration, but I was already cataloging possibilities. If Thorne had somehow acquired early evidence of Egyptian astronomical knowledge... evidence that certain parties might prefer to remain hidden...

"My dear Dr. Bell," Lady Blackwood's voice cut through my analysis, "you look quite done in from your journey. Shall we show you to your rooms? You'll want to rest before dinner —we have quite the gathering planned!"

A voice answered from behind me. "Then I'm not too late?"

The voice mingled with a scent that made my heart stutter —sandalwood and leather and something uniquely him. I didn't need to turn around to know who had just entered the Salon.

Benedict Quinn's voice rolled through the room like warm honey. "I believe the lady is cataloging all the ways she might scientifically justify avoiding my gaze. Though I must say, Dr. Bell, your method of classification seems to have overlooked the most obvious specimen of all—the way you still catch your breath when I enter a room."

I kept my spine straight as I turned, summoning every lesson in composure my mother had ever drilled into me.

Benedict Quinn lounged in the doorway, devastating as ever in a perfectly tailored suit that somehow managed to suggest the savage beneath the sophisticate.

Well, perhaps savage was too strong, but maybe... powerhouse in pinstripes?

The easy set of his shoulders still carried the quiet authority of a man who'd seen danger and didn't flinch from it.

And eight months of carefully neutral correspondence hadn't dulled the impact of those eyes one bit.

"Mr. Quinn." My voice remained steady. "I wasn't aware you'd be joining us."

His smile was pure sin. "Didn't get my reply to your message at Shepheard's? How disappointing. Though perhaps not as disappointing as your determination to pretend our last meeting ended with a handshake."

Color rose to my face before I could marshal it—the taste of whiskey on his lips, the strength in his hands as they tangled in my hair, the way the sunlight had turned the sands of my Giza digsite to gold...

"I remember our last meeting ended with you promising to maintain professional boundaries," I managed.

"Did I?" He pushed off from the doorframe with casual grace. "How uncharacteristically rigid of me. Though I seem to recall you were rather more flexible about boundaries that morning."

Lady Blackwood was watching this exchange with undisguised delight, while Montague suddenly seemed fascinated by the hieroglyphs on the far wall.

"Lady Blackwood," I trained my voice into a determined brightness, "you didn't mention you knew Benedict Quinn."

Her eyes sparkled. "Ah, my dear, but neither did you. And when he telegrammed yesterday with the most charming request to join our party, how could I resist?"

Quinn crossed the salon and kissed Lady Blackwood on each cheek. "And thank you for keeping my arrival a secret, my lady."

He nodded in Montague's direction. "Good to see you, sir."

Montague dipped his head in return. "Yes, it's been a while. Not since all that shocking business at the Symposium." He turned a half-smile on me. "And all of Dr. Bell's remarkable detective work."

The memory of that night—and how it had ended—fell heavy between Quinn and me. His eyes held mine, and for a moment I was back there: the crack of gunfire, Hawke's body on the floor, the mystery figure in the violet hat disappearing into the chaos.

"Yes," Quinn said softly. "Dr. Bell has many remarkable

qualities. Though I suspect we've only scratched the surface of what she's capable of."

The weight of everything unsaid, everything unresolved between us, settled like stone behind my ribs. Eight months of questions without answers. Eight months of wondering if I could trust him, if I could trust myself around him.

I'd spent those months trying to file away our kiss under *Professional Complications: Archaeological Romance (ill-advised)* but it kept sliding out of that neat mental drawer, refusing to be cataloged so simply, resisting my usual retreat into scientific classification when emotions threatened to overwhelm logic.

Lady Blackwood clapped her hands, startling me from my thoughts. "Well! Shall we show Dr. Bell to her rooms? The solstice is only three days away, and we have so much to discuss!"

CHAPTER TWO

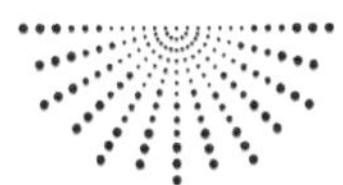

The garden path crunched beneath our feet as Annie and I sought refuge from Quinn's unexpected arrival. Lady Blackwood's attempts at an Egyptian pleasure garden provided welcome shade, though the reflecting pools needed attention.

"So," Annie's eyes sparkled with mischief, "that's why you were so eager to accept Lady Blackwood's invitation. You knew he'd find you here."

Misguided Assumption by Companion (Common), notable characteristics: completely incorrect.

I twirled the parasol Lady Blackwood has insisted on and traced my fingers along a limestone bench. "I came because Lady Blackwood mentioned Thorne's blue-pigmented artifact. After eight months of dead ends with Operation Indigo..."

"Mmhmm." Annie adjusted her hat. "Nothing to do with a certain antiquities dealer who just happened to arrive moments after us?"

"I left word at Shepheard's purely as a courtesy." The climate wasn't solely responsible for my flush. "Besides, Mother made it quite clear during those endless summer soirées that a proper New York debutante doesn't chase after mysterious men with questionable backgrounds in antiquities."

Annie snorted most unbecomingly. "And that's exactly why you're back in Egypt instead of waltzing your way through your parents' Christmas dinners and gala."

"I'm here to continue my work." But even I could hear the defensive note in my voice. "Mother and Father may consider archaeology an unsuitable profession for their daughter, but—"

A burst of angry voices from the front drive cut me off.

"It's nothing compared to your disregard for the integrity of the provenance of these artifacts—"

Two men rounded the corner of the house, clearly in the middle of a heated argument.

"—and your absurd theories about stellar alignments makes you a laughingstock!" The younger man's cultured voice dripped with disdain.

The gruffer, somewhat older voice countered. "The calculations are irrefutable, Foster! The solstice will prove—"

Annie and I exchanged glances. Apparently, Dr. Jasper Thorne, and at least one critic, had arrived.

We stepped onto the crushed limestone path that led toward the voices. The argument grew louder as we approached, though neither man noticed our emergence from behind the towering palms.

I adjusted my parasol, using the moment to study the pair ahead. The older man's gesticulations sent papers fluttering from his overstuffed journal, while his younger companion maintained a pose of arrogant condescension.

Annie cleared her throat delicately, and both men startled and turned toward us.

Specimen: Dr. Jasper Thorne (Academic, Late-middle-aged), Notable Characteristics: Wild gray hair, threadbare tweed despite heat, clutching leather satchel like a talisman.

The other man, in his early thirties and extremely handsome, wore an expensive cream-colored linen suit, and carried himself with a forced casual air.

"Dr. Thorne." Quinn's voice came from behind me as he emerged from a nearby archway, extending a hand toward the older man. "Benedict Quinn. I believe we met briefly at the Egyptian Museum last spring."

Quinn's presence shifted the atmosphere. He positioned himself between me and the younger man, a move that appeared accidental but felt deliberate.

I stepped aside, to get a better look at the blonde-haired stranger.

Annie quirked her eyebrows but then slipped toward the front door and into the estate.

"Ah yes, Mr. Quinn." Thorne brightened, clearly eager for a new audience. "Then you must hear about my discovery. The winter solstice alignment at Karnak isn't merely architectural—it's part of a vast network of ancient observatories!"

The other man's exaggerated eyeroll spoke volumes. "More fantasies about your mysterious 'Stellar People' who supposedly preceded the Egyptians?"

Quinn's voice lost its humor. "That's enough, Foster." The words landed like a quiet slap, calm but edged with steel. "You can disagree without sneering." For an instant, his usual charm dropped away and something harder showed beneath—then, just as quickly, he eased back, the faintest ghost of a smile returning. "We're all here for the same purpose, aren't we? To learn."

The younger man—Foster, it seemed—half bowed to Quinn. "Ah, Mr. Quinn, and so charming to find you here as well."

"Yes!" Thorne seemed oblivious to the tension. "You must see what I've learned! The evidence is in the mathematics!" Thorne flipped open a journal, pages dense with calculations. "The temple alignments follow a precise seventy-year cycle that matches an unknown planetary orbit. The ancient texts speak of 'the time when the sky gods return'—clearly astronomical predictions!"

I couldn't help interjecting. "But surely the Egyptian astronomical knowledge developed organically through their own observations?"

"Exactly!" Foster jabbed a finger at me. "Finally, someone

with sense." His smile held something predatory. "Harrison Foster. And you are?"

"Dr. Clarissa Bell." I noted how his gaze sharpened at my name.

"Dr. Bell is an expert in pigment authentication," Quinn said smoothly, though his eyes remained fixed on Foster. "I'm certain she'd be fascinated by the blue pigments in the Astral Sphere, Dr. Thorne."

More than fascinated, truth be told, as it was the reason I'd accepted Lady Blackwood's invitation.

Thorne's face lit up. "Yes! The sphere's markings contain precise astronomical calculations, painted in what appears to be Egyptian blue—though some suggest it's actually lapis lazuli. When properly aligned during the solstice—"

"It will prove nothing except your own delusions," Foster cut in. "You're seeing patterns where none exist."

The tension crackling between these men felt deeper than mere academic disagreement.

Quinn's stance remained aloof, but I recognized the alertness in his posture—the same readiness I'd seen before trouble struck.

But his attention kept drifting from Thorne's enthusiastic gestures to study my reactions. Each time our eyes met, that same electric awareness sparked between us. I forced myself to focus on cataloging the complex dynamics between the men.

"Come now, everyone!" Lady Blackwood swept into the garden, again like a purple silk hurricane. "It's much too hot for arguing outdoors. Let's continue this fascinating discussion in the Salon."

The Salon's "Christmas-meets-Ancient-Egypt" decor seemed even more dramatic in the waning afternoon light. Lady Blackwood coordinated our seating arrangements like a general deploying troops for battle. Jasper Thorne positioned near the Egyptian artifacts that lined the marble mantle, Harrison Foster deliberately separated from Quinn by the width of a Persian carpet whose patterns echoed the painted murals.

Dr. Montague wandered in and took a seat near the decorated palm tree, settling himself to appear absorbed in the evening newspaper while maintaining a clear view of the entire room.

"Miss Bell, do sit here." She patted the striped damask of a settee positioned very close to Quinn's chair and angled to catch the last rays of sun. The light would illuminate the faces of those seated opposite. Perfect.

The room's competing scents assaulted my overdeveloped nose—cypress boughs, frankincense, and the ghost of morning's coffee. Like the rest of Lady Blackwood's curated chaos, it served to unsettle and intrigue. The question was: had she engineered this gathering as purposefully as she'd arranged its setting?

"This calls for a celebration!" Lady Blackwood beamed at Thorne. "You did bring your special faience cup, didn't you? The one you always use to toast your discoveries?"

"Of course!" Thorne patted his worn leather satchel. "Eighteenth Dynasty, you know. The perfect vessel for marking momentous occasions."

"Momentous delusions," Foster muttered, just loud enough to hear.

Quinn's hand brushed my elbow as he leaned close. "Our friend Foster seems rather fixated on discrediting Thorne."

I suppressed a shiver at his proximity. "Perhaps he's just concerned about academic integrity."

"Perhaps." Quinn's quiet voice held an edge of skepticism. "Though I've known Harrison Foster to overlook far greater concerns when profit was involved."

The tension between them was impossible to miss. "Previous dealings?"

"Let's just say Mr. Foster's definition of legitimate antiquities acquisition differs somewhat from mine."

Considering Quinn's dubious definition, that was saying something.

Before I could probe further, Thorne moved to the window. The setting sun painted the desert in shades of flame and shadow as he raised one trembling hand toward the horizon.

"Time grows short," he announced with theatrical gravity. "In four days, the winter solstice will reveal what they've all dismissed as impossible. The Astral Sphere's true purpose, the ancient knowledge encoded in its surface..." His voice dropped to a near-whisper. "The return of the Stellar People."

Foster's derisive snort cut through the dramatic moment. "I suggest we all stock up on Egyptian coffee before then. It'll be a long night of waiting for imaginary astronomical beings."

But something in Thorne's intensity gave me pause. Beyond his wild theories, I sensed genuine fear beneath his bombastic exterior. His fingers clutched his satchel white-knuckled, as if protecting something far more valuable than a ceremonial cup.

I caught Quinn watching me catalog these details, a familiar half-smile playing at his lips. He knew my methods too well—how I constructed mental files of every oddity, every contradiction, every subtle tell that might later prove significant.

Whatever lay behind Thorne's theories and Foster's antagonism, I couldn't shake the feeling that we were all being drawn into something far more complex—and dangerous—than a mere academic dispute about ancient astronomy.

As if reading my thoughts, Quinn moved closer. "Trust your instincts, Clarissa," he murmured. "They've rarely led you wrong."

Except, perhaps, when it came to him.

Eight months of impersonal letter-writing had done nothing to resolve the central question: could I trust a man who'd kissed me with such devastating honesty one moment, then maintained such ambiguous life details the next?

Back in his presence again now, I inspected each word for hidden meaning, each gesture for proof of sincerity or deception. *Evidence of genuine affection: sustained eye contact, protective positioning, willingness to validate my investigative instincts.*

Evidence of manipulation: professional charm, calculated proximity, expertise in reading behavioral cues.

The problem was that both interpretations fit the available data perfectly. And without proof—without some scientific method to distinguish authentic emotion from practiced seduction—how could I possibly know which was real?

My time in Egypt last winter had taught me that people were complex, capable of containing contradictions. But in some ways, that lesson had left me paralyzed. If everyone could be both simultaneously trustworthy and deceptive, honorable and opportunistic, how did one ever choose whom to believe?

I needed certainty. I needed evidence. I needed something more reliable than the treacherous flutter beneath my ribs whenever he drifted within arm's length.

CHAPTER THREE

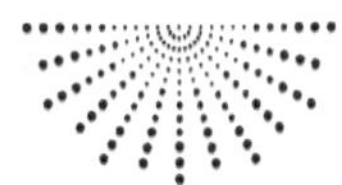

The winter sun sank lower, shadows lengthening across the Salon, reminding us all that the shortest day of the year would soon be upon us. As twilight crept in, the atmosphere seemed to shift, taking on an edge of foreboding that even Lady Blackwood's enthusiastic hospitality couldn't quite dispel.

The prospect of a four-day house party with this assortment of people suddenly loomed long.

Just before the four o'clock, another automobile arrived in the front drive. My perch at the window afforded me the first look at the new arrivals.

Two figures emerged—as different as a granite obelisk and a chubby sphinx.

Specimen 1: New Arrival (Female, Egyptian), Notable Characteristics: Commanding presence despite petite frame.

Her European-cut traveling suit in midnight blue, adorned with subtle lotus embroidery at collar, suggested a fusion of cultures and attention to symbolic detail. She moved with the fluid grace of someone at home in her own skin. Striking features, I thought. Intelligence tempered with warmth, though there was iron beneath the surface—evident in how she subtly adjusted her stance when the man beside her stepped too close.

Specimen 2: New Arrival (Male, British), Notable Characteristics: Precisely arranged chestnut hair and round gold spectacles magnifying sharp eyes scanning surroundings.

His fleshy build was wrapped in a charcoal suit that spoke of good breeding.

Lady Blackwood was at my side a moment later, peering through the window at the arriving guests.

"Ah, now we are all here." She inclined her head toward the foyer, calling out. "Freddie, see our arriving guests into the Salon and retrieve their luggage."

The young man materialized in the doorway—Freddie, I presumed—his pressed shirt and precise manners compensating for the slight shabbiness of his clothes. Something in his deferential posture reminded me of the display of lesser artifacts in my father's study—items positioned to suggest wealth while masking their own depreciation.

Lady Blackwood swept forward to greet the newcomers. "Dr. Mujahid, Professor Whitmore! You've made excellent time from Cairo."

The woman—Dr. Mujahid—removed her gloves with elegant efficiency. "The train was unexpectedly punctual. Though I suspect that had more to do with Professor Whitmore terrorizing the conductor with his pocket watch than any improvement in the rail service."

Whitmore adjusted his spectacles, managing to look both apologetic and entirely pleased. "Precision in all things, my dear."

Lady Blackwood performed the introductions with her brand of scattered thoroughness. I filed away the subtle tells—how Yasmin Mujahid's polite smile tightened almost imperceptibly at Thorne's effusive greeting, the way Whitmore's gaze cataloged each person in turn while appearing to focus solely on Lady Blackwood's chatter.

A dark-haired young woman—Laila, according to Lady Blackwood's introductions—appeared with a tea service. She moved through the room like a shadow, though I noticed how she deliberately avoided Foster's side of the settee.

I did appreciate how the tea service merged British tradition with Egyptian hospitality. The silver tray held delicate bone china alongside small brass cups for Turkish coffee. Freshly baked date cookies and slices of orange-scented semolina cake shared space with traditional cucumber sandwiches. The scent of Earl Grey mingled with cardamom and mint.

"Ah, Freddie, do help Laila with that tray."

"Right you are, m'lady!"

I bit back a smile at the unexpected London East End accent, which seemed so out of place.

Lady Blackwood's voice dropped to a confiding whisper as she leaned closer to me. "Freddie is a distant cousin's boy. I brought him with me to Egypt for the season. Unfortunate business in London. But he's making a fresh start here, poor dear."

Thorne had already cornered Dr. Mujahid near the fireplace. "You must let me show you the astronomical calculations. The alignment of the temple axis clearly indicates—"

"Really, Jasper." Yasmin's tone suggested she'd weathered similar enthusiasms before. "We've discussed your... creative interpretations of the evidence."

Foster smirked from his position by the window. "Creative is certainly one word for it."

I caught Quinn watching this exchange with attention, though his posture remained deliberately casual. He'd taken up a position that kept both Foster and the door in his line of sight —a habit I'd noticed during our previous adventures. It made me wonder, not for the first time, exactly what his antiquities dealings had involved before we met.

Foster reached for a piece of baklava on the tea tray with exaggerated leisure. Honey clung to the flaky pastry as he set it beside his cup, then proceeded to add milk and sugar to his tea with meticulous care. The silver spoon clinked against fine china with each deliberate stir, the sound cutting through the tension like a metronome.

I noticed how his eyes never left the Astral Sphere, even as he appeared absorbed in his cup.

"Do you have enough tea, sir?" Laila's voice was barely above a whisper as she approached Foster with a pot in one hand and tray in the other. Her hand trembled slightly, causing the teapot lid to rattle.

"Yes." His reply was curt, but his fingers brushed the edge of her sleeve as she withdrew—a gesture so subtle I might have missed it had I not been watching closely. The girl's face remained blank, though her steps quickened as she retreated.

Freddie, still hovering nearby, also tracked this exchange, with sharp eyes that belied his servile posture. He steadied a plate of delicate almond macarons threatening to slide from Laila's overcrowded tray. The pastries had been arranged in a precise pattern alongside stuffed dates and tiny spinach fatayer, their shapes echoing the Egyptian motifs that decorated the salon.

I filed the notable characteristics of "Afternoon Tea in the Salon" under *Complex Web of Unspoken Messages*.

Lady Blackwood clapped her hands for attention. "Now then, shall we discuss the arrangements for the solstice? We'll want everything perfectly positioned for Jasper's demonstration."

The Salon hummed with competing conversations as Thorne unfurled an elaborate star chart across the mahogany side table. His fingers traced celestial paths with reverent intensity.

"The convergence occurs once every seventy years—when the celestial bodies align precisely with the temple's central chamber. The Astral Sphere acts as a focal point, gathering and channeling these cosmic energies."

The Astral Sphere itself sat beneath glass nearby, where Thorne had reverently placed it. The stone was etched with intricate markings that seemed to shift in the lamplight. Something about its presence made the hair at the nape of my neck prickle.

Foster leaned over the table, squinting at the artifact as though his gaze might uncover fresh scandal.

"Astral *Sphere*, is it?" he said, one corner of his mouth curling. "Is it just me, or is this a disc? But I suppose *Astral Dinner Plate* lacks a certain gravitas."

Dr. Thorne's jaw tightened by a millimeter. "The terminology reflects its celestial mapping function, not its—"

"—shape, yes, clearly." Foster's tone carried mock deference. "Heaven forbid I mistake a cosmic saucer for a star chart. And cosmic energies? Really, Thorne. Next, you'll be telling us your 'Stellar People' descended from the heavens to build the pyramids."

"The evidence speaks for itself." Thorne's normally precise voice took on an edge of zealotry. "The astronomical knowledge encoded in these ancient structures far exceeds what was supposedly possible for that era. Unless, of course, they had... guidance."

Quinn drifted closer to where I sat near the window, then slid onto the seat beside me.

"Might we discuss privately that matter we spoke of in Cairo?" Quinn's voice was pitched for intimacy.

There was no "matter" we needed to discuss. He wanted to get me alone.

I wasn't ready for that.

Before I could respond, Lady Blackwood materialized before us. "Clarissa dear, you simply must see these photographs from the Valley dig site."

The interruption carried the weight of intention rather than coincidence. Her bright smile didn't quite mask the sharp assessment in her eyes as she steered me away.

Across the room, Dr. Mujahid and Whitmore had withdrawn to a corner, heads bent in conversation. Their words were too low to catch, but the tension in Yasmin's shoulders spoke volumes.

"The alignment isn't merely astronomical." Thorne's voice

rose with evangelical fervor. "It represents a confluence of forces beyond our modern understanding. The ancients knew secrets we've only begun to glimpse."

Behind his newspaper, Montague's eyes tracked each speaker in turn. The paper itself hadn't turned a page in twenty minutes.

"And I suppose these 'forces' explain why your last research paper was thoroughly discredited?" Foster's words fell like stones into still water.

Lady Blackwood's laugh tinkled with forced lightness. "Really, Mr. Foster. We needn't dwell on such unpleasantness."

"Indeed." Thorne's smile had vanished completely. "Curious how eager you are to tear down the work of actual scholars, just to bolster your own shady dealings, not to mention your shady associates, Foster."

Whitmore's head snapped up at this, his gaze meeting Yasmin's in a loaded exchange.

The grandfather clock struck the hour, its chimes unnaturally loud in the tension-thick air. Through the window, the early darkness was claiming the grounds, transforming the glass into a mirror that reflected our gathering like figures in a tableau—each person frozen in their own private drama.

Foster dismissed Thorne's barb with a silent shrug.

"It doesn't matter." Thorne caressed the glass case housing the Sphere. "In four days, the sunrise alignment will prove everything. When the forces gather, there can be no more doubt."

Dr. Mujahid's hands clenched briefly.

Quinn's expression remained neutral, but his fingers drummed once against his leg.

Even Lady Blackwood's smile faltered for a heartbeat.

The lamplight struggled to chase away the desert night now, casting shadows that seemed to reach toward the Sphere with grasping fingers. Saturday's solstice suddenly felt less like an astronomical event and more like a gathering storm.

Thorne smiled, his teeth gleaming in the lamplight. "The

alignment of forces cannot be denied. The truth will emerge...
whether some wish it to or not."

Lady Blackwood rose to her feet, demure elegance
personified.

"Each of you has been specially invited to join the festivities
for this exciting event this week." She forced a smile around the
Salon. "We may not all see eye-to-eye, but certainly we can
respect and learn from each other."

She crossed the room toward the foyer, then turned with
another tight smile. "And now I believe it best if we each retire
to our private rooms." She waved a vague hand toward the
stairs. "But please do join me at eight o'clock in the Dining
Room, for our first celebratory dinner."

With that, she exited, leaving a beat of silence in her wake,
and the various players still scattered around the Salon.

Annie materialized at the door, her eyes on me. "Shall we
prepare for dinner, miss?"

Before I could respond, Quinn leaned into my shoulder. "A
moment first, Dr. Bell?"

The warmth in his tone coaxed a tremor up my spine, but I
kept my voice steady. "I really should freshen up before
dinner."

"It won't take long." His fingers brushed my upper arm.
"Unless you're still cataloguing reasons to avoid being alone
with me?"

Annie's strategic retreat told me whose side she was on in
this battle.

I led him into the foyer, marshaling my defenses, then
turned to face him. "Very well. What pressing matter requires
immediate discussion?"

His eyes held mine. "Eight months of letters, and you still
won't admit why you really came back to Egypt."

"Oh, I'm happy to admit it." I cocked my head and smiled.
"Two words..." I leaned close, bringing my lips to his ear.

I was rewarded by his sharp intake of breath.

For all his practiced charm, that involuntary sound
betrayed something raw beneath the polish.

"Two words?" His voice was low and smooth.

"Mmhmm. Operation Indigo."

CHAPTER FOUR

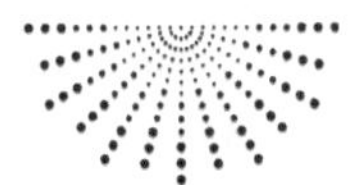

As usual, Annie outdid herself, transforming my travel-worn appearance into something approaching respectability for dinner. The drop-waisted midnight blue chiffon evening dress had survived its journey from New York remarkably well, though the heat made me question the wisdom of bringing anything but muslin to Egypt.

At least the private bedchamber Lady Blackwood had assigned boasted surprisingly modern amenities, including a proper vanity mirror and excellent lighting that had allowed Annie to wage war on ten hours of train dust.

Now, gliding one hand down the banister of the grand staircase, and gripping a tiny beaded purse in the other, I caught snippets of conversation drifting from the dining room. Lady Blackwood's voice rose above the others, directing servants with the precision of a conductor orchestrating a symphony.

The dining room itself presented yet another study in cultural collision. Massive mahogany furniture that must have survived a tortuous journey from England now sat beneath elaborate Egyptian revival chandeliers. Their crystal drops cast prismatic patterns across damask tablecloths and Wedgwood china, while gilt-framed hunting scenes shared wall space with hand-painted hieroglyphic borders that told the story of Isis and Osiris which, ironically, was a story not at all fit for polite society, let alone dinner.

"Dr. Bell!" Lady Blackwood swooped forward to claim my arm. "You must sit here, between Mr. Quinn and Professor Montague."

Quinn pulled out my chair with a look that skimmed my dress from shoulder straps to hem, followed by a look that sent my carefully labeled thoughts skittering out of their drawers.

On my other side, Montague offered a gentlemanly nod while Lady Blackwood settled herself at the head of the table beside him.

The excessive number of candles—clearly meant to create atmosphere—succeeded mainly in raising the room's temperature to nearly unbearable levels. A gust of desert wind rattled the French doors leading to the terrace, making the flames dance and sending shadows skittering across the walls.

Laila appeared at my elbow with the first course, a lentil soup whose aroma carried hints of cumin and coriander. Behind her, Freddie managed the wine service with a concentration that didn't quite mask his unfamiliarity with formal dining. His hands shook slightly as he filled Dr. Thorne's ceremonial cup—positioned prominently beside his place setting like some sort of talisman.

"A perfect evening for revelations, wouldn't you say?" Thorne's voice carried an edge of feverish excitement that set my teeth on edge.

Quinn's hand brushed mine as he reached for his water glass. "Some revelations require perfect timing." His tone carried layers of meaning that had nothing to do with astronomy, but as usual his subtle flirtations barely made sense to me.

Beside me, I could feel his arm was coiled tension—refined manners masking something far less tame.

I focused on analyzing the room's occupants, as scientific observation always steadied my nerves.

Under Observation: one barely tolerating antiquities dealer (likely dangerous), one overexcited astronomer (possibly unhinged), and a hostess whose energy suggests pharmaceutical assistance at play.

But even my most rigorous classification systems seemed inadequate for the undercurrents of tension flowing beneath the surface of polite dinner conversation.

"Finished dissecting us all?" Quinn asked under his breath. "Should I be flattered or frightened?"

I bumped his knee with my own but did not answer.

The soup course continued with small groupings of conversation around the long mahogany table. I chatted with Dr. Montague about the upcoming dig season's plans at Giza and tried to ignore Quinn's leg pressed against my own.

The soup bowls had barely been cleared when Lady Blackwood straightened in her chair, tapping her crystal water glass with a silver spoon.

"Since we represent such a distinguished gathering of scholars and experts, perhaps we might each share a brief introduction? Something about our interests and specialties?"

A subtle collective wince rippled around the table. Even the most enthusiastic academic rarely welcomed the command to perform like a trained seal.

"I'll begin." Lady Blackwood's smile didn't quite reach her eyes. "As your hostess, and carrying on my late husband's passionate interest in Egyptian archaeology, I'm thrilled to support groundbreaking research like Dr. Thorne's astronomical studies."

At the opposite end of the table, Thorne practically vibrated with eagerness for his turn.

"Mr. Foster?" Lady Blackwood nodded toward the left side of the table.

Foster lounged back in his chair, managing to look both elegant and insolent. "Harrison Foster, antiquities acquisition specialist." His smile carried an edge. "I help ensure significant artifacts find their way to... appreciative collectors."

Quinn's barely audible snort spoke volumes about his opinion of Foster's methods.

Pot calling kettle black?

Professor Whitmore adjusted his spectacles. "Reginald Whitmore, Regional Documentation Committee of the Royal Geographical Society." His precise tone suggested measured revelations.

Lady Blackwood smiled down the table. "And the lovely Dr. Mujahid?"

Yasmin's chin lifted slightly. "I am an archaeologist, but also cultural advocate for independent Egypt. My work centers on bringing attention to Egyptian achievements throughout history." Her gaze flickered toward Thorne. "And I prefer to ground my theories in demonstrable evidence."

Harrison Foster leaned closer to her, murmuring something that made her shoulders tense. The crystal chandelier caught the rigid angles of her shoulders.

Beside me, Montague waggled his fingers at the group. "Nigel Montague, here." His kind voice carried warmth. "Currently Interim Curator at the Graeco-Roman Museum in Alexandria, though I'm particularly fascinated by the intersection of Greek and Egyptian traditions."

Quinn's turn came next. "Benedict Quinn. I... deal in the recovery and protection of artifacts that too often vanish into the wrong hands." His hand brushed my knee under the table. "Among other interests."

I shifted away from his touch. Why were these candles so hot?

"Dr. Clarissa Bell." I aimed for professional detachment. "My work focuses on pigment authentication in ancient artifacts, but I'll be working at the Giza plateau site this season, under Dr. Bradford. Hopefully doing a bit more than pottery-sorting." I smiled, and the guests chuckled politely.

"Also, solving crime," Quinn murmured, low enough that only I could hear.

"And Dr. Thorne?" Lady Blackwood prompted, as servants began distributing the fish course.

"Jasper Thorne, former professor at Oxford, former Fellow of the Royal Geographic Society."

Quinn leaned in. "That's quite a bit of 'former.'"

I nudged him with my elbow.

"As I'm sure you all know, I've spent considerable time both in India and here in Egypt. But of course, my true credentials lie in unlocking the ancient mysteries encoded in temple architecture." He smiled expansively at the group, as though he were the host rather than Lady Blackwood. "In four days, the winter solstice alignment will prove what they've all dismissed —that a civilization of remarkable astronomical sophistication preceded the ancient Egyptians!"

Yasmin leaned forward. "Perhaps you could share some of the academic response you've received from your recent paper, Dr. Thorne. I believe it was titled, 'The Forgotten Architects: Celestial Wisdom of the Ancients.'"

The room fell into awkward silence, other than the whistle of wind outside the doors. Everyone at the table knew Thorne's career had basically imploded after publication, with reviewers dismissing it as pseudoscientific speculation.

Montague studied his wine glass with sudden fascination while Whitmore developed an intense interest in his napkin.

A particularly fierce gust of wind rattled the French doors, making several people jump. The candles flickered wildly, transforming the gilt-framed hunting scenes into dancing shadows that seemed to reach toward each of us.

Yasmin pushed away from the table and laid her napkin delicately across the chair. "Lady Blackwood, I beg your forgiveness, but I'm afraid the travel has given me quite a headache. I believe I will retire for the night."

"Of course, dear. Shall I send Laila up—"

"No, thank you. I only require a night's rest. Thank you."

She slipped out, just as the fish arrived—perfectly cooked but thoroughly overshadowed by the increasing tension crackling through the room like static before a storm.

"Excellent fish." Montague's conversational detour had all the subtlety of a camel in a china shop.

Quinn turned his head to whisper in my ear. "Enjoying the floor show?"

"Oh yes. Nothing says 'festive dinner party' quite like academic bloodsport."

The meal proceeded in tense snippets of conversation, broken only by the clink of silverware and the increasing howl of wind outside. Foster kept glancing at the doorway through which Yasmin had disappeared, while Thorne grew more agitated with each passing moment, his movements becoming jerky and unpredictable.

Finally, as servants cleared the main course plates, Thorne lurched to his feet, ceremonial cup clutched in both hands.

"My friends!" His voice carried an edge of desperation. "Before dessert, we must mark this momentous gathering!"

Lady Blackwood brightened. "Ah yes, your lovely faience cup! Do tell everyone its history."

"Eighteenth Dynasty." Thorne raised the vessel reverently. "Found in a forgotten corner of a noble's tomb in the Valley of the Kings. See how the glaze catches the light? The ancients knew secrets of craftsmanship we've barely begun to understand."

"Are you certain that's a cup you've got there, my dear man?" Foster laughed. "Perhaps it's a sphere? A vase? A canopic jar? I know how you like to use alternate names."

A snide reference to the Astral Sphere / Disc, no doubt.

Foster was obnoxious, but he wasn't wrong. I didn't think I could bring myself to call Jasper's prize Astral Artifact a "sphere," either.

But I studied his cup with professional interest, especially given our investigation into both Egyptian blue pigment and the rarer lapis lazuli that had some kind of connection to Operation Indigo. This blue-green faience glaze did possess remarkable clarity for its age.

Thorne ignored Foster, his eyes gleaming. "Join me in a toast!" He stood, cup in hand. "To the truth that cannot be denied. To the wisdom of the ancients, waiting to be revealed. To the alignment of forces that will prove them all wrong!"

He raised the cup high.

The rest of us reached for our wineglasses, holding them

aloft with varying degrees of enthusiasm. Harrison Foster looked like he'd rather swallow sand than toast Thorne's theories.

Thorne brought the cup to his lips with a flourish, and the rest of us sipped and set down our glasses.

The first taste made him pause, brow furrowing. By the second swallow, his face had contorted in pain.

The cup slipped from his fingers, shattering against the polished mahogany table. Green-glazed shards scattered like fallen stars across the pristine damask table runner.

Lady Blackwood gasped.

But there was something wrong with Thorne's face.

I went cold, shock compressing into a clinical focus as I cataloged his symptoms.

Thorne clutched his throat, eyes bulging. His lips had taken on a distinctive bluish tinge that had nothing to do with the spilled wine or any ancient pigment.

"Dear God," Montague whispered, half-rising from his seat.

Thorne's legs buckled. He toppled sideways, crashing into a side table laden with dessert plates. The sound of shattering porcelain mixed with the howling wind as his body hit the floor.

Lady Blackwood's scream pierced the chaos.

Whitmore lunged forward, then kneeled to check for a pulse.

But the peculiar cherry-red color of Thorne's face told me everything we needed to know.

Death by Poisoning (Cyanide), Notable Characteristics: Rapid onset, distinctive coloring, flecks of white foam on lips.

"Nobody touch anything!" Quinn's voice cut through the pandemonium. He was already on his feet, positioning himself between me and Foster, who had jumped from his chair, away from Thorne.

Montague hurried to comfort Lady Blackwood, who had collapsed into helpless whimpering. "Someone fetch a doctor, though I fear..."

"Yes, someone needs to alert the authorities." Whitmore still bent over Thorne's prone form.

I forced myself to study the scene with detachment, even as my heart hammered against my ribs. The scattered pieces of the ceremonial cup drew my eye. Someone needed to retrieve those shards.

But a more urgent question pressed forward: who had known about Thorne's habit of using that specific cup for celebrations? And who had access to it before this fatal toast?

CHAPTER FIVE

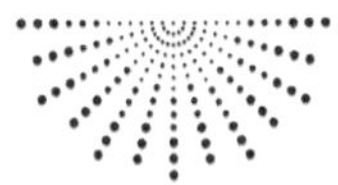

Through the ringing in my ears, I catalogued the chaos unfolding in Lady Blackwood's dining room.

Murder Scene Aftermath (Initial), Notable Characteristics: Controlled panic descending into disorder.

Servants materialized in the doorway, drawn by Lady Blackwood's continued sobbing. Winters, the estate agent, loomed behind them. Laila's hands trembled violently, and a cup from the coffee service she carried crashed to the floor, sending more pottery skittering across Egyptian carpets.

Quinn positioned himself between the body and the door, where Foster was already edging toward escape. "Leave him as you found him, Whitmore. The police will need to examine everything exactly as it is."

"Simply checking for a pulse," Whitmore announced smoothly. "Though I fear there's nothing to be done."

His concern for the victim's pulse would have been more convincing if he wasn't simultaneously rifling through the man's pockets with the efficiency of a professional pickpocket.

Before I could object, he'd withdrawn a folded paper and tucked it into his own jacket.

Lady Blackwood's hysteria crescendoed. "We can't leave him here—not in the Dining Room! What will people say?"

Voices echoed through the room as the assembled party argued, talking over one another with increasing volume.

"He should be moved to a private room upstairs!" Foster jabbed his finger toward the ceiling.

"No." Lady Blackwood cut in, drawing herself up. "The Library is much simpler, and can be locked. We'll keep him there until the authorities arrive."

Apparently in Lady Blackwood's world, a corpse in the Library was somehow more socially acceptable than one in the Dining Room. She fixed the others with a stern look until heads nodded in agreement.

Quinn cleared his throat. "Freddie, Winters—careful now." He directed the estate agent and the young footman as they bent to lift Thorne's body.

The dead man's head lolled back as they raised him, his arms swaying. His fingers remained frozen in a claw-like grip, the same position they'd been in when he'd last clutched his cup.

The servants inched sideways through the doorway, trying not to bump the corpse against the frame as they maneuvered toward the Library.

While the others fussed over the macabre procession, I leaned over the scattered ceramic fragments, collecting each shard into a linen napkin, to protect my hands from any remaining residue. That distinctive bitter-almond smell wrinkled my nose. Definitely cyanide.

Annie materialized at my elbow with an evidence box she'd fashioned from an empty biscuit tin. Her hands stayed steady as she held it out to collect the ceramic shards, though her face had gone quite pale.

"A bit more exciting than New York society events," she whispered.

The understatement nearly made me laugh, but the sound caught in my throat as Quinn's hand settled on my shoulder.

"Careful with those fragments," he murmured. "They may tell us more than we expect."

I handed off the biscuit tin to Annie, who trotted off to secure them in my room for the police.

Then opened my linen-covered palm to show Quinn the one piece I'd kept back.

He nodded. "Poison, you think?"

"You can't smell it? The cyanide?"

He half-smiled. "No. But it doesn't surprise me that you can." He pulled a handkerchief from his pocket. "Let's not make off with the table linens, in case the servants are counting."

I transferred the fragment to his handkerchief, then wrapped it, the monogrammed "BEQ" tucked on top. I'd have to ask about that "E" sometime. For now, I tucked the wrapped fragment into my purse, and we followed the others into the Library.

The room embodied everything the British Empire aspired to. Towering mahogany bookshelves reached fourteen feet high, their deep burgundy wood gleaming with years of polishing. A coffered ceiling featured hand-painted Egyptian motifs in gold leaf, while tall arched windows with bronze latches stretched nearly floor-to-ceiling, their weighted tapestry curtains in deep emerald drawn against the night.

Familiar scents wrapped around me. Predominant notes of aged leather and paper, hints of beeswax from polished wood, subtle traces of incense, and the faint metallic tang of brass fixtures warming in the light. Plush Tabriz carpets in rich jewel tones muffled our footsteps as we entered.

Lady Blackwood swooped in clutching a tapestry embroidered in greens and golds. "We must cover him, at least." The tapestry rippled like a banner as she snapped it outward and draped it over Thorne's body.

We stood staring at the prone figure, all of us silent at last.

After some minutes, the groups divided into factions. Foster shepherded Lady Blackwood toward the Salon, his solicitous manner at odds with the calculated glances he kept casting toward the Library door.

Whitmore drifted after them, pausing to adjust his glasses and glance backward.

Quinn watched them go, his jaw tight. "That man's played this scene before."

"Which man?"

"Take your pick."

Montague settled into a leather armchair in the Library, his keen eyes missing nothing despite his pose of elderly exhaustion.

Quinn prowled the perimeter of the room like a caged lion in evening wear, while I positioned myself near the doorway, arms folded and leaning against the wall.

It seemed necessary to hold vigil, to keep track of the body and the comings-and-goings of the guests. But would I stand here all night? How long would the police take to reach the estate, here on the outskirts of Luxor?

The fireplace remained unlit, but a series of candles across the mantlepiece cast strange shadows across the tapestry-shrouded form on the oriental carpet.

A floorboard creaked overhead, making us all start.

"Dr. Mujahid is still absent," Quinn noted softly. His hand brushed my elbow as he passed, a gesture somehow both protective and questioning.

The touch sparked an absurd urge to lean into his strength, and his smile was invitation and warning in equal measure. He paused, as if he sensed my desire. "Perhaps we might pool our observations? Over brandy?"

Before I could reply, raised voices erupted from the Salon. Foster's cultured tones clashed with Lady Blackwood's barely controlled hysteria.

Quinn's expression darkened. "Shall we see what that's about?"

Montague followed as we filed into the Salon, in time to hear Lady Blackwood's tiny sob. "The scandal! What will people say?"

"Perhaps less than you fear, my lady," Montague murmured, though she didn't hear him.

Yasmin Mujahid had returned downstairs and sat in a chair on the far side of the Salon.

At my raised eyebrows, she smiled sadly. "I heard the commotion and came to check. Lady Blackwood has told me what happened."

We found our seats again, in much the same places as we'd held during the afternoon's tea service.

Lady Blackwood called for Winters and instructed him to lock the Library and leave the corpse to rest alone until the police arrived.

Silence fell again, until a piercing scream shattered the peace.

Annie.

Quinn reached the Dining Room first, with me close behind. The French doors banged against the wall, desert wind whipping the curtains into frenzied shapes. Annie stood frozen, hand pressed to her chest.

"Just the wind." She shook her head, red-faced. "It caught me by surprise when the doors blew open."

But her other hand clutched Thorne's battered satchel. Papers spilled from its worn leather confines as she thrust it toward me. "I came back for this."

I shuffled quickly through the jumble of astronomical calculations and temple diagrams, but a sheet of papyrus stood out. The block letters were in English, not hieroglyphic.

The phrase made the hair rise on my neck:

Those who deny the gods their due shall feed the jackals before dawn.

Quinn's shoulder pressed against mine as he read. The solid weight of him at my side steadied my racing thoughts—before sending them skittering where they oughtn't go.

"A curse?" His voice held the same skepticism I felt. "Rather theatrical."

"Unless that's precisely the point." The pieces began shifting in my mind, forming a pattern still too nebulous to name.

My fingers traced the threatening papyrus, sorting each

detail of the past hour. As Quinn observed, there was a deliberate theatricality to it all—the curse, the ceremonial cup, even the timing— like an elaborately staged play.

We returned to the Salon, the papyrus in hand.

"Do be cautious, Clarissa." Quinn's voice was low as entered. "Our killer is still among us."

"I've just rung off after speaking to the authorities." Whitmore's crisp voice carried into the Salon, followed by the man himself. "They won't arrive until morning. Given that the victim is British, they seem disinclined to rush." He shrugged. "They insist we all remain here, of course. They want to speak to us tomorrow."

Glances went round the room, each of us studying the others in turn.

At least until morning, we were all trapped here together. The living, the dead, and whoever had decided Jasper Thorne's theories needed silencing.

CHAPTER SIX

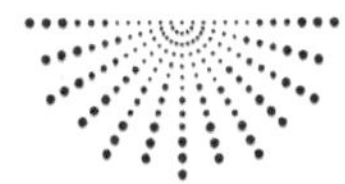

*D*awn crept over Lady Blackwood's estate like an archaeologist approaching an unstable dig site—cautiously, and with good reason to fear what might collapse.

I stood at the window to the Salon again, watching the long drive leading from the estate to the main road and the shafts of sunlight hitting the Theban dessert's angular hills to the west.

So, I was watching when the first police officers arrived with all the enthusiasm of sleepy desert lizards seeking shade.

They puttered through the house, with desultory questions and an apparent disinterest in examining the actual crime scene.

Clearly, they'd already filed this under "Dead Englishman, Natural Causes" and were simply going through the motions.

Until Inspector Hassan swept in.

Antiquities Inspector (Egyptian), Notable Characteristics: Commanding presence despite average height, impeccably tailored European suit that somehow enhanced rather than masked his Egyptian heritage, and eyes that missed absolutely nothing.

I'd met him last summer at Giza, when our scribe's palette—still missing—first disappeared.

He stood in the open doorway when he began his interrogation. "I understand Dr. Thorne was in possession of an artifact of significant cultural importance." His clipped tones carried both authority and warning. "The so-called 'Astral Sphere.' Where is it?"

"Astral *Disc*," Foster said, deliberately, as Hassan took notes. "Just to avoid confusion with all the other mystical geometry floating about."

"If you call it that one more time," Yasmin muttered, "I may find religious justification for violence."

Lady Blackwood fluttered forward. "Oh, but surely that's not relevant to poor Jasper's... unfortunate passing?"

Hassan's gaze could have stripped paint from limestone. "Everything is relevant, Lady Blackwood. Including why an English academic was carrying an artifact that rightfully belongs to Egypt."

"Of course, Inspector. Let me show you to Dr. Thorne's room." Lady Blackwood gestured toward the stairs. "The sphere must be among his belongings."

As they ascended, the crunch of tires on gravel drew my attention to the drive. Another motorcar pulled up, its gleaming black paint incongruous against the dusty landscape.

The automobile door opened, and my heart stuttered.

Richard Sullivan stepped out, looking exactly as he had the day I'd broken our engagement—perfectly tailored suit, chestnut-brown hair catching the morning light, and that devastating smile that had once made my knees weak.

Now it just made my stomach clench.

I gripped the doorframe. "What in the—"

Quinn was beside me in a flash, peering over my shoulder. "Who is it?"

"It's... Richard. My fiancé. Former."

Richard was already across the drive and pushing into the house.

"Well, if it isn't the cleverest Jane in Egypt. Still diggin' up dusty old dead fellas, doll?"

He swept toward me with the confidence of someone

who'd never doubted his welcome. "I see I've succeeded in surprising you, baby! Cat's got your tongue, eh?"

Nearly a year since I'd broken our engagement, and he still acted as though it had been a minor lovers' quarrel rather than a fundamental clash of worldviews.

Quinn's casual pose shifted subtly. Anyone else might have missed it, but I recognized his pre-pounce stillness. The predator beneath the gentleman—alert, assessing, ready to strike if needed.

My stomach churned again. "Richard, how on earth did you know I was here? And—and what are *you* doing here?"

Richard brushed a kiss to either side of my face, a calculated affectation that set my teeth on edge. As though he were born on this side of the pond. "Your Dr. Bradford at Giza told me where to find you and gave me Lady Blackwood's details."

Behind us, Hassan and Lady Blackwood were descending the main staircase.

"Ah, this must be the lady herself." Richard pivoted around me and crossed to clasp Lady Blackwood's hands. "Thank you so much for allowing me to crash your lovely party and surprise my dear, dear Clarissa."

"Former 'dear,'" I muttered, though only Quinn stood close enough to hear.

His lips twitched.

Inspector Hassan's attention had locked onto Richard like a compass finding magnetic north. "And you are?"

"Richard Sullivan, real estate acquisition. I'm helping some keen New York cats snap up some nifty properties over here. This King Tut business has everyone hopped up about Egypt!" He offered his hand to Hassan. "Including Armand Bell."

My father's name dropped into the tension like a stone into still water.

"How fascinating." Hassan's tone suggested it was anything but. "And your arrival, mere hours after Dr. Thorne's death, is pure coincidence?"

"Dr. Thorne—a death, you say?" Richard's brows shot upwards. "I'm afraid I'm at a loss. I was already headed to surprise Clarissa. When I reached Giza and learned she'd come to Luxor, I contacted Lady Blackwood immediately."

"To surprise me." My voice dripped skepticism. "Because that worked so well last time."

The last "surprise" had involved him announcing our engagement to New York society before actually proposing. Mother had been thrilled. I had been... less so.

"Actually," Richard's smile turned ingratiating, "I came hoping to discuss your future. Time for you to quit playing in the sand and come back to civilization. To the bright lights, where the real action is. This ridiculous archaeology jazz has gone far enough, baby."

Quinn moved before he seemed to think, stepping too close to Richard. "Watch your tone." The words were quiet, but there was iron beneath them. For a heartbeat, the charm dropped away and something far more dangerous looked out of his eyes—then just as quickly, he reined it back, smile restored. "Clarissa decides where she belongs."

"Where exactly do *you* think I belong, Richard?" Ice crept into my tone.

"New York, of course! We can put this Egyptian adventure behind you. I'm happy to support your little hobby while I establish business connections here, but—"

"You knew he was coming?" I rounded on Lady Black-wood, accusation sharpening my tone.

Her lips quirked and she shifted her glance from me, to Quinn, then to Richard. "Any friend of yours, my dear..."

By which she clearly meant that watching a triangle of two different men showing up to surprise me was too intriguing to resist.

Quinn stepped away from Richard to stand beside me, his presence both reassuring and confusing. The memory of our kiss in Giza warred with Richard's reappearance, creating an emotional tangle that defied my usual categorization.

Richard didn't miss Quinn's subtly possessive posture. His eyes narrowed and he glanced at me, as if to gauge my reaction.

Hassan cleared his throat. "I must ask each of you to move

into the Salon. As well as anyone else who was present last night."

We all filed in, with Annie, the servants Laila and Freddie, and Winters bringing up the rear, after Whitmore, Montague, and Foster had been summoned.

A quick count showed twelve of us, ranged around the Salon in various positions of ease (notably Foster) and terror (mainly Laila).

Hassan stood with his back against the cold fireplace, scowling.

"Where is the Astral Sphere?"

I shot a look at Lady Blackwood. "It wasn't in Dr. Thorne's bedroom?"

She shook her head. "I'm afraid not. We searched thoroughly."

Dr. Montague crossed his legs and tapped a finger against his chin. "Are you suggesting Thorne was murdered for that ridiculous artifact?"

"But why would he be?" I couldn't keep quiet. "Why not simply steal it? It wouldn't be necessary to kill him."

Hassan swept the room with his piercing eyes. "Who has noticed something out of the ordinary? Someone acting strangely."

I nearly laughed. Who wasn't strange at this gathering?

Laila raised a hand, half-bowing as though Hassan were royalty. Although, since the extraordinary finds began pouring of out Tutankhamun's tomb earlier this year, the Antiquities Department practically *had* been elevated to royalty in Egypt.

"What is it?" Hassan barked in her direction.

"It's nothing, I'm certain. But outside... with the kitchen scraps and garbage..."

"Yes?"

She shrugged. "Apricot pits."

A beat of silence followed the unexpected statement.

Then Hassan harrumphed. "No time for silliness, foolish girl—"

"Many, many apricot pits. Most of them ground up. But we have not served apricots."

Lady Blackwood was frowning. "How odd. We have trees, of course, but they are not in season. We haven't had fresh apricots since June."

Hassan sighed, the sound more angry than amused. "Can we return to—"

"Cyanide!" It was my turn to interrupt.

All eyes turned in my direction. "The poison that killed Thorne. It was likely cyanide, from his obvious physical reaction. And cyanide can be extracted from apricot pits." I swung toward Quinn, who would be tracking with me. "Only a small amount from each pit, of course. It would take 'many, many apricot pits' to extract enough cyanide to kill someone."

Quinn was shaking his head. "Why so elaborate?"

Foster slammed a hand down on the end table at his side. "Because that's how the ancient Egyptians did it! Or how an ancient Egyptian god would do it, if he were taking revenge on a crazy old man who'd crossed him!"

"The curse!" Lady Blackwood's voice rose with hysteria. "Just like the papyrus said! The gods have taken their revenge on poor Jasper!"

I'd made the mistake of sharing the threat we'd found in Thorne's satchel with the entire group last night.

Foster shuddered. "Yes, first that threatening note, now this? Perhaps we should all leave before—"

"Nobody leaves." Hassan's voice cracked like a whip. "Particularly not those who arrived under suspicious circumstances."

His pointed look at Richard made my heart thud.

Richard raised his hands. "I've no intention of going anywhere. But I wasn't even here last night when Jasper-whatever-his-name-is met his Maker. You can't pin this rap on me!"

"Yes, your late arrival is a convenient excuse. The police will need to investigate further, to determine if you are telling the truth."

Hassan's ill-founded accusations made little sense, but I guessed it didn't matter. We were all on the suspect list.

What had last night seemed merely shocking was rapidly becoming personally dangerous.

I'd come to investigate Operation Indigo. But could I ignore a different crime altogether, especially when it involved my fiancé?

Former. Former fiancé.

CHAPTER SEVEN

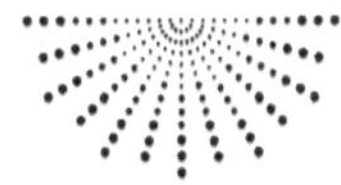

CHAPTER 7

The police departed with Thorne's body as the morning sun climbed higher, baking any lingering drama from the scene with its merciless heat. I handed over my biscuit tin of ceramic shards, explaining about the cyanide poisoning and its telltale signs.

All but one piece, that is. The small fragment with the most intact faience glaze remained tucked in my pocket. The police had plenty of cup fragments to analyze.

Ethical Compromise (Minor), Notable Characteristics: Rationalization of evidence tampering for greater good.

Inspector Hassan remained behind after the police left, still prowling the Salon like an impatient cat.

"Now." He planted himself before the fireplace, forcing us all to orient toward him like compass needles. "Someone will explain to me exactly what this 'Astral Sphere' is, and what Dr. Thorne intended to do with it."

The gathered suspects exchanged glances, a silent game of scholarly chicken to see who would speak first.

"It's a remarkable artifact," Lady Blackwood ventured, "with astronomical markings that—"

"Astronomical nonsense," Foster cut in. "The ravings of a desperate man trying to rebuild his ruined reputation."

Yasmin's eyes flashed. "At least he attempted academic research, however misguided. Unlike some who simply profit from our heritage."

"Now, now." Montague raised his hands in a placating gesture that drew all eyes to him. "Perhaps we should explain systematically."

Quinn's shoulder brushed mine as he shifted position. "Quite right. Starting with how Thorne acquired this supposedly remarkable object."

The room fell silent again. Lady Blackwood suddenly found the pattern of her Persian carpet fascinating, but her face had taken on a flush.

"The sphere belonged to Lady Blackwood's late husband." Montague's voice was gentle, as though he feared upsetting her. "He was... passionate about astronomical alignments at ancient sites."

"'Obsessed' is more accurate." Lady Blackwood's smile was forced. "Though not without reason."

Hassan's scowl deepened. "Continue."

The story emerged in pieces, each person adding their own perspective like artists working on a collaborative painting. Though in this case, the artwork resembled something closer to a child's finger-painting.

Thorne believed the winter solstice alignment at Karnak Temple was evidence of an advanced pre-Egyptian civilization he called "The Stellar People." The name alone made me want to break something, preferably over his posthumous head.

No, that was unkind. The man was dead, after all.

"The temple alignment follows a precise seventy-year astronomical cycle," Whitmore explained, adjusting his spectacles. "Thorne believed this corresponded to the orbital period of an undiscovered planet."

"Known to these hypothetical pre-Egyptian astronomers,"

Foster added with a smirk. "But somehow missed by every subsequent civilization."

"The triple planetary conjunction occurring during this winter solstice wasn't coincidental," Montague continued, ignoring Foster's interruption. "According to Thorne, the temple builders encoded mathematical formulas into the temple's proportions."

Yasmin's laugh held no humor. "Yes, because surely the Egyptians couldn't have managed such calculations on their own. It must have been mysterious predecessors who did all the real work."

"The ancient texts speak of 'the time when the sky gods return,'" Lady Blackwood insisted, her voice taking on an edge of Thorne's fevered conviction. "Jasper believed these were an advanced race!"

I caught Quinn stifling what might have been either a laugh or a groan.

"And the sphere?" Hassan's patience was clearly wearing thin.

"Ah yes, the centerpiece of his theory." Montague's kind voice took on a scholarly tone. "A blue-pigmented artifact covered in astronomical markings."

Really, I needed to get a look at that sphere.

"Thorne planned to position it at Karnak Temple during the solstice sunrise in three days," Lady Blackwood explained, warming to her role as chief enthusiast. "He believed the markings would interact with the alignment to reveal coordinates of other ancient observatories around the world!"

"All connected," Foster drawled, "in a vast network created by his imaginary 'Stellar People.'"

"That's why I arranged this gathering," Lady Blackwood continued, shooting Foster a quelling look. "So, Jasper could demonstrate his theories to influential figures in archaeology."

"And now both Thorne and the sphere are gone." Hassan's voice cut like a blade. "How convenient."

"Not so convenient for Thorne," Quinn murmured.

I bit back a completely inappropriate laugh. Trust Quinn to find gallows humor in a murder investigation.

"The theory was controversial," Whitmore offered, his precise tone suggesting this was a dramatic understatement.

"Controversial?" Yasmin surged to her feet. "It was colonial erasure at its finest! Dismissing Egyptian achievements by crediting everything to some mythical earlier civilization. As though we couldn't possibly have developed astronomical knowledge ourselves!"

"And why, exactly, did Lord Blackwood give this artifact to Jasper Thorne?"

Hassan was holding onto the thread well, considering the chaotic delivery of the information.

Lady Blackwood's jaw tightened. She opened her mouth, then closed it again.

"Charles—Lord Blackwood—gave it to him—" Montague continued when she remained silent. "On his deathbed, I believe?"

"Yes." Lady Blackwood's voice had sharpened considerably. "Apparently, Charles told him, 'This belongs with someone who truly understands its significance.'"

Hmmm. Was she more upset about losing her husband or losing the artifact?

Hassan scowled. "So. A valuable Egyptian artifact was gifted to a foreign academic by a dying British aristocrat who had no clear right to it in the first place."

Lady Blackwood's spine stiffened. "My husband's collection was legally acquired—"

"Was it?" Hassan's tone could have dehydrated the Nile. "Regardless, the police must be persuaded to investigate more thoroughly."

His lip curled as he glanced around the room. "This 'Astral Sphere,' as you dramatically call it—a ludicrous name fit for those sensational newspaper stories about curses and revenge— must still be in this house. Someone here has it."

Tension in Drawing Room (Acute), Notable Characteristics: Collective guilty shuffling, averted gazes.

"Perhaps," Hassan continued with deadly softness, "the police should search everyone's belongings."

No one objected, though the chorus of uncomfortable throat-clearing suggested several people might have reasons to prefer their luggage remain private.

"An excellent suggestion," I said brightly, earning several startled looks. "In fact, why not start with whatever Professor Whitmore removed from Thorne's jacket pocket last night?"

The resulting silence was profound enough to be measured in geological time.

Whitmore's hand twitched toward his own jacket before he caught himself. His mask of academic detachment cracked just enough to reveal something darker beneath.

"I'm certain I don't know what you mean, Dr. Bell."

"No?" I smiled with all the warmth of a cobra. "How fascinating. Because I distinctly remember watching you rifle through a dead man's pockets with rather impressive expertise."

The corner of Quinn's mouth twitched upward, and I felt an absurd flutter of pride at his approval.

Hassan's eyes narrowed to obsidian chips. "Professor Whitmore? Your response?"

For a long moment, the only sound was the Yasmin's shoe tapping against the floor.

Then Richard's voice cut through the tension: "I say, all of this is much more exciting than anything happening in New York. Clarissa, no wonder you can't get enough of this place!"

I could feel Quinn's silent laughter beside me.

Some things, it seemed, never changed. Including Richard's impeccable timing for saying exactly the wrong thing at exactly the wrong moment.

CHAPTER EIGHT

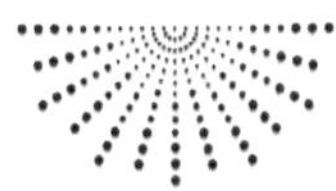

The sunlight streaming through Thorne's bedroom window did little to dispel the unsettling atmosphere. Even his possessions seemed restless, scattered across every surface as though searching for escape.

"Someone's been here before us." Quinn's voice carried the same conclusion I'd reached. He crouched to examine scuff marks on the floor where the heavy wardrobe had clearly been moved and inexpertly replaced.

"Hassan and Lady Blackwood, searching for the Astral Sphere perhaps?" But even as I suggested it, something felt off about the scene. The disarray was too... thorough.

"Notice how the papers are stacked?" Quinn gestured to the desk. "Deliberately messy, as though someone wanted it to look like casual disorder."

I nodded, cataloging the details. Books on shelves slightly askew, dresser drawers not quite flush. "Like when my mother's maid 'straightens' my research notes and tries to make them look 'charmingly disheveled.'"

His laugh poured slow and rich, smoothing the edges off the room. "Somehow I doubt your notes have ever been charming. Brilliant, maddening, possibly dangerous—but never charming."

"You forgot 'thoroughly correct.'"

"Never that either."

His voice dropped to a timbre that narrowed the distance between us. The ever-present scent of him, sandalwood and leather and something uniquely Quinn, wrapped around me like an embrace. Sometimes my sense of smell was a curse.

Focus, Clarissa.

"Whitmore, perhaps? His explanation downstairs, about looking for identification in Jasper's pockets after he collapsed, didn't exactly have the ring of truth."

"Agreed."

"These astronomical calculations..." I rifled through the papers, grateful for the distraction. "They're actually quite sophisticated, despite his theories. And look—notes about the blue pigment on the sphere."

Quinn leaned closer, his chest brushing my shoulder. "Interesting timing, given our Operation Indigo investigation. Another artifact with potentially significant blue pigment, another death."

"But what's the connection?"

"I think Thorne may have stumbled onto something far more dangerous than ancient astronomy." His breath stirred the hair at my temple. "Whether he knew it or not."

The memory of our last investigation together rose unbidden. The mystery of my stolen scribal palette, my mentor Dr. Sutherland's murder, and that moment in Giza when professional boundaries had blurred beneath the desert sun.

I reached for a higher shelf, and Quinn's hand settled on my waist, steadying me. The touch sent energy skittering across my skin.

"You never answered my letters properly," he murmured. "Eight months of correspondence, and not one mention of that morning in Giza."

"We agreed to keep it professional." But my voice sounded unconvincing even to my own ears.

"Did we?" His fingers traced idle patterns at my hip. "I remember a rather different kind of agreement being reached."

"Quinn..." The warning in my tone was undermined by the way my breath caught as he moved closer.

"I've missed watching you catalog everything in sight." His voice dropped lower, intimate. "The way your mind works, always sorting and filing. Tell me, Clarissa, how do you classify this?"

He gently turned me to face him, and his other hand came up to brush a strand of hair from my cheek. The room suddenly felt entirely too small. Every point of contact between us sparked with awareness.

"Under *Ill-Advised Investigative Collaborations,*" I managed, looking away from his eyes.

"Really?" His smile held dangerous promise. "I'd have filed it under *Unfinished Business.*"

The space between us crackled with tension, his hand still cupping my face. I should step away. Should maintain the boundaries we'd agreed upon. Should remember that Richard was somewhere in this house, complicating everything.

Instead, I found myself leaning into his touch.

"Clarissa."

The way he said my name... like a prayer and a promise.

His restraint felt dangerous, like a man holding back more strength than he dared show.

"I've thought about you every day since Giza. Every morning I've awakened, every deal I've negotiated, every sunset over the dig sites."

"Quinn..." The protest died as his thumb traced my lower lip.

"Tell me you haven't thought about it, too. About us."

The honest answer would destroy my composure. Because I had thought about it—about him—far more than my "professional distance" should allow. The way he'd kissed me that morning, desperate and tender and entirely consuming. The strength of his hands, the heat of his mouth, the way he'd whispered my name—

"I came back to Egypt for Operation Indigo," I said instead, though the words felt hollow.

"Of course you did." His smile held dangerous affection. "Always the dedicated scholar. But you left word for me at Shepheard's."

"Simple courtesy." The repetition of this claim was beginning to feel false.

"That's all?" He leaned closer, backing me against the desk.

Breath snagged as his hands planted on either side of me, hemming me in against the desk. "Richard's arrival complicates things."

"Hmm, yes." Something dark flickered across his features. "Interesting timing, don't you think? Arriving mere hours after a murder?"

"You suspect Richard?" The idea was absurd. Wasn't it?

"I suspect everyone, Clarissa. It's kept me alive thus far." His voice carried an edge I'd rarely heard before. "But your former fiancé's sudden appearance, claiming he wants to whisk you back to New York? After you only left there days ago?"

"He mentioned business interests. Something about the Tutankhamun discovery making Egypt fashionable."

"Convenient." Quinn's jaw tightened. "And his interest in your father's 'acquisition' work?"

Before I could answer, his nearness crowded out rational thought—the clean scent of his soap, the solid line of him.

"Clarissa." Barely a whisper now.

His head dipped toward mine, and I forgot everything else —Richard, the investigation, the proper behavior expected of Oxford-trained archaeologists. There was only Quinn, and the spark between us, and the memory of how perfectly I'd fit in his arms that morning in Giza.

Our lips were a breath apart when the door burst open.

"There you are, baby!"

I jumped, startled, and clutched at Quinn's shirt. His hands dropped automatically to steady me, fingers splaying across my waist with intimate familiarity.

Richard stood framed in the doorway, his smile bright and proprietary. If he noticed our compromising position, he gave no sign.

"I've been looking everywhere for you! Though I should have guessed you'd be playing detective." He strode into the room with the confidence of someone who'd never questioned his welcome anywhere. "Hello there, Quinn, was it? Fancy finding you here, too."

Quinn's hands remained at my waist a heartbeat longer than strictly necessary before he stepped back, his expression shuttering into polite neutrality.

"Mr. Sullivan." His tone carried ice. "Brilliant."

"Isn't it just?" Richard's grin widened as he moved to my side, his hand settling possessively on my upper arm. "Though, I have to say darling, this whole murder business is rather sordid. Surely someone else can handle the unpleasant details?"

I twisted away from his touch. "I'm perfectly capable of conducting an investigation, thank you."

"Of course you are! That marvelous mind of yours." He beamed at me like I was a clever child who'd just recited her alphabet. "But really, Clarissa, is this the sort of thing you want to be involved in? What would your mother say?"

"My mother," I said through gritted teeth, "is in New York. Where you should be."

"Ah, but that's where you're wrong!" Richard's eyes sparkled with triumph. "I'm here on business. Very important business that could benefit us both."

Quinn shifted away, leaning back against the window frame. The gesture appeared casual, but I recognized the alertness beneath his urbane exterior.

"What sort of business?" I asked, though something in Richard's manner made my stomach clench.

"Well, that's what I wanted to discuss privately." Richard shot a meaningful look at Quinn. "Family matters, you understand."

The dismissal was clear, and Quinn's smile turned razor-sharp. "Of course. How thoughtless of me to intrude on such an intimate reunion."

He moved toward the door with fluid grace, pausing only

to brush my shoulder with his fingertips—a touch so brief it might have been accidental.

"Clarissa." His voice carried layers of meaning. "Do be careful."

Then he was gone, leaving me alone with Richard and the uncomfortable weight of everything unsaid between himself and me.

Richard watched the door shut with satisfaction. "I don't like that fellow. Something shifty about him, don't you think? All that mysterious antiquities dealing—probably not entirely legitimate."

The irony of Richard questioning anyone's legitimacy wasn't lost on me, but I filed it away for later analysis.

"What do you want, Richard?"

His smile softened, taking on the boyish charm that had once made my heart flutter. Now it only made me wary.

"Can't a man want to see the woman he loves? Especially when she's gotten herself mixed up in murder and mayhem in foreign countries?"

"Former woman," I corrected automatically. "And I can take care of myself."

"Can you?" His hand found mine, tightening around my fingers. "Because from where I'm standing, it looks like you're playing with fire. And not just with mysterious antiquities dealers."

CHAPTER NINE

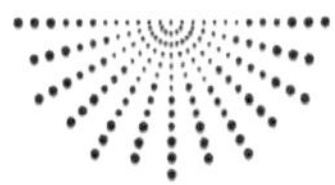

I bristled at Richard's familiar touch and pulled my hand free. "My personal relationships are none of your concern."

"Aren't they?" Richard's expression grew serious. "Clarissa, I came here to bring you home. Your father's worried sick, and frankly, so am I. This archaeology business was supposed to be a brief adventure, not a permanent life change."

The breezy and pretentious slang he'd lately adopted had slipped from his voice like a discarded mask. What remained was something rawer, almost pleading. But still, the familiar frustration reared its head. Dead pharaohs told more interesting stories than Richard's same-old retread, that my life's work was merely a phase to be outgrown.

"Last I checked, Richard, you were the son of my father's business partner. Since when are you on Armand Bell's payroll?"

He moved to the window, his silhouette backlit against the harsh Egyptian sun. For a moment, he looked exactly as he had that summer afternoon when he'd first called on me at Father's Newport house—confident, handsome, utterly certain of his place in the world.

"Do you remember that morning at the Frick Collection?"

His voice carried a wistful note I'd rarely heard before. "You spent thirty minutes explaining the brushwork in that Whistler portrait, and I thought I'd never heard anything more fascinating in my life."

Despite myself, the usual fondness flickered somewhere deep. I did remember—how earnestly I'd lectured him about pigment analysis while he listened with apparent rapt attention.

"You said you were going to revolutionize art authentication," Richard continued, turning from the window with that boyish smile. "Make all the old museum directors sit up and take notice. And look at you now—digging in sand like an Egyptian laborer! Is this truly what you mean to do with your life?"

The comment hit closer to home than I cared to admit. "My work is respected."

"Is it, though?" Richard stepped closer, his expression growing concerned. "From what I can see, you're still playing second fiddle to men who take credit for your insights. Like that Quinn fellow."

My spine stiffened. "Benedict has never—"

"Hasn't he?" Richard's voice dropped to the intimate tone he'd once used to share secrets. "Think about it, Clarissa. Eight months of letter-writing, and what do you have to show for it? Meanwhile, he's traveling freely, making deals, building his reputation while you return to sort pottery sherds in the desert."

Richard had clearly been speaking with my parents. But the observation stung because it held an uncomfortable grain of truth. While Quinn's letters had been entertaining, our investigation had yielded frustratingly little progress.

"That's not how scholarly collaboration works." I hated the uncertainty that had crept into my voice.

"Is it collaboration?" Richard moved closer, his hand finding my elbow. "Or are you doing the intellectual heavy lifting while he reaps the benefits? Remember Professor

Fairchild at Oxford—how she published your research without any credit?"

Of course I remembered.

But I'd been naive then, trusting a mentor who'd seen my work as a stepping stone to her own advancement.

"Benedict isn't Rosamund Fairchild."

"Perhaps not." Richard's thumb stroked my arm through the fabric of my sleeve. "But what do you actually know about Quinn's background, darling? His business dealings, his funding sources, his real agenda?"

The questions he posed were ones I'd asked myself countless times during those long months of correspondence. Quinn's letters were charming, flirtatious, occasionally insightful—but rarely revealing about his actual work or methods.

"He was helpful in my previous investigation—"

"Or has he been managing you?" Richard's voice carried gentle concern, but his words landed like poisoned arrows. "Stringing you along, staying close so he has access to research, perhaps?"

"That's..." I started to protest, then stopped.

"I know this is difficult to hear." Richard's other hand stroked my face with familiar tenderness. "But I've seen how brilliant you are when you're thinking clearly, without distractions."

The comparison made me flush with confused irritation. I had been proud of that work, proud of my independent analysis before Quinn's magnetic presence had... what? Compromised my scholarly objectivity?

"You're suggesting Quinn is deliberately misleading me?"

"I'm suggesting that a man who makes his living in the gray areas between legal and illegal antiquities dealing might have his own agenda." Richard's voice remained gentle, but something hard underlay his words.

A cool prickle climbed my neck as unwelcome doubts slipped under my guard. Quinn's mysterious funding sources. His expertise in whatever topic I happened to be researching.

The way he'd deflected my questions about his past with charm and flirtation.

"Besides," Richard continued, his thumb tracing my cheekbone, "what kind of man pursues an engaged woman? Even a temporarily estranged one?"

"We aren't temporarily estranged," I protested weakly. "I broke our engagement."

"You weren't thinking clearly." His smile held fond confidence. "We both said things we didn't mean. But that doesn't give him the right to take advantage of your emotional vulnerability."

The casual dismissal of my decision should have rekindled my anger. Instead, exhaustion washed over me. The weight of constantly defending my choices, my work, my right to make my own decisions.

"I just want what's best for you, darling." Richard's hands framed my face now, his touch achingly familiar. "Your father does too. We both know how extraordinary you are, how much you could accomplish with the right support. But this Quinn character... a woman of your caliber deserves better than mysterious men with questionable ethics."

"His ethics aren't—" But was I defending Quinn or trying to convince myself?

"Clarissa, you're brilliant, but you've always been too trusting. Too willing to see the best in people who might not deserve it. It's one of the things I love about you, but it also leaves you vulnerable to manipulation."

There it was. The familiar pattern I'd learned to recognize too late during our engagement. *Compliment my intelligence, then immediately undermine my judgment. Make me feel special, then suggest I'm naive. Frame control as protection.*

If only I could publish a paper on the mating habits of condescending men. The field work alone would merit a grant.

"So then, what are you suggesting I do?"

"Come home." Richard's voice filled with warm conviction. "To people who genuinely care about your welfare. Your father has connections that could advance your career properly, legitimately. No more shadowy dealings or mysterious benefactors. No more uncertainty about whether someone's helping or using you."

The offer hung between us like a lifeline—or a trap. Safety, certainty, the familiar comfort of a world where my place was clearly defined, even if that place felt increasingly constraining.

"I can't just abandon my work here."

"You're not abandoning anything," Richard assured me. "You're choosing to focus your talents where they'll be properly appreciated. Where you won't have to wonder whether your research partner has ulterior motives."

His words wrapped around the doubts I'd been trying to ignore, giving them shape and substance. Was I really that naive? That easily influenced by a charming smile and practiced seduction techniques?

The thought made me burn with humiliation—and something dangerously close to anger at Quinn for making me question my own judgment once again.

A bell chimed somewhere in the house, calling us to the midday meal.

I shook off the angst. "Perhaps we should rejoin the others. Inspector Hassan already seems to suspect your timing."

Richard's face darkened for just a moment before the charming mask slipped back into place. "Of course. Though I do hope we'll have time to discuss your future properly. Away from all these distractions."

His gaze lingered on the door through which Quinn had vanished, and I realized the battle lines had been drawn.

Yes, people are complex, capable of containing contradictions. Richard genuinely believed he was helping me. He truly thought his protective instincts justified his controlling behavior. Both things were simultaneously true.

But here was the lesson I was still learning: understanding his motives didn't mean I should trust him with my decisions.

CHAPTER TEN

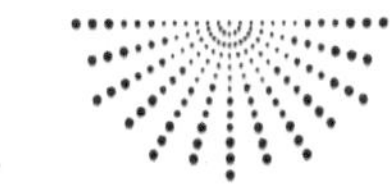

The dining room had undergone a remarkable transformation since last night's deadly dinner party. Gone were the formal place settings and dripping candles. In their place, Lady Blackwood had engineered a more casual affair—a buffet arranged along the mahogany sideboard, with platters of grilled lamb, rice pilaf studded with almonds, and delicate pastries that would have been perfectly appetizing if not for the lingering specter of murder.

I'd attended livelier funerals. Without the buffet.

The servants moved with the nervous energy of cats in a thunderstorm. Laila arranged and rearranged the serving spoons with trembling hands, while Freddie polished specks off already gleaming silver.

I filled my plate with deliberate calm, selecting items that required no cutting implements. Call it overcautious, but dining with potential murderers had made me wary of anything sharper than a butter knife.

It did rather simplify menu choices. Nothing with bones, shells... Pudding it was.

I turned to sit, and saw two figures approaching from opposite directions with the determined stride of territorial animals converging on the same watering hole.

Richard materialized at my right elbow with the smooth efficiency of a practiced maître d', his hand already reaching for the chair back nearest the window.

"Right here, darling." His smile radiated proprietary confidence as he pulled out the seat with flourish. "Perfect lighting to show off your beauty."

Before I could respond, Quinn's voice drifted from my left shoulder like smoke from expensive tobacco.

"Actually, Dr. Bell? I believe we were in the middle of discussing those pigment samples?"

I turned to find him standing several chairs down the table from Richard's selection, his posture casual.

At the head of the table, Lady Blackwood watched this territorial standoff with barely concealed delight. Her eyes sparkled with the same anticipation I'd seen in Cairo audiences watching cobra-and-mongoose demonstrations.

Clearly, she had no intention of assigning seats and spoiling her entertainment.

"Gentlemen." I surveyed both options. "How thoughtful of you both to be so concerned about my seating arrangement."

The standoff escalated as neither man moved. Richard's hand remained on his chosen chair while Quinn's fingers drummed once against the seatback—which meant he was calculating odds and angles.

I selected the chair directly between their offerings and settled myself with deliberate grace, leaving them to flank me like competing bodyguards.

"There." I spread my napkin with satisfaction. "Diplomacy in action."

Richard recovered first, sliding into the seat on one side, while Quinn claimed the other.

The other guests trickled in to fill plates at the sideboard and seats at the table.

Yasmin caught sight of our triangular arrangement and raised one eloquent eyebrow.

Lady Blackwood settled into her chair with the satisfied air of a theater director. "Now then, isn't this cozy? Nothing like good company to lift our spirits after yesterday's unfortunate events."

Her deliberate understatement would have made me laugh if I weren't trapped between two men radiating enough tension to power the electric lights at Shepheard's Hotel.

We'd barely begun the meal when Laila appeared again in the doorway, her face flushed with what appeared to be equal parts exertion and terror.

Freddie followed, bearing a tray and setting it on the table.

"Lady Blackwood, ma'am." She executed a quick curtsy. "I must report a small incident in the kitchen."

"Oh?" Lady Blackwood settled her fork beside her plate. "Nothing serious, I hope?"

"A fire, ma'am. Very small, very contained. Only the bread for this afternoon's service was affected." Laila's voice dropped to barely above a whisper. "But ma'am... it was only the bread shaped like ankhs that burned. The regular loaves were untouched, sitting right beside them in the same oven."

A collective intake of breath circled the table like a contagious yawn.

"The curse!" Freddie crossed himself with enough vigor to qualify as exercise. *(Was he even Catholic?)* "The gods are angry about Dr. Thorne's theories!"

Harrison Foster leaned forward. "Gosh, perhaps we *should* all take these ancient warnings more seriously. After all, mysterious deaths, missing artifacts, and now selective divine intervention in the kitchen?"

"Divine intervention?" I couldn't keep the skepticism from my voice. "Or perhaps uneven oven temperatures and the basic properties of different bread shapes affecting heat distribution?"

"You didn't see it, miss." Laila's eyes were wide as saucers. "Perfect ankh shapes, all of them, burned black as charcoal. The curse paper said the gods would take their revenge, and now—"

"Now we have a minor baking mishap," I interrupted

firmly. "Which can be explained by any number of rational factors, starting with—"

"What if Jasper disturbed something that should have remained hidden?" Lady Blackwood's voice rose with mounting hysteria. "What if the Astral Sphere was meant to stay buried? What if his theories about the Stellar People offended the actual gods?"

What was it with everyone's preoccupation with curses? Why did rational thought abandon educated minds like rats fleeing a sinking ship, at the first sign of anything unpleasant?

"This is absolutely ridiculous!" The words burst out before I could stop them. "A man was poisoned with cyanide extracted from apricot pits by a very human murderer with very earthly motives. It has nothing to do with supernatural vengeance or divine retribution or whatever mythological explanation you're constructing to avoid facing reality!"

My outburst sent ripples of shocked silence around the table. Every face turned toward me with expressions ranging from wounded reproach to open fascination.

Great. Now I was the voice of reason against mounting superstition.

Into the awkward silence following my outburst, Richard's voice dropped like honey from a silver spoon.

"Of course, Clarissa is right to demand rational explanations." He cut his lamb like it was surgery, each movement calculated. "My own extensive research into Egyptian sea routes has taught me the importance of evidence-based conclusions."

Quinn's fork paused halfway to his mouth. "Fascinating. I wasn't aware real estate acquisition required knowledge of Ptolemaic maritime commerce."

The temperature in the room seemed to drop several degrees.

"Naturally, any serious property investment in Egypt demands thorough historical research." Richard's smile could have cut glass. "One must understand the cultural significance of sites before making recommendations to discerning clients.

Unlike certain… freelance operators who seem to work without institutional oversight."

Specimen: Masculine Verbal Combat (Escalating), Notable Characteristics: Archaeological terminology weaponized for maximum damage.

"Indeed." Quinn's voice carried the deceptive calm of a cat tensing before the leap.. "Though some of us prefer fieldwork to drinks party theorizing. There's something to be said for actually getting one's hands dirty in service of scholarship."

"Oh, I'm sure your hands see plenty of action." Richard's tone suggested this wasn't entirely a compliment. "Though one does wonder about the mysterious funding sources behind such… unconventional methods. Don't legitimate scholars generally rely on institutional backing rather than private arrangements?"

The verbal thrust hit its mark. A muscle jumped in Quinn's jaw, though his smile never wavered.

"True. Though private funding allows for more… flexible approaches to ethical acquisition. Fewer committee meetings about whether preserving artifacts is more important than procedures."

"Ethical acquisition?" Richard laughed, the sound carrying just enough disbelief to sting. "How refreshingly modern. In my experience, collectors who operate outside established channels often find themselves explaining their methods to uncomfortable authorities."

Quinn set down his fork. "Speaking of uncomfortable authorities, how exactly did you manage to travel from New York to Egypt with such remarkable timing? One might almost think you'd been planning this trip for some time."

"One might think many things." Richard's hand found mine on the table, his thumb stroking the back of my hand. "Though I'd be more curious about antiquities dealers who seem to appear wherever certain attractive archaeologists happen to be conducting research."

I retrieved my hand and folded my napkin into a narrow band, then placed the knife blade neatly on it.

"Perhaps," I forced lightness into my voice, "we might discuss something else?"

Around the table, our audience watched with the fascinated horror of spectators at a gladiatorial match. Montague had given up all pretense of eating, while Lady Blackwood's eyes sparkled with malicious delight. Even Foster had stopped smirking, apparently recognizing that the entertainment had evolved into something more dangerous.

Lady Blackwood finally clapped her hands like a theater director calling for scene change.

"Enough scholarly debate!" Her voice cut through the charged atmosphere. "All this intellectual sparring is giving me quite the headache. Tonight, we shall have dancing—something to lift our spirits after yesterday's dreadful events!"

She beamed around the table as though she'd just announced the cure for malaria rather than an evening of forced merriment in a house that still contained a murderer.

"Dancing?" Foster's eyebrows climbed toward his hairline. "Given the circumstances, isn't that rather—"

"Rather necessary," Lady Blackwood interrupted firmly. "We cannot allow tragedy to completely overwhelm civilized behavior. Music, movement, celebration of life—these are the proper responses to death's intrusion."

I seized the momentary lull in masculine territorial disputes to assert some agency over my own investigation.

"Actually, I was hoping to visit Karnak Temple this afternoon. The connection between Thorne's theories and the winter solstice alignment seems worth examining, particularly if we're to understand his murder."

The words had barely left my mouth when both men erupted in simultaneous objection.

"Absolutely not!" Richard's hand slammed down on the table hard enough to make the water glasses jump. "Clarissa, you cannot seriously consider wandering around ancient ruins with a killer on the loose!"

"Far too dangerous," Quinn agreed, his rare harmony with Richard somehow more alarming than their previous antagonism. "Until we know who murdered Thorne and why, you shouldn't be anywhere near those temple sites."

I stared at them both with growing incredulity. "I beg your pardon?"

"Darling, be reasonable." Richard's voice took on the patronizing tone that had once made me throw a teacup at his head. "What if the killer followed the same logic? What if they're waiting at Karnak, knowing you'd want to investigate Thorne's astronomical nonsense?"

"He's right," Quinn said, the words seeming to pain him physically. "The temple complex is too sprawling and complicated, too many hiding places. If someone wants to silence witnesses or eliminate threats to their plans—"

"Then I'd be a sitting duck." The phrase tasted bitter on my tongue. "So, I must abandon my own investigation for my safety?"

"It's not abandonment," Richard insisted. "It's basic self-preservation. Let the authorities handle the dangerous work while you focus on—"

"On what?" I interrupted. "Arranging flowers? Planning dinner parties? Choosing appropriate dance partners for this evening's entertainment?"

The frustrated edge in my voice seemed to surprise both men. Quinn's expression shifted toward something that might have been remorse, while Richard's confidence flickered momentarily.

"We only want to protect you," Quinn said quietly.

"From what? Making my own decisions about my own research?" I pushed back from the table, my chair scraping against the floor with satisfying violence. "How remarkably thoughtful of you both to manage my choices so I don't have to trouble myself with independent thought."

Lady Blackwood's dramatic sigh drew all attention back to the head of the table.

"Well! Perhaps we might all benefit from some rest before tonight's festivities? Dancing always goes more smoothly when tempers have had time to cool."

She rose from her chair with regal finality, effectively ending the meal and our argument.

Between Richard's protective possessiveness and Quinn's strategic caution, my role had somehow shifted from lead investigator to protected asset. The evening's planned activities loomed before me less like entertainment and more like an elaborate distraction—another performance where I'd be expected to dance to someone else's choreography.

The question was whether I'd allow them to lead, or if I'd finally insist on choosing my own steps.

Even if those steps led directly into danger.

CHAPTER ELEVEN

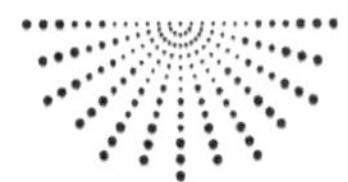

*I*n the end, my decision was made for me, as I had no way of reaching Karnak on my own, and Lady Black-wood would not arrange an auto for me.

By evening, she had transformed the Salon into what could charitably be called a "festive gathering space," though the overall effect of the Christmas-meets-Ancient-Egypt decor, which had seemed merely eccentric in daylight, now appeared positively grotesque in the flickering candlelight. The decorated palm tree cast shadows that resembled grasping claws, while the gilt Egyptian gods seemed to leer from their perches among the cypress boughs. Even the scent of frankincense, meant to evoke sacred mystery, now carried undertones of funeral preparation.

"Music!" Lady Blackwood clapped her hands with manic enthusiasm. "We simply must have music. Freddie, wind the gramophone!"

The poor boy fumbled with the mechanism. The scratchy opening notes of "Yes! We Have No Bananas" filled the air—a tune so relentlessly cheerful it bordered on offensive.

Inspector Hassan had returned, and stood near the fire-place once more like a disapproving sphinx, his presence a constant reminder that we were all potential murderers rather than holiday guests. He'd come to ask more questions, but somehow acquiesced to Lady Blackwood's insistence he stay for "protection" and ask his questions later.

I suspected she simply found the drama irresistible.

"Surely we could manage something more... appropriate?" Montague suggested gently.

"Nonsense!" Lady Blackwood's voice pitched higher. "Poor Jasper would have wanted us to celebrate life. And the solstice approaches—we must mark these momentous days!"

A reckless idea crossed my mind. If we were all going to pretend this was a normal social gathering rather than a murder investigation, why shouldn't Egypt's most rigid antiquities inspector join the charade?

I approached him with what Mother would have called "inappropriate determination"—which is to say, the kind that gets things done.

"Inspector Hassan." I extended my hand with my brightest smile. "Could you spare a dance? Even official guardians need occasional entertainment."

His expression suggested I'd just proposed we raid the British Museum while dressed as dancing girls.

"Dr. Bell," he replied, each word carved from ice, "I am not here for... entertainment."

"Oh, come now. One dance won't compromise Egyptian governmental authority. Besides, you might overhear something useful if you actually moved around the room instead of glowering at everyone from over here."

Something flickered in his eyes—surprise, perhaps.

"I do not dance."

"Hmm. Well, your loss, Inspector." I tilted my head, studying him. "Though I suspect you'd be quite good at it. All that rigid posture and controlled movement—perfect for a waltz."

For just a moment, I could have sworn I saw the corner of his mouth twitch.

Small victories.

Richard materialized at my elbow with two glasses of champagne, having somehow procured evening wear that fit him perfectly. The man could locate a decent tailor in the middle of the ocean.

"May I have this dance, doll?" His smile held all the charm that had once made New York debutantes swoon at cotillions. "For old time's sake?"

Before I could decline, Quinn appeared on my other side, equally elegant in black tie that emphasized his dark hair and those fascinating brownish-gold eyes.

"I believe the lady promised me the first dance." His tone remained perfectly cordial while managing to suggest Richard might spontaneously combust if he pressed the issue.

"Actually, I haven't promised anyone—"

"Oh, but darling," Richard interrupted, sliding his arm around my waist with practiced ease, "surely you remember how beautifully we danced at the Astors' Christmas ball? Right before our engagement announcement?"

The reminder hit like a slap. That ball, where he'd swept me onto the dance floor and whispered sweet promises about our future while Mother beamed from the sidelines. Two weeks later, I'd discovered his "promises" included managing my inheritance and steering my "little archaeological hobby" toward something more socially acceptable.

Quinn's jaw tightened almost imperceptibly. "Engagement announcement? How fascinating. I wasn't aware Dr. Bell was in the habit of making promises she didn't intend to keep."

"She keeps the promises that matter," Richard replied smoothly, guiding me toward the makeshift dance floor as Freddie switched the gramophone's tune to a waltz. "Don't you, sweetheart?"

My feet moved automatically through the familiar steps, the muscle memory from countless society functions overriding my desire to plant my heel firmly on Richard's instep. His hand pressed possessively against my back, exactly as it had during those long-ago evenings when I'd mistaken his confidence for strength.

"You look beautiful tonight," he murmured, leading me through a turn that brought us dangerously close to where Quinn stood watching. "That dress always was my favorite."

The emerald green beaded chiffon had been Richard's choice, purchased during our engagement for a Metropolitan Opera gala. I'd worn it tonight because Annie had packed it, not from any sentiment. Though watching Quinn's eyes darken as they tracked the dress's lines made me grateful for the selection.

A moment later, Quinn cut in with the smoothness of a professional dancer—or a man accustomed to taking what he wanted.

"May I?" He didn't wait for Richard's permission, simply stepped between us and claimed my hand.

The difference was immediate and startling. Where Richard had guided with presumptuous familiarity, Quinn moved with attention to my preferences. His touch remained light but sure, his steps perfectly matched to mine without the subtle pressure to follow his lead.

"Enjoying the performance?" His voice carried gentle irony as he spun me away from Richard's glowering presence.

"Which one? The forced festivities or the territorial display?"

He chuckled. "I suppose both are equally performative." He pulled me closer as we navigated around Foster, who was attempting to charm Dr. Mujahid with stories of his latest acquisitions.

The waltz ended, but before Quinn could release me, Richard appeared again.

"My turn," he announced, already reaching for my waist. "We have so much to catch up on. Like our spring wedding plans."

I felt Quinn stiffen beside me. "Wedding plans?"

Richard's smile turned smug. "Didn't she mention? We've decided to make it official this spring. Haven't we, darling?"

Heat flooded my face—part fury, part mortification. "We most certainly have not—"

Quinn's hand fell away from mine, his expression neutral. "How... definitive."

"Well, when you know, you know." Richard's arm snaked around my waist again, proprietary and confident. "Besides, this little Egyptian adventure has run its course. Time for Clarissa to come home and focus on more suitable pursuits."

Quinn watched my face, reading every emotion with uncomfortable accuracy. I could see him filing this interaction under some mental category—probably *Professional Partnership (Terminated)* or *Romantic Complications (Resolved)*.

The thought of losing his respect, his partnership, his— whatever this was between us—made my breath catch.

"Richard," I said, my voice carrying the granite Mother had trained into me for dealing with presumptuous suitors, "we need to talk. Privately."

But even as I spoke, I caught Hassan's sharp gaze tracking our conversation with the intensity of a hawk spotting prey.

"Later," I turned from Richard, as Lady Blackwood began her hand-clapping again.

"Entertainment! We must have entertainment. Who among us possesses hidden talents worth sharing?"

The collective groan was nearly audible, though everyone maintained proper social facades.

"Mr. Foster," she declared, "I've heard you're quite accomplished with the playing cards?"

Foster rose with the smooth confidence of a man accustomed to performance. He produced a card deck from his jacket pocket—suspiciously convenient—and proceeded to execute a series of tricks that involved making cards vanish, reappear, and generally behave in ways that defied both physics and my patience.

"The Queen of Hearts," he announced with a theatrical flourish, pulling the card from behind Yasmin's ear.

Yasmin did not appear amused.

"Marvelous!" Lady Blackwood applauded. "Who will be next?"

Montague stood with the self-conscious dignity of a

scholar drafted into unwanted performance. "I suppose I could offer a brief passage from *The Odyssey*? The original Greek, naturally."

What followed was rather beautiful—his voice taking on a rhythmic quality as ancient Greek rolled from his tongue with obvious affection. Even without understanding the words, one could hear the poetry in them, the way Homer's lines had been crafted for oral recitation across millennia.

"Book Five," he concluded modestly. "Odysseus departing Calypso's island."

"How perfectly lovely," Eleanor beamed and studied each of us, searching for her next victim.

I didn't make eye contact, which might have been dangerous.

"Dr. Mujahid, what about you?"

Yasmin hesitated, then smiled. "I could tell a brief folktale? One my grandmother shared about a clever mouse who outwitted a cat."

She launched into the story with surprising flair, her voice shifting seamlessly between characters. The mouse squeaked with high-pitched cunning, the cat rumbled with pompous authority, and an old village woman cackled with knowing wisdom. Each voice was distinct, perfectly pitched, utterly convincing.

I found myself genuinely entertained despite the absurdity of our situation—sitting in a house with potential murderers, listening to a children's story.

"The mouse, you see," Yasmin concluded in the old woman's creaky voice, "understood that cleverness comes in small packages, while arrogance comes in large ones."

The room applauded with genuine appreciation.

Hassan still stood near the French doors, and his expression suggested he'd reached the end of his considerable patience.

I drifted his direction. "Inspector Hassan, not in the mood for entertainment?"

"This is intolerable." His voice cut through the music as he addressed the room at large. "All of you flitting about as though you agree with the local police, that Thorne's death was by 'natural causes brought on by excitement.'"

Lady Blackwood's fan fluttered more rapidly. "Surely that's... a good thing? Perhaps poor Jasper simply had a weak heart—"

"A weak heart that happened to fail immediately after consuming cyanide? The same evening a priceless artifact disappears from his possession?"

Quinn slipped beside me with a glass of lemonade, his movements casual but his eyes alert. "What exactly are you proposing we do, Inspector?"

"I am proposing to do what the local authorities will not." Hassan's gaze swept over each of us in turn. "I will investigate this matter myself, starting with the missing Astral Sphere. Someone in this room knows where it is."

Foster laughed, the sound sharp as breaking glass. "You're an antiquities inspector, not a detective. What makes you think—"

"What makes me think? A man is dead, and Egypt's cultural heritage has been stolen." Hassan stepped closer to Harrison Foster, who suddenly found his champagne glass fascinating. "Two crimes that often go together in my experience."

Richard chose that moment to rejoin our little group, sliding his arm around my shoulders with the presumption of ownership. "Now see here, old fellow. You can't seriously suspect any of us. We're all respectable people."

"Respectable people," Hassan repeated, his tone suggesting he'd found something unpleasant on his shoe. "How reassuring. And what, Mr. Sullivan, makes you particularly respectable?"

The question hung in the air like incense smoke, heavy and accusatory. Richard's arm tightened around me.

"I represent prominent American business interests," Richard replied. "My connections are impeccable."

"Your connections." Hassan's smile held no warmth.

"How interesting. Tell me, do these connections include an interest in Egyptian antiquities?"

The atmosphere in the room shifted. Even the gramophone chose that moment to wind down, leaving us in a silence broken only by the whisper of desert wind and the distant cry of night birds.

I moved away from Richard, stepping close to Quinn.

Quinn's fingertips brushed mine, a touch so brief it might have been accidental.

I squared my shoulders; the room came back into proportion.

"Actually," Quinn's eyes glinted like obsidian blades, "Mr. Sullivan's connections to the antiquities trade are quite well-documented."

He produced a telegram from his jacket with the flourish that rivaled Foster's card tricks. The yellow paper crackled as he unfolded it, and I caught a glimpse of the Western Union header.

Richard Sullivan (Revised Classification), Notable Characteristics: Potential antiquities dealer, possible connection to Father's business interests, suspicious timing of arrival.

Richard's face went the color of limestone. "Now wait just a minute—"

"The telegram is quite clear." Quinn's tone remained conversational as he read aloud. "'Acquire sphere at any cost. Discretion essential. Funding arrangements confirmed. A. Bell.'"

The words hit me like a physical blow. Acquire... for my father.

Richard reached to snatch the telegram from Quinn's fingers. "You've been snooping through my—"

"You—" My voice came out as barely a whisper. "You didn't come here to win me back."

Richard's hand fell away from the telegram. "Clarissa, darling, listen to me—"

"You *do* work for him. And you came for Father's artifact

collection." The pieces clicked into place. "This was never about us. It was only about business."

"Both things can be true!" Richard's composure finally cracked, revealing the desperation beneath his polished exterior. "I do love you, Clarissa. But yes, your father asked me to handle some business while I was here. The two aren't mutually exclusive."

Hassan stepped forward, his presence suddenly far more threatening than that of a mere antiquities inspector. "So, you admit to having business interests in Egyptian artifacts, Mr. Sullivan?"

"I admit to facilitating legal transactions between willing parties," Richard shot back, though sweat beaded on his forehead despite the evening's coolness. "There's nothing illegal about that."

"Legal perhaps," Hassan's smile resembled that of a crocodile spotting unwary prey. "But when combined with your arrival mere hours after Dr. Thorne's murder, and the subsequent disappearance of the very artifact mentioned in your telegram... well. That creates what we call 'compelling circumstances.'"

The spectators in the room were silent but taking it all in. Lady Blackwood's fan worked overtime as she fanned herself with increasing desperation. Dr. Mujahid and Professor Whitmore exchanged loaded glances. Foster's earlier smirk had vanished completely, replaced by what looked suspiciously like relief that Hassan's attention had shifted elsewhere.

But all I could focus on was the betrayal that burned like acid. Not just Richard's betrayal—though that was crushing enough—but the implications for my father's reputation, my family's honor, and my own judgment.

How could I have been so blind?

"Now see here," Richard sputtered, his lawyer instincts finally kicking in after being thoroughly blindsided. "You can't seriously believe I would murder someone over an artifact. I'm a businessman, not a—"

"Killer?" Hassan's eyebrow arched. "How reassuring. Though I notice you don't deny wanting the Astral Sphere."

"Of course I wanted it!" Richard's eyes flashed. "Armand Bell has been collecting Egyptian artifacts for twenty years. When he heard about Thorne's discovery through his contacts—"

"Father has contact with Dr. Thorne?" This revelation felt like discovering an extra chamber in a tomb you thought you'd completely mapped.

Richard's face paled. "Not... directly. But word travels in collector circles, and when someone claims to have found something that could revolutionize our understanding of ancient astronomy—"

"So, Father sent you to acquire it." I filed this under *Family Betrayals (Mounting Evidence).* "What were your instructions exactly? What exactly does 'acquire the sphere at any cost' mean?"

"Nothing like that!" But Richard's protest lacked conviction. "I was already here in Egypt—for business, and that—personal matter we discussed—when you telegrammed your father that you'd be visiting Luxor and meeting Dr. Thorne. He simply wanted me to make an offer. A generous offer. Completely legitimate."

Hassan stepped closer, and I noticed how Richard instinctively backed away. For an antiquities inspector, Hassan had a remarkable presence.

"And when Dr. Thorne refused your generous offer?" Hassan's tone could have etched glass.

"You *knew* I never got the chance to make it!" Richard's voice pitched higher with desperation. "I only arrived this morning, hours after the man was already dead!"

"So you say. But I, for one, do not believe you."

I glanced at my evening bag on a nearby chair, still holding the piece of Thorne's cup I'd kept wrapped in Quinn's monogrammed handkerchief.

This wasn't about social embarrassment or romantic

complications. A man was dead. And my family's reputation hung in the balance.

"Then I'll prove Richard's innocence myself," I heard myself say, my voice carrying more confidence than I felt. "And clear my father's name in the process."

Quinn's smile was barely visible, but I caught it. Admiration, mixed with something that might have been jealousy, flickered in his eyes.

Richard stared at me as if I'd sprouted hieroglyphs. "Clarissa, you can't be serious. Leave this to the professionals—"

"The professionals have already dismissed the murder as natural causes," I cut him off, my fury finally finding its voice. "And you—you lied to me from the moment you arrived. About your reasons for coming, about your feelings, about everything."

Quinn slid to my side. "Dr. Bell has already solved one murder conspiracy this year. Her methods are... unconventional, but effective."

The warmth in his voice when he said my name sent heat spiraling through me, even as Richard's face darkened with something between jealousy and rage.

Lady Blackwood clapped her hands, the sound sharp as breaking pottery. "How thrilling! A real investigation, right here in my home!"

Her enthusiasm for the dramatic was beginning to concern me. Anyone that excited about having a murder investigation conducted in their drawing room either had nerves of steel or an alarming disconnect from reality.

Possibly both.

A year ago, I would have stepped back. Let the authorities handle it. Worried about propriety and reputation and what Mother would say if the Bell family name appeared in the newspapers connected to anything as sordid as murder.

But a year ago, I hadn't stood over Dr. Sutherland's body, hadn't watched Eli Hawke die in a spray of gunfire, hadn't learned that the academic world I'd trusted contained shadows deep enough to hide conspiracy and corruption.

A year ago, I wouldn't have been capable of this.

I pulled the ceramic shard from my bag. The faience glaze caught the candlelight, seeming to pulse with ancient secrets.

"This cup killed Dr. Thorne. I think someone in this room planned his murder, stole the Astral Sphere, and is now watching us all dance around the truth like fools."

I looked directly at Hassan, then at each face in turn. "Well, I'm done dancing. The real investigation starts now."

CHAPTER TWELVE

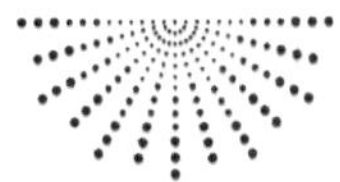

The Salon felt different in the aftermath of my declaration—less like an impromptu ballroom and more like a courtroom where I'd just announced my intention to prosecute half the jury.

I'd escaped quickly, and Quinn followed me from the Salon, his evening shoes clicking against marble. I'd expected him to argue against my investigative pronouncement, to join Richard's chorus of protective objections. Instead, he'd simply nodded once and murmured, "After you, Dr. Bell."

Now he leaned against the mahogany table where Thorne had died mere hours ago, his black tie slightly askew and his eyes holding that dangerous glint I'd learned meant trouble—usually the exciting kind.

"Brilliant performance back there." Approval threaded his voice. "Though I have to ask—did you plan that dramatic revelation, or was it pure improvisation?"

I shrugged. "I suppose I may have been... slightly dramatic."

"Slightly?" His laugh was all smoke and velvet. "Clarissa, you just declared war on a roomful of suspects while holding a piece of evidence like Excalibur. It was magnificent."

The way he said my name sent entirely unprofessional

thoughts skittering through my mind. I busied myself examining the half-wrapped ceramic shard until the world narrowed back to glaze, pigment, and measurable facts.

"We should focus on the investigation." I held up the fragment. "Someone in that salon likely murdered Jasper Thorne, and Richard's arrival has complicated everything."

"Has it?" Quinn's tone carried layers I couldn't quite decipher. "Or has it clarified things?"

Before I could ask what he meant, he moved closer, his presence filling the space between us with that familiar hum of awareness.

He bracketed my hand with his—precise, unhurried—and set the shard down. "You deserve better than men who see you as a means to an end, Clarissa. Your brilliance, your passion for the truth—those aren't tools to be exploited."

The intensity in his voice made my breath catch. We were supposed to be investigating a murder, not examining the wreckage of my romantic judgment.

"We should catalog what we know," I said, though I didn't pull my hand away from his touch. "The cyanide from apricot pits, the missing sphere, Richard's telegram about acquiring artifacts—"

"Your father's involvement," Quinn added gently.

The reminder hit hard. "Father asked Richard to acquire the sphere. That means..." I couldn't finish the sentence. That means my family's reputation was now tied to this murder investigation.

Quinn's thumb stroked across my knuckles. "It means we clear both their names by finding the real killer. Your investigative instincts were right in Giza, and they're right now."

"Even when those instincts led me to trust the wrong people?"

"Especially then." His free hand traced my cheek with devastating gentleness. "Because despite everything Richard put you through, despite what Fairchild did at Oxford, you haven't let betrayal make you cynical. You still believe in justice, in truth, in the possibility that people can be better than their worst impulses. That courage is what makes you extraordinary."

The words wrapped around my heart, healing wounds I hadn't fully acknowledged. When Quinn spoke to me like this —seeing past my analytical armor to the vulnerable woman beneath—it felt more intimate than any physical touch.

And I hated how much I wanted to believe those words.

Here was Quinn again, asking me to believe in his sincerity based solely on... what? The intensity in his eyes? The consistency of his attention?

That wasn't evidence. That was hope masquerading as logic.

Why couldn't people come with authentication certificates?

"Quinn," I whispered, and the distance between us seemed to evaporate like morning mist over the Nile.

His eyes darkened as they dropped to my lips. "Tell me to stop, Clarissa. Tell me this is just investigative partnership and I'll step back. But if there's any chance—"

"If that's how you feel, then why did you maintain such distance in your letters?" The question had tormented me through the endless New York summer and fall.

"Because you asked me to." His smile held regret. "Because you said we needed professional boundaries, and I thought respecting your wishes was more important than my own desires. Because I was terrified that pushing too hard would drive you to stay in New York permanently."

The honesty in his confession tightened my throat. "I thought you were indulging in casual flirtation. That I was just... another distraction."

"Clarissa." He lifted our joined hands, pressing a kiss to my knuckles. "You are many things—brilliant, maddening, courageous to the point of recklessness—but you have never been a distraction. You're the reason I wake up every morning excited to solve the next puzzle, to uncover the next truth. You're—"

"The reason you're in Luxor at all?" I finished, hope fluttering like a caged bird.

"The reason I'm anywhere." His voice carried such conviction. "I told Lady Blackwood I was coming to discuss antiquities, but the truth is simpler. Wherever you are, that's where I want to be."

"We should..." I started, then forgot what we should do when his thumb traced my lower lip.

"Should what?" His voice held gentle amusement.

"Investigate," I managed weakly. "Murder. Evidence. Rational thought processes."

"Dr. Bell," he murmured, "I do admire your commitment to thorough research."

Before I could formulate a suitably witty response, reality reasserted itself. We were standing in a dining room where a man had been murdered, holding evidence in a case that could destroy my family's reputation, while a houseful of suspects waited mere yards away.

"Right then." I leaned back with scientific determination, though Quinn didn't let go. "Systematic review of suspects and their motives. Starting with whoever had access to Thorne's ceremonial cup."

Quinn's smile suggested he was cataloging the pink in my face and the slight breathlessness in my voice. "Excellent plan. Though I suspect our investigation may have more... complications than strictly professional partnerships typically involve."

"I'll risk it," I said with more confidence than I felt.

"Good." He released me with obvious reluctance. "Because I have a feeling this case is about to get considerably more dangerous."

We relocated to the far end of the dining room, away from the French doors where servants might overhear. The table where Thorne had died stretched between us like a mahogany conference table.

I spread my mental files across its polished surface—not literally, of course, though the impulse to create a physical evidence board was strong.

"Let's start with opportunity." I pulled out a chair and settled into analytical mode, grateful for familiar scholarly territory. "Who knew about Thorne's habit of using that specific cup for ceremonial toasts?"

Quinn leaned against the sideboard, his evening jacket catching lamplight in a way that was distracting. "Well, for one, Lady Blackwood, obviously. She specifically asked if he'd brought it to dinner."

"Which suggests she planned the toast in advance." I filed this under *Premeditation (Possible)*. "But would she really murder a guest in her own dining room? The scandal alone..."

"Unless the scandal was preferable to whatever Thorne represented." Quinn's voice carried thoughtful consideration. "What do we actually know about her relationship with him? Beyond her enthusiastic support for his theories?"

I tapped my fingers against the table, organizing details. "Montague mentioned that Lord Blackwood gave Thorne the Astral Sphere on his deathbed. But Lady Blackwood seemed... conflicted about that gift."

"Conflicted enough to kill for it?"

"Possibly. Though she's hardly the only one with question-able motives." I counted off on my fingers. "Foster clearly despised Thorne's theories and had that overeager interest in the sphere. Yasmin appeared genuinely offended by his colonial attitudes. Even Professor Whitmore seemed uncomfortable with the whole demonstration."

Quinn moved to the window, his reflection ghostlike in the dark glass. "Don't forget Professor Whitmore's mysterious pocket-rifling last night. Whatever he removed from Thorne's jacket, he considered it important enough to steal from a corpse."

"In front of witnesses," I added. "Which suggests either remarkable boldness or complete panic."

"Or professional expertise." Quinn's tone sharpened. "Whitmore's movements were too smooth, too practiced. Like he'd done it before."

The observation sent a chill down my spine. "You think he's not actually an academic?"

"I think Professor Whitmore may have more complex

loyalties than his Royal Geographical Society credentials suggest." Quinn turned back to face me. "His questions about the sphere's location, his immediate offer to contact authorities, his expertise in handling crime scenes—it all feels rather too convenient."

"You think he wants the same thing everyone else seems to want—the Astral Sphere itself?"

"Or something to do with Operation Indigo?" Quinn's smile held no humor. "Another blue-pigmented artifact, another suspicious death, another academic with questionable credentials. The patterns are starting to feel familiar, don't you think?"

"We need a strategy." I tapped my chin. "We can't just accuse everyone and hope something sticks."

"What do you suggest? Interrogate each suspect until someone confesses?"

"Actually, yes." I turned to face him, bringing us close enough that I could smell his cologne mingling with the lingering scent of dinner candles. "But more subtly. We need information about who had access to apricot pits, who knew about the cup, and most importantly—"

"Who has the sphere now," he finished.

"Exactly. It's too large to hide indefinitely, and Hassan will eventually search everyone's belongings. We need to know, who had access to Thorne's room before dinner? Who knew enough about cyanide extraction to plan this method? And most importantly—" I pulled back to meet his eyes, struck by a sudden realization. "Why use such an elaborate poison when a simple knife would have been more efficient?"

Quinn's eyes sharpened with interest. "Because the method itself was part of the message. The curse note, the apricot pits, even the ceremonial cup—someone wanted this to look supernatural."

"To hide very human motives." I felt the familiar thrill of discovery. "Which means our killer is either genuinely superstitious or deliberately manipulative."

"My money's on manipulative. The question is—manipulating whom? The local police who dismissed it as natural causes? The suspects who might flee in superstitious terror?"

"Or us," I realized with growing excitement. "What if the elaborate staging was designed to draw attention away from the real motive? Make us focus on curses and ancient vengeance instead of modern greed?"

"Didn't you say Lady Blackwood invited you here to analyze some of her pieces? Maybe we start there, to see what else we can learn from her."

"Excellent idea."

We headed back to the Salon, but the group had dispersed. Dr. Montague informed us that Lady Blackwood was catching up on some paperwork at her private desk in the Antiquities Room.

I smiled at Quinn. "Perfect."

As we headed toward Lady Blackwood's Antiquities Room, the sound of a muffled voice drifted through the partially open door.

Quinn's hand found my elbow, drawing me to a halt.

"—one way or another." Lady Blackwood's voice carried a desperate edge I'd never heard before, but it sounded as though she were speaking to herself.

"Getting back what belongs to me. Never have been given away in the first place—"

The rustle of papers accompanied the mumbling, as though she were rifling through documents with increasing desperation.

I knocked softly against the doorframe and entered to find Lady Blackwood hunched over her desk, surrounded by scattered papers.

She looked up with startled guilt, quickly shuffling documents into neat piles.

"Oh! Dr. Bell, Mr. Quinn. I was just... organizing Jasper's... papers." Her laugh held a brittle quality. "He was not the most organized of scholars."

I slid into the room, trying to focus on the woman and not the treasure trove of artifacts lining the space. "I'm rather surprised the police left all that behind for you to... organize."

"Yes, well." She smoothed her hair. "We were good friends, after all."

"Were you? I got the impression earlier that you weren't pleased with your husband's gift of the Astral Sphere to Dr. Thorne."

She dropped back into her chair with a forced smile. "Well, better Jasper than someone like Harrison Foster, I suppose."

"Yes, his behavior tonight seemed rather aggressive."

Her face hardened immediately. "Foster is a vulgar opportunist who mistakes charm for breeding." The venom in her tone was startling. "The man has no respect for proper scholarship or cultural preservation."

Quinn ran a finger along a palm-sized heart scarab of dark green stone, its smooth back worn by centuries and its underside incised with faint markings. "Then why invite him to your celebration?"

Lady Blackwood's hands stilled on the papers. "I... well, one must maintain certain professional courtesies. As you know, Benedict, the antiquities community is quite small."

But her evasive tone suggested far more complex motivations than simple politeness.

First thing tomorrow, it would be time to have a more direct conversation with Harrison Foster.

CHAPTER THIRTEEN

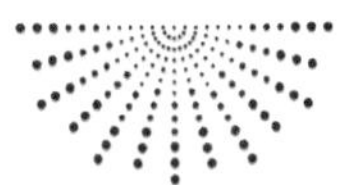

The Servants' Wing occupied an entirely different universe from Lady Blackwood's main house—one where functionality trumped aesthetics and honest work took precedence over dramatic posturing. Whitewashed walls reflected practical electric bulbs rather than atmospheric candlelight, while sturdy wooden furniture bore the honorable scars of daily use rather than the polish of museum pieces.

Annie guided me through a maze of back corridors with the expertise of someone who'd spent considerable time mapping the estate's hidden arteries. Her usual lady's companion demeanor had shifted into something more purposeful—less decorative, more strategic.

"The staff quarters are just through here," she murmured, pausing at a heavy wooden door. "Though I should warn you, they're not accustomed to entertaining guests from the main house."

We entered a common room dominated by a long oak table scarred with decades of meal preparation and evening conversations. The space hummed with quiet industry—Laila bent over a basket of linens with needle and thread, while silver gleamed under Freddie's methodical polishing. At the head of the table,

93

Winters reviewed household accounts with the focused intensity of a general planning a campaign.

The moment we appeared, all activity ceased. Laila's needle froze mid-stitch, Freddie nearly dropped a serving spoon, and Winters looked up from his ledgers with the expression of a man discovering exotic wildlife in his parlor.

"Blimey! Miss Clarissa—I mean, Dr. Bell, your ladyship!" Freddie scrambled to his feet, managing to knock over his polish tin in the process. "We weren't expecting—that is, should I fetch—oh, where's me manners? Me mum would box me ears proper!"

His flustered stammering was endearing, but Annie chose that moment to step forward with a smile that could have powered the electric lights.

"Please, don't let us interrupt your work," she said, her voice carrying warmth that transformed the awkwardness. "We're simply checking on laundry arrangements, and I thought Dr. Bell might appreciate seeing how efficiently the household operates."

The diplomatic fiction allowed everyone to relax slightly, though I noticed how Freddie's attention remained fixed on Annie with the single-minded focus of a moth discovering flame.

"'Course, Miss Evanwood," he managed, his earlier panic settling into nervous energy. "Though I ought to mention, the silver's near done for, and this morning's bread came out a right treat, despite yesterday's bit of bother, and perhaps you'd fancy a look at the pressing room, or maybe—"

He was babbling, the Cockney accent and phrases nearly too thick to follow. More tellingly, Annie was listening to every word with rapt attention, her usual composed mask slipping to reveal genuine interest.

Good heavens. My supremely competent companion was developing feelings for Lady Blackwood's flustered footman. In the middle of a murder investigation.

Some days I felt like an archaeologist who'd accidentally

enrolled in a French farce. And somehow, I appeared to be the only person taking attendance.

I leaned against the doorframe, watching Annie work her brand of social magic. I wanted to verify some details about our guests from those who saw and heard everything. But my usual direct approach—march in, demand answers, analyze responses—tended to scatter people like startled scarabs. I really must work on that. Annie understood something I'd somehow missed during my Oxford education: people responded better to genuine concern rather than scholarly interrogation.

"It must be terrifying," she continued, settling herself on a wooden stool with practiced grace, "working in a house where such dreadful things have happened. How are you all managing?"

The simple question unlocked a flood of responses. Laila's needle resumed its steady rhythm, but her voice carried tremors.

"We keep expecting... something else to happen," she admitted. "First Dr. Thorne, then the strange fires in the kitchen, and now Inspector Hassan asking questions like we might all be murderers ourselves."

Winters set down his pen with the deliberate care of someone trying not to appear nervous. "The staff has been... unsettled. Some of the local girls are talking about leaving before the solstice."

"Load of old codswallop, that is," Freddie declared, though his swagger wobbled a bit. "Mind you, I'll give you this much —the whole business does give a bloke the willies. Ancient temples, mysterious whatsits, people droppin' dead when the stars line up—sounds like somethin' you'd read in one of them cheap horror rags down the market."

Annie's laugh tinkled like silver bells. "Oh, you must be quite well-read to make such literary comparisons!"

Freddie shrugged, and knocked over his polish tin again, sending the cloth flying toward Annie's feet. As she bent to retrieve it, their fingers brushed, and I swear the temperature in the room rose several degrees.

Romantic Subplot (Accelerating), Symptoms include flushed cheeks, nervous stammering, and a total disregard for professional decorum. Prognosis: terminal.

At this rate, they'd be planning their wedding before we solved the murder.

Freddie fell into fresh spasms of nervous energy. "Well, I do read a bit," he stammered, puffing up like a peacock. "Got meself a subscription to *Pearson's Weekly*—very educational, that is. And I borrowed a book from the vicar once. Nearly finished it too, 'cept it had all these long words that gave me a proper 'eadache."

"Of course," I interjected before Freddie could compose poetry about Annie's helpful nature, "with all the comings and goings this week, it must be difficult to keep track of everyone's movements."

The servants exchanged glances, and I recognized the moment when decision crystallized. They were going to trust us with information—or at least trust Annie, which amounted to the same thing.

"Mr. Foster arrived quite early," Laila offered. "Before the afternoon tea service. Said he wanted to 'survey the architecture' of the estate."

"So, he didn't arrive at the same time as Dr. Thorne?" The argument Annie and I had witnessed in the front drive seemed to take place when the two men arrived together.

Winters shook his head. "Came early and spent hours wandering the grounds." His tone drifted into obvious disapproval. "Never staying in any one place long enough for proper conversation. Most peculiar behavior for a guest."

"That ain't the peculiar bit though," Freddie said, his jitters settling right into proper storytelling mode. "Round about teatime, didn't he turn up in the kitchen askin' about local grub and such—Egyptian dishes, he said. But his questions..." He paused for effect, clearly pleased with his audience. "He wanted to know about Dr. Thorne's green cup, specific-like.

Called it a 'charming' local tradition—charming!—and asked if loads of the guests had the same sort of bits and bobs."

The hair on my neck rose. "He knew about Thorne's cup before dinner?"

"Oh yes," Laila confirmed. "Even asked if Dr. Thorne always used it for special occasions."

But I was already cataloging this under *Premeditation (Confirmed)*. Foster hadn't stumbled onto Thorne's habits by accident—he'd researched them deliberately.

Freddie's storytelling momentum had hit full stride, and I recognized the gleam in his eye—the same expression Annie wore when she'd cornered particularly juicy gossip at New York society luncheons.

"But the proper weird bit," he continued, lowering his voice, "was when the bloke started asking about the horti-business... the garden stuff. Says he's dead keen on 'ancient Egyptian botanical knowledge'—posh words or what?—and wants to know what sort of dodgy remedies we might be growing round here."

Annie leaned forward, her interest apparently genuine rather than investigative. "How intriguing! Were you able to help him?"

"Well, I mentioned Lady Blackwood's apricot trees, though they're well past it now, ain't they? Haven't seen hide nor hair of fruit since June." Freddie's face scrunched with concentration. "But blimey, Mr. Foster got all excited about that, didn't he? Wanted to know what 'appened to all the old fruit, whether we kept the stones for anythin' useful, like."

My pulse quickened. "And do you?"

"Oh yes," Winters interjected matter-of-factly. "The gardener dries and grinds them for rat poison. Most effective deterrent for the storage rooms, though you need quite a quantity to make it worthwhile. Takes dozens of pits to produce enough powder for proper pest control."

I felt a familiar thrill, like hieroglyphs revealing their meaning. Our charming antiquities dealer had essentially received a tutorial on cyanide extraction disguised as a gardening lesson.

If Foster had been any more obvious in his research, he might have simply requested a copy of "How to Poison a Dinner Companion."

The revelation seemed to settle over the servants' quarters like a morning fog rolling off the Thames—cold, clammy, and thoroughly unwelcome.

Laila's needle had stopped moving entirely. "That's... that's why I came to tell you about the ground-up pits we found. I feared Mr. Foster... that he used our rat poison to..."

"We don't know anything for certain yet," Annie said quickly.

"But we served the dinner," Laila whispered, her face draining of color. "What if he blames us for not stopping it? What if he thinks we know too much now that we've told you about the apricot pits?"

Freddie's protective instincts kicked in with admirable speed. "Oi, don't you worry yourself, Laila love. That pillock ain't gonna lay a finger on any of us, is 'e? Besides, Miss Evanwood and the good doc'll sort this mess, won't ya?'"

The touching faith in his voice hit me with unexpected responsibility. These people had trusted us with information that could prove dangerous—information that made them witnesses rather than mere bystanders.

"We'll be watchful," I promised, though even as I said it, I realized how inadequate the assurance sounded. "And you should all be wary too. Don't be alone with any of the guests, especially not Mr. Foster. And if anyone asks what you've told us..."

"We'll say nothing," Winters declared with the firmness of a man who'd spent his career managing household crises. "Staff loyalty is absolute, Dr. Bell. You have our word."

Annie rose from her stool, and I caught the reluctant way her eyes lingered on Freddie's earnest face. "We should return before we're missed. But please, all of you—stay together when possible. There's safety in numbers."

As we prepared to leave, Freddie called after Annie with the desperation of a man who'd just discovered treasure and feared it might vanish.

"Oi, Miss Evanwood! 'Ere, if you ain't too busy... fancy 'aving a look at Lady Blackwood's roses? They're bloomin' lovely this time of morning, they are!"

The servants' quarters suddenly felt warmer, despite the growing certainty that we were all in more danger than when we'd arrived.

Annie's face bloomed crimson, a sight so rare I nearly catalogued it under *Natural Phenomena (Unprecedented)*. Her usual composure wavered as she glanced between Freddie's hopeful expression and the door leading back to the main house.

"That's very kind of you, Freddie," she managed, her voice carrying an unfamiliar breathlessness. "Perhaps this evening, when the light is better for proper appreciation?"

Freddie's face lit up like the Luxor Temple at sunrise. "Brilliant! I mean—yes, miss. I'll see they're lookin' their best for you. Maybe trim back some of the dead 'eads, give 'em a proper tidy-up."

"That would be lovely." Her smile had enough sunshine to melt the Sphinx. "I do so admire a man who takes pride in his work."

The poor boy looked ready to faint from pleasure.

As for me, it was time to face my number one suspect.

CHAPTER FOURTEEN

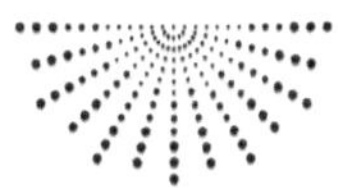

After extracting Quinn from the main house—where he'd been enduring Richard's increasingly pointed questions about our "investigation" while maintaining the diplomatic smile of a man defusing unexploded ordnance—I shared what the staff had revealed about Foster's suspicious behavior.

"Right then." Quinn adjusted his jacket. "Time to have a proper chat with Mr. Foster."

We began our search of the house, starting with the obvious locations. The Salon stood empty except for the lingering scent of champagne and social warfare. The Library contained nothing more threatening than Montague's abandoned newspaper. Even Foster's assigned bedroom yielded only the evidence of meticulous packing—his clothes arranged with the obsessive care of a man who believed proper collar starch could solve any crisis.

"Where does a man go to lurk mysteriously after committing murder?" I mused as we checked the final upstairs room.

Quinn's laugh carried the warm approval that knocked my composure half a step sideways. "In my experience, guilty men prefer outdoor spaces. Easier to run if cornered."

"Speaking from professional experience with guilty men, are we?"

"Extensive experience." He winked. "Though I find innocent archaeologists far more intriguing."

We descended toward the garden entrance. Through the French doors, I could see the stone pathways winding between palms trees and flowering jasmine, the cultivated paradise bleached by the midday sun.

And from the deeper pathways came the unmistakable sound of voices—low, urgent, and decidedly heated.

"Found him," Quinn murmured against my ear, sending shivers down my spine.

We moved through the garden pathways with stealth, the scent of jasmine wrapped around us like expensive perfume attempting to mask something rotten underneath.

We positioned ourselves behind a robust date palm that provided excellent concealment. The voices were clearer now.

"You promised this would be different. You said you'd changed." Yasmin's voice carried the disappointment reserved for men who'd failed spectacularly. "That you weren't simply using me."

Foster's reply held a casual intimacy. "I never lied to you about what this was, Yasmin."

"You're right. I shouldn't have expected you to be a decent human being."

I glanced at Quinn.

His eyebrow arched, silently asking if I was cataloging this revelation.

I nodded once. Oh, I was cataloging it all right. These two had a relationship that predated our little house party by more than polite introductions had suggested.

I leaned forward, unfortunately rustling the date palm's lower fronds.

Yasmin's head snapped up. "We're not alone."

She stepped away from Foster.

Foster spun around, and the transformation was remarkable. His charming mask didn't so much slip as shatter completely, revealing something underneath that made my skin crawl.

"Dr. Bell, Mr. Quinn." His voice carried polished menace. "How long have you been enjoying the sunshine?"

Quinn materialized between me and Foster.

"Long enough," Quinn replied, his tone suggesting Foster might want to reconsider any sudden movements.

Yasmin backed further into the shadow of a palm, and the desert wind chose that moment to send jasmine petals drifting around us like confetti at the world's most awkward garden party.

Foster recovered with the impressive speed of a con artist caught mid-swindle but determined to complete the transaction.

"Dr. Mujahid and I were discussing the tragic circumstances of poor Thorne's death. Such a shock to us all."

Quinn's stance remained deliberately casual. "How thoughtful of you both to conduct grief counseling in the shrubbery."

"Grief makes people seek solitude," Foster replied smoothly, apparently deciding to brazen through the situation with maximum audacity. "Surely you understand the need for... private reflection after such tragedy."

I frowned. "Yet your 'reflection' seemed to involve considerable finger-pointing and hostility."

Foster's jaw tightened almost imperceptibly. "You misunderstood what you overheard."

"Did we?"

"Perhaps," Foster continued with renewed confidence, "you should be questioning Professor Whitmore instead. His behavior last night was far more suspicious than anything I've done."

The deflection was so smoothly executed it deserved credit. "What sort of suspicious behavior?"

Foster produced a folded paper from his jacket, as though reluctant. "I was planning to share this with Inspector Hassan in the morning."

He unfolded what appeared to be a letter. "I suspected Whitmore's explanation about checking Thorne's pockets, so I searched his room. Found this correspondence, suggesting our esteemed professor had been making threats."

Yasmin's eyes widened, though whether from surprise or performance anxiety remained unclear.

Quinn folded his arms across his chest. ""How remarkable. You just happened to conduct an unauthorized search of another guest's belongings and discovered incriminating evidence."

"Professional curiosity." Foster shrugged. "When I saw Whitmore going through a dead man's pockets with such practiced efficiency, well... one develops suspicions."

I extended a hand. "May we examine these so-called threats? For authentication purposes, of course."

Foster's grip tightened on the letter. "I'm sure Inspector Hassan would prefer to handle the evidence personally."

"Hmm. I'm sure you're right."

Foster cleared his throat. "Well, no point in skulking about in gardens when the Egyptian gods have cursed us all. Shall we return to the house? Together?"

I smiled on him. "An excellent proposal. Though I do hope this letter of yours survives the journey back. Evidence has such an unfortunate tendency to disappear when it's not properly... supervised."

Foster's predatory smile chilled me. "Oh, I'll take very good care of it. Very good care indeed."

CHAPTER FIFTEEN

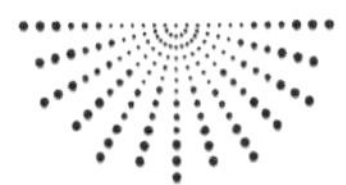

The Library's mahogany shelves stretched into shadows beyond the lamplight, creating pools of scholarly intimacy that felt more menacing than romantic. Professor Whitmore sat hunched over Lady Blackwood's massive partner desk like a monk illuminating manuscripts, though his urgent scribbling suggested less holy pursuits.

"Professor Whitmore." I stepped into the circle of lamplight. "We need to discuss what you removed from Dr. Thorne's jacket last night."

It was our first chance to catch the man alone, and I was taking full advantage.

His pen froze mid-sentence, an ink droplet falling to the paper. Behind his round spectacles, his eyes darted toward Quinn, who had positioned himself near the door.

Whitmore's hand moved instinctively toward his own jacket pocket, a gesture so reflexive it practically screamed guilty conscience. "Perhaps you've forgotten, I've already explained all this to Inspector Hassan?

Academic Condescension (Desperate Variety), Notable Characteristics: Patronizing tone masking obvious distress.

"My memory remains quite intact, thank you." I moved closer to the desk, noting how the papers scattered across its surface had been hastily covered. "As does my eyesight. Your pocket-search technique was admirable—almost professional in its execution."

Whitmore's academic composure developed hairline cracks. His fingers drummed against the desktop.

"Really, Dr. Bell, these accusations are quite unseemly. Perhaps we should discuss this with Inspector Hassan present?"

"Excellent suggestion," I replied brightly. "I'm sure he'd be fascinated to hear about the paper that's been found in your belongings, which you took from Dr. Thorne. A letter, I believe, that proves you were making threats against Thorne."

It was a bluff, since the paper was still in Foster's greedy hands and we couldn't be certain of what it truly contained, if anything. But I let it hang there until it did its work, the silence stretching like a taut wire until Whitmore registered indignant surrender. He reached into his jacket.

"That's absurd. And exactly the opposite of the truth. I wasn't pressuring Thorne. I was investigating him." He withdrew a small bundle of papers. "I was monitoring Dr. Thorne's... questionable associations."

Quinn shifted closer. "Questionable how?"

"His correspondence revealed liaisons that could compromise British interests." Whitmore's voice took on the clipped precision of a military briefing. "The man had been in contact with German archaeological societies whose research funding raised considerable red flags."

He unfolded one of the letters, revealing dense text peppered with astronomical calculations and technical diagrams. "Site surveys along strategic locations near the Suez Canal, Dr. Bell. Mapping exercises disguised as academic research."

I leaned forward to examine the correspondence, noting the impressive quality of the paper and the distinctive watermark. "These look quite official."

"Because they are." Whitmore snatched the papers away from my attention. "Thorne was either a willing collaborator or dangerously naive about who was bankrolling his expeditions. German 'cultural preservation societies' with remarkably generous funding for British scholars researching Egyptian defensive positions."

Quinn's expression remained neutral, though I caught something flickering in his eyes—recognition, perhaps, or calculation.

"So, you appointed yourself patriotic watchdog?" I asked.

"Someone had to." Whitmore straightened his spectacles with righteous fervor. "The man was either treasonously deliberate or stupid. Either way, he posed a threat to Crown interests."

I filed this under *Motives for Murder (Patriotic Variety)*, though something about Whitmore's performance felt rehearsed rather than spontaneous.

"How terribly convenient," I murmured, "that someone so interested in national security was on the scene for the fateful dinner party."

Whitmore's demeanor shifted like quicksilver, his defensive academic posture transforming into something altogether more unsettling. His spine straightened, and when he spoke again, his voice carried fervent conviction. "Loose lips sink ships—surely even amateur investigators understand basic operational security."

The phrase raised all sorts of flags. This wasn't the bungling professor who'd fumbled with his spectacles during dinner; this was someone familiar with intelligence procedures that stretched beyond academic experience.

"Operational security?" Quinn's voice was like flint. "Rather specific terminology for a geographical society fellow."

"Some of us understand that scholarship and patriotism are inseparable." Whitmore's gaze flicked between Quinn and me. "Thorne forgot which country gave him his education, his opportunities, his very freedom to pursue these ridiculous theories. The man was a walking security breach."

I cataloged the transformation with growing unease. His methodical nature, which had seemed academic during our earlier interactions, now revealed itself as something more sinister. Could this same thinking extend to planning elaborate murders?

"You tried to warn him, I suppose?" I kept my voice level despite the chill creeping up my spine.

"Repeatedly." Whitmore's laugh held no humor whatsoever. "Including in the note you saw me pull from his pocket. The fool thought I was jealous of his astronomical nonsense. Couldn't comprehend that some things matter more than personal recognition or scholarly glory."

"And when warnings proved insufficient?" Quinn asked, though something in his tone suggested he already knew the answer.

Whitmore's eyes gleamed behind his spectacles. "Sometimes individual sacrifice becomes necessary for the greater good. Thorne's death may have prevented casualties on a much larger scale."

The easy way the man spoke of murder astounded me—the detached efficiency of an accountant balancing ledgers, weighing one life against hypothetical strategic advantages.

But what truly chilled me was how his gaze kept sliding toward Quinn, as though seeking some form of professional understanding—or approval. As if they shared common ground in this shadowy world of national interests and calculated sacrifices.

"How patriotic of you," I said, my voice dripping with distaste. "But even if Dr. Thorne was sharing information unwisely, that hardly justifies poisoning him at a dinner party. Rather extreme, wouldn't you say?"

His smile reminded me of a mathematics professor explaining elementary arithmetic to particularly slow students. "My dear Dr. Bell, your feminine sensibilities are understandably delicate, but warfare requires difficult decisions. Thorne's elimination may have prevented German agents from accessing strategic intelligence about British defensive positions."

Feminine sensibilities? I mentally filed this under *Reasons to Feed Professor Whitmore to Crocodiles*, a category that was expanding by the minute.

"So, you admit you considered Dr. Thorne expendable?" I pressed.

"I admit I will aways prioritize British interests over one man's delusions." His gaze sharpened behind those spectacles. "Though your amateur detection is admirable, Dr. Bell, it's becoming potentially dangerous. Some investigations are better left to professionals."

The threat hung in the air. Quinn straightened slightly, his casual pose shifting toward something more aggressive.

"Dangerous how?" I asked, steadying my voice while my balance threatened to tilt.

Whitmore's attention swiveled to Quinn. "Surely Mr. Quinn understands the... complications that arise when civilians interfere with sensitive operations? Call her off before she stumbles into something beyond her comprehension."

Call me off? Like I was an overeager spaniel chasing pheasants through someone's prize garden?

"I'm sitting right here," I informed them both with the icy politeness Mother had perfected for managing presumptuous dinner guests. "Perfectly capable of managing my own comprehension, thank you."

But something passed between the two men—a flicker of recognition that made my analytical instincts tingle. Quinn maintained his cool exterior, yet his silence felt weighted with unspoken knowledge.

Whitmore leaned forward across the desk, his voice dropping to confidential tones. "Some stones are better left unturned, Dr. Bell. Your enthusiastic investigation could expose operations that extend far beyond one scholar's unfortunate death."

His mask finally slipped completely, revealing something cold and calculating beneath the academic veneer. "You have no idea what you're meddling with, young lady. I suggest you return to pottery classification and leave complex matters to those qualified to handle them."

The dismissal stung, precisely because it echoed every condescending professor who'd ever suggested my proper place was cataloging artifacts rather than discovering them. But it also confirmed my growing suspicion that Professor Whitmore possessed both the fanatical conviction and methodical care necessary to plan Thorne's elaborate murder.

Quinn finally spoke, his voice like ice. "I think we've heard enough. Professor."

I hadn't heard nearly enough, but something about Quinn's demeanor had me concerned. As though he needed to get me out of the Library before someone said—or did—something fatal.

I turned to leave the Library, pausing only to hear Whitmore's parting words, lobbed at my back like a final attack.

"Be very careful, Dr. Bell. Curiosity kills more than just cats."

CHAPTER SIXTEEN

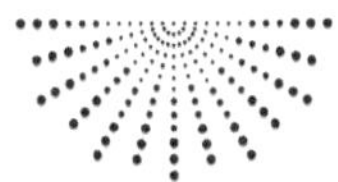

The hallway stretched before me like a timeline—ancient Egyptian motifs giving way to British colonial excess, all of it now seeming as artificial as Whitmore's academic facade. My mind buzzed.

"Quinn, we've found our killer," I announced, turning to find him waiting by the carved mahogany banister, his expression unreadable in the lamplight.

Before I could launch into my triumphant analysis, his hand closed around my elbow with unexpected urgency.

"Not here," he murmured, guiding me swiftly up the staircase. "Too many listening ears."

He pulled me into what I assumed was his assigned bedroom, closing the door with practiced stealth. The space mirrored my own quarters—four-poster bed, French doors opening to a narrow balcony overlooking the desert night—but somehow felt entirely different with Quinn's presence filling it.

I began pacing immediately, my investigative excitement refusing to be contained by mere walls.

"Whitmore practically confessed! The way he discussed individual sacrifice—that's exactly the fanatical mindset required to justify murder." My evening shoes clicked against the polished wood. "His access to Thorne's correspondence, his patriotic delusions about German archaeological conspiracies. It all fits perfectly."

Quinn remained by the door, but instead of sharing my enthusiasm, his expression grew increasingly troubled.

Why was he not appreciating my brilliant deductive reasoning?

"Clarissa," he said quietly. "You need to drop Whitmore as a suspect. Immediately."

The words hit me like a slap.

"What do you mean, drop him?"

Quinn's flat refusal stopped me mid-pace, like I'd walked into an invisible wall of pure masculine obstinacy.

"He confessed!" My voice pitched higher with indignation. "The man discussed murder like it was crop rotation!"

"He did nothing of the sort." Quinn's tone carried a maddening calm. "You're seeing what you want to see because Foster pointed you in this direction."

"Foster?" I whirled to face him, my beaded dress catching lamplight like accusations. "This has nothing to do with Foster's letter-waving. Whitmore's own words condemned him!"

Quinn moved to look through the French doors, his silhouette dark against the gauzy curtains stirring in the desert breeze. "You're connecting dots that don't form the picture you think they do."

"Then explain it to me!" Frustration crackled through my voice. "Earlier you agreed Whitmore seemed suspicious. Now suddenly he's above reproach? What changed between the Library and here?"

His shoulders tensed beneath his evening jacket. When he spoke, his voice carried gravity that made my analytical excitement falter.

"Because pursuing Whitmore could get you killed."

The words settled over the luxurious bedroom like a burial shroud.

"Killed?" I managed, my pacing momentum finally

arrested completely. "Quinn, what exactly aren't you telling me?"

He opened the doors, and I caught his reflection in the glass. For the first time since I'd known him, Benedict Quinn looked genuinely concerned.

For a long moment, the only sound was desert wind threading through gauze curtains like whispered secrets finally demanding to be heard.

Then Quinn turned from the doors, and something in his expression gave me a flicker of premonition.

"Because Whitmore is British intelligence," he said quietly. "And so am I."

The admission hit me with the force of a limestone block tumbling from temple heights.

"You're..." I groped for words while my brain frantically reshuffled every interaction we'd ever had. "You're... what?"

He sighed. "I should have seen it earlier. Clearly, he knows my position. That subtle comment about civilians interfering with operations—he was signaling me. Why I wasn't informed by my superiors of the presence of another agent here, though—"

"Another agent?" My blood pressure was rising by the second. "Another agent?! So, you've been lying to me. About everything. Your antiquities dealing, your background, your reasons for being in Egypt..."

"Not about everything." He moved away from the doors. "Not about what matters between us."

I laughed, the sound sharp. "What *matters*? How can I possibly know what matters when I don't know who you are?"

Personal Devastation (Acute), Notable Characteristics: Complete reorganization of reality required.

"Benedict Quinn, antiquities dealer with mysterious funding sources and expertise in whatever I happened to be researching." My voice dripped with bitter comprehension. "Of course. Richard was right. You were too good to be true."

"Clarissa—"

"No wonder you always knew exactly what questions to

ask, exactly which contacts to pursue. You weren't helping with my investigation—you were conducting your own."

Quinn ran a hand through his hair—a gesture I'd once found endearing but recognized as frustration.

"This changes things. Thorne wasn't treasonous, just catastrophically naive."

He was really going to focus on our investigation, when he'd just dropped this bombshell on me?

"His astronomical research provided perfect cover for German intelligence teams surveying British defensive positions along the Suez Canal." He moved closer, though I retreated toward the bed. "Those 'cultural preservation societies' funding his expeditions? Must have been military reconnaissance disguised as academic grants."

My scientific mind was reframing the months of our correspondence with horrifying efficiency, but I still chose to follow the investigative lead. "So, Whitmore was actually preventing espionage, not committing murder."

"Most likely monitoring communications, tracking funding sources, documenting which sites were being surveyed under archaeological pretexts." Quinn's proof made my skin crawl. "Standard counterintelligence work. But Whitmore wouldn't have killed Thorne over any of it. And I don't think he has anything to do with Operation Indigo."

"And you?" The question tasted bitter. "Whitmore was here for Thorne. But what's your standard work, exactly? Are *you* part of Operation Indigo?"

"No! If someone in the British government is truly behind these thefts, then my superiors know nothing about it. I'm here to prevent sensitive sites and pieces from falling into hostile hands. Among other things."

Among other things. The casual phrase encompassed a universe of deception I'd been too besotted to notice.

"When you said you facilitated 'ethical preservation of cultural artifacts'..." I began.

"I meant it. Just not in the way you assumed." His attempt

at a smile fell flat. "My cover story contained enough truth to be believable."

"Believable?" I sat heavily on the bed's edge, my legs suddenly unsteady. "Your entire personality was a cover story."

The betrayal cut deeper than Richard's lies ever had. Richard had simply been selfish and presumptuous. Quinn had been professionally deceptive—which somehow felt infinitely worse.

The revelation hung between us, impossible to ignore. Quinn moved closer, close enough that I could smell his cologne mingling with the flower-scented night air drifting through the French doors.

"What about us?" My voice carried equal measures hurt and fury. "Was seducing the naive archaeologist part of your assignment specifications?"

"Everything I've felt for you has been genuine." His hand reached toward my face, then stopped mid-gesture as though he'd remembered his new honesty policy. "The assignment was tracking the antiquities thefts and forgeries—what we now know as Operation Indigo. You became something entirely unplanned."

I wanted to believe him. God knew, I wanted to believe him.

But what proof did I have? What evidence could possibly distinguish genuine affection from professional manipulation when both looked identical from the outside? He'd been trained to be convincing, trained to read people, trained to make them trust him. That was literally his job.

And my track record of judging people's sincerity was, objectively speaking, abysmal.

I stood abruptly, putting the width of a Persian carpet between us. "How tremendously flattering. I've been upgraded from 'assignment' to 'complication.'"

"Clarissa—"

"No, let me properly catalog this." I began pacing again, my mind seizing control from my wounded heart. "Mysterious antiquities dealer with perfect timing, extensive contacts, and expertise. Obviously too coincidental to be romance."

"It started as professional interest," he admitted, his mask finally dropping completely. "But somewhere between listening to you lecture me about pigment authentication while completely ignoring your own safety and watching you solve Dr. Sutherland's murder—it became something else entirely."

The rawness in his voice hurt somehow.

"Prove it," I challenged.

"I'm risking my entire career by telling you the truth." His smile held rueful frustration. "My superiors would have me transferred to Scotland Yard's filing department if they knew I'd compromised operational security for a woman who thinks proper fieldwork involves charging headfirst into danger while taking meticulous notes."

Despite everything, something unspoken stirred behind my ribs at his exasperated fondness.

Quinn moved to the mahogany armoire, suddenly looking every inch the professional spy rather than the charming rogue I was falling for.

Yes, falling for. No sense denying it. Now that it meant nothing.

"And all these months I've been in New York? You've been... what? Investigating?"

"Unsuccessfully, but yes. With Eli Hawke's death, the trail went cold. I've gotten nowhere. But listen... with Whitmore eliminated as a suspect, we need to refocus our investigation." His voice carried a new authority that caught me off guard. "Your former fiancé's arrival remains suspicious. That telegram about acquiring artifacts suggests your father's collection activities extend beyond casual antiquing."

I bristled at his clinical assessment. "Are you redirecting suspicion to protect Whitmore, or because you genuinely believe Richard murdered someone over a stone sphere?"

"Both." Quinn's honesty was becoming almost as irritating as his previous deceptions. "Richard Sullivan's timing is either remarkably coincidental or perfectly calculated. Arriving hours after Thorne's death, carrying explicit instructions to acquire the very artifact that's now missing..."

"You're suggesting my former fiancé is a killer because he's punctual and follows Father's business instructions?"

"I'm suggesting," Quinn replied, "that men who lie about their romantic intentions often lie about other things as well."

"Well," I observed sweetly. "I suppose it takes one to know one."

Quinn's laugh held genuine appreciation. "You are mistaken, Dr. Bell. I have never lied about my romantic intentions. Richard's intentions appear to be for profit and patriarchal control. While my deceptions were for King and Country."

"Ah yes, much more noble motivations for lying."

The desert wind stirred the curtains, creating dancing shadows across Quinn's face that somehow made him look both dangerous and devastatingly attractive. Which was absolutely not what I should be cataloging at this moment.

"This changes things between us, Quinn. You know it does. And if we are to continue working together, it's as equals. No more protective lying, no more managing me for my supposed benefit, and definitely no more treating me like a delicate specimen who might shatter under pressure."

Quinn's smile held genuine respect. "Agreed. Though my cover limits how much I can share about ongoing operations."

"I don't need your operational secrets," I replied crisply. "Just honesty about this investigation. And perhaps advance warning before you plan to dramatically overturn my entire understanding of reality."

"I'll pencil it into my intelligence briefing schedule."

Despite everything, his dry humor caused a flutter in me. Which was inconvenient but apparently unavoidable.

"We solve this murder, clear my father's name, and expose whoever actually poisoned poor Thorne." I moved toward the door, needing distance from the intimate atmosphere of his bedroom. "Then we determine what, if anything, survives between us after all this duplicity."

"And if I said I'd prefer to determine that right now?" His voice carried heat.

I paused with a shaking hand on the doorknob. "I'd say you've lost credibility privileges, Mr. Quinn. You'll have to earn back the right to make such suggestions."

His laughter followed me into the hallway, low and promising and entirely too appealing for my peace of mind.

CHAPTER SEVENTEEN

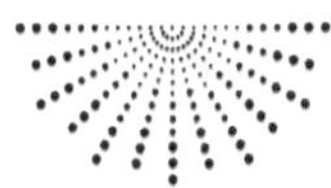

The Antiquities Room at night resembled a jeweler's private vault more than a scholar's collection space. Glass cases reflected lamplight like still water, transforming Lady Blackwood's treasures into something almost ethereal. The ventilated atmosphere provided blessed relief from the desert heat, though the metallic tang of the ventilation system couldn't quite mask the scent of ancient materials and preservation wax.

Richard stood before a display case containing Egyptian artifacts, taking notes with the focused intensity of a man cataloguing assets rather than admiring artistry.

Just the man I'd come to see.

"Admiring Lady Blackwood's remarkable collection," he said without looking up as we entered. "Your expertise would be valuable here, Clarissa."

Quinn positioned himself between Richard and the door. I approached the display cases, noting how Richard's attention lingered on pieces with blue pigmentation—exactly the type connected to Operation Indigo.

"Actually, Richard," I said with my best academic tonality, "we'd like to discuss *your* expertise. Specifically, your experience with Egyptian artifact acquisition."

His pen paused mid-notation. "I'm not sure what you mean."

Quinn produced the leather portfolio he'd brought from his room and spread documents across the nearest surface with efficiency.

I looked over his shoulder to see shipping manifests, customs declarations, correspondence bearing my father's letterhead—paperwork that made my stomach clench with growing dread. Where had Quinn acquired all this evidence?

"Armand Bell's collection activities are far more extensive than you initially suggested, Mr. Sullivan." Quinn's tone carried the deadly calm of a prosecutor.

I'd known since last spring that he had his suspicions about my father, but it stung to see how much paperwork his misgivings involved.

Richard straightened and crossed to the desk. His confident mask slipped as he scanned the documentation. "I don't know where you acquired these private papers—"

"The scope is remarkable," Quinn continued, ignoring Richard's protest. "Multiple dealers, questionable export channels, acquisition that operates well outside Egyptian antiquities law."

I studied the manifests with growing horror, recognizing my father's signature on many transactions.

Family Reputation (Catastrophically Compromised), Notable Characteristics: Potentially criminal smuggling operation.

"This isn't about one artifact, is it?" The words tasted bitter as comprehension dawned. "It's about an entire network."

Richard's shoulders sagged.

"Good grief," I whispered, sinking into the nearest chair. "Father isn't just collecting—he's running a smuggling operation. How many laws are being broken? How many Egyptian families are being cheated?"

Richard slumped against the display case, his polished facade finally surrendering to exhaustion. "Fine. I will explain.

Yes, your father assigned me to acquire multiple pieces, not just the sphere." His voice carried the defeated tone of a man whose perfectly pressed shirt had finally wrinkled. "But it's not what you're making it sound like."

"Then enlighten us," I said, though my chest tightened with dread.

"Bell believes the political situation here is... unstable. He wants to preserve important pieces in American collections before they're lost to revolutionary sentiment." Richard's justification emerged with the practiced ease of a speech he'd rehearsed many times. "We're protecting these artifacts from people who don't understand their true value."

The arrogance in his tone made my hands clench. "Their true value? To whom, exactly?"

"To civilization, Clarissa! To proper scholarship and preservation." He gestured toward the gleaming cases around us. "Look at Lady Blackwood's collection—beautifully maintained, properly documented, accessible to serious researchers. Compare that to some dusty tomb or overcrowded government warehouse in Cairo."

A flash of memory, the vast underground facility beneath the Egyptian University asserted itself. And along with it, Quinn's identical justification several months ago.

"My business truly does involve evaluating properties for wealthy Americans," Richard continued. "But yes, I also identify artifacts that might become... available through estate sales or desperate sellers."

"Available." I repeated the distasteful specimen of a word. "How delightfully euphemistic."

"And yet, the scope suggests institutional corruption rather than individual collecting," Quinn observed, his professional assessment making Richard flinch.

Richard's laugh held no humor. "You make it sound like we're tomb raiders with sterling silver shovels."

The irony, again. I'd once accused Quinn of something quite similar.

"My family's reputation is thoroughly compromised." My voice emerged barely above a whisper.

"Clarissa, baby, you're being dramatic." Richard moved toward me with the cautious approach of someone attempting to calm a spooked horse. "Your father is a respected business-man. These are legal transactions between willing parties. Not some sort of smuggling ring."

My anguish over Father's actions warred with decades of love and loyalty.

"Your father may not understand the full implications," Quinn said gently. "But someone is coordinating this on a much larger scale."

"How reassuring," I managed. "Father's merely an unwit-ting participant in international artifact smuggling. What a comfort that will be when he's arrested."

The silence lengthened while I contemplated whether proper filial duty required visiting Father in prison or if I could simply changed my name and flee to Australia.

I sank into the nearest chair, my legs suddenly unsteady. "All those artifacts in his study. The pieces he showed me as a child, teaching me about provenance and authentication..." My voice cracked slightly. "How many were stolen?"

"Clarissa—" Richard began.

"Don't." I held up one hand. "Just... don't."

Quinn moved closer but didn't touch me, respecting my need for space. "Your father's actions don't define you. Your work, your integrity—those are yours alone."

"Are they?" The question tasted bitter. "How many of my professional connections came through Father's network? How many opportunities were offered because someone owed him a favor? Was anything in my career earned, or was it all just... tainted?"

The room felt too small, too warm despite the ventilation system. I'd spent years trying to prove I was more than just Armand Bell's daughter, that my scholarship stood on its own merit. And now I had to face the possibility that everything I'd built rested on a foundation of illegal acquisition and cultural exploitation.

"I must know one thing, Richard. Did Father arrange for me to work with Dr. Sutherland?" The questions tumbled out. "Have I been a pawn in Operation Indigo from the very beginning?"

Richard looked genuinely bewildered. "Operation what now? Clarissa, what are you talking about?"

His confusion seemed authentic, suggesting he was merely a well-dressed cog in a machine whose full scope he didn't comprehend. Which somehow made it worse—my former fiancé wasn't even competent enough to be a proper criminal mastermind.

"The possibility that I've been manipulated from the beginning," I continued, my voice rising with each word, "that my scholarly independence was just an elaborate illusion while Father pulled strings behind every opportunity, every connection, every—"

"Clarissa." Quinn's hand found mine, steady and sure. "Your brilliance is entirely yours. Whatever your father's schemes—your mind, your insights, your courage—those belong to you."

My breath shallowed at the sincerity in his voice. But here was a professional spy offering reassurance about authenticity. The irony would have been amusing if I weren't having an existential crisis.

Richard straightened his tie. "If we're discussing questionable dealers, Harrison Foster's methods make your father look like a choir boy."

"How so?" Quinn's attention sharpened like a hawk spotting prey.

"Foster's been pressuring collectors to make immediate decisions. Claims political instability makes quick acquisition necessary." Richard's distaste was evident. "I think he's specifically targeted Lady Blackwood, pressuring her for pieces his backers desperately want."

My focus tightened as well. "What sort of pressure?"

"I overheard them talking last night. He implied she might need to sell items quickly to cover unexpected expenses. Seemed to know something about her finances that she wouldn't want public. Sounded to me more like blackmail disguised as helpful business advice."

"Did you find Foster's methods effective?" Quinn asked.

"Distasteful but efficient," Richard admitted. "Though I wondered what exactly Foster had on Lady Blackwood that made a woman of her standing so... accommodating."

"I do hope you're not suggesting anything improper about my collection, Mr. Sullivan."

Lady Blackwood's voice carried the crystalline authority of polite menace. She swept into the Antiquities Room with yellow silk rustling, her keen eyes immediately cataloging our positions around her precious artifacts.

"Lady Blackwood!" Richard straightened with the guilty efficiency of a schoolboy caught raiding the biscuit tin. "We were just... admiring your remarkable pieces."

"Were you indeed?" There was enough chill in her smile to preserve mummies without natron. "How fascinating that such admiration requires quite so much paperwork."

She gestured toward Quinn's scattered documents with one elegantly gloved hand.

I attempted diplomatic deflection. "Richard was sharing insights about current market conditions for Egyptian artifacts."

"Market conditions." Lady Blackwood's laugh tinkled with dangerous sweetness. "How delightfully commercial of you all. Though I must say, examining my private collection at midnight suggests rather more than casual market research."

The conversation had acquired the delicate tension of a poorly supported excavation—one wrong move and everything would come crashing down.

"Eleanor, perhaps these questions could wait until morning?"

Professor Montague materialized in the doorway like a

scholarly guardian angel. "You've had quite enough stress for one evening."

Hmm. *Eleanor*? I filed this under *Romantic Developments (Unexpected)*, noting how he positioned himself between Lady Blackwood and our investigative tribunal like a knight defending his castle.

"Nigel, how thoughtful." Lady Blackwood's relief was palpable as she moved closer to him, her earlier defensive brittleness softening. "Though I'm perfectly capable of handling a few questions about my collection."

"Of course you are." His voice carried gentle fondness. "But surely business discussions can wait for civilized hours?"

Quinn and I exchanged glances. The depth of feeling in Montague's tone had transformed our academic colleague into something altogether more protective.

"Lady Blackwood's integrity is beyond question." Montague stepped closer to her. "If there are concerns about business arrangements, surely they should be directed toward the appropriate parties."

The man was clearly besotted.

Lady Blackwood raised her hands in mock surrender. "I have no secrets. If you want to know the truth, then yes, I hoped this gathering would pressure Jasper to return Charles's sphere. It rightfully belongs to this estate."

The admission gave me analytical whiplash. Richard's insinuations about Foster's blackmail had nothing to do with Jasper Thorne.

"I thought if his Solstice demonstration failed spectacularly," she continued, her voice gaining strength as she warmed to her theme, "he might donate the Astral Sphere back to avoid further embarrassment. Public humiliation has remarkable persuasive powers."

I blinked. "You set up this house party to intentionally embarrass your guest?"

"I choreographed a controlled social experiment," she corrected with dignity that would have impressed a dowager empress. "Entirely different thing."

Montague circled the woman with his arm. "Eleanor's methods may have been... indirect, but her motives were entirely understandable."

Quinn murmured against my ear: "Note how she needed Thorne alive for maximum humiliation potential."

Which rather elegantly eliminated Lady Blackwood from our suspect list—since dead men tell no embarrassing tales at failed public demonstrations.

CHAPTER EIGHTEEN

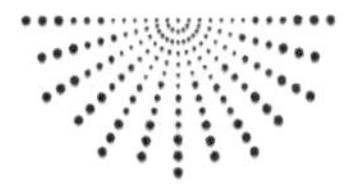

$\mathcal{A}$nnie swept through the Servant's Wing common room ahead of me, like a benevolent whirlwind, distributing smiles with the efficiency of a postal service.

"Freddie!" Her voice carried genuine warmth that made the young man's face glow. "I do hope you slept well despite all this dreadful business."

Annie's Social Strategy (Masterful), Notable Characteristics: Genuine affection disguised as investigative technique, or possibly the reverse.

"Much better now you're here, Miss Evanwood," Freddie managed, his earlier stammering replaced by something approaching confidence. "Though I'll admit, we're all still a bit rattled by Monday's... unpleasantness."

Laila looked up from her needlework. "Miss Evanwood's kind to check on us. Some of the main house guests haven't exactly been... considerate about how all this affects the staff."

Winters emerged from behind his ledgers. "Indeed. It's refreshing to encounter visitors who understand that those of us in service have eyes and ears, not just hands for carrying trays."

"We were hoping," Annie continued, "that you might help

us understand exactly what happened to Dr. Thorne. For everyone's safety, of course."

Three pairs of eyes focused on us with the intensity of scholars examining newly discovered papyri.

"About time someone asked the right people the right questions," Winters declared.

"Those apricot pits Laila mentioned a couple of days ago," I began, "the ones that had been ground up—do you know who is responsible for that particular... horticultural project?"

Freddie scratched his head, looking genuinely puzzled. "Well, we don't keep the pits here. But if it weren't December, it'd be old Tarik from town. Comes by in the summer for the pest control, he does. Been tendin' this place since before Lady Blackwood arrived, I reckon."

My heart sank. "So he's not connected to any of our guests?"

"Lord no!" Freddie laughed. "Tarik wouldn't know a house guest from a house cat, beggin' your pardon. Keeps to himself, does his work, takes his payment, and scarpers back to Luxor quick as you please."

Quinn's slight exhale beside me suggested he was reaching the same disappointing conclusion. Our case against Foster's apricot pit cyanide extraction was crumbling.

Laila shook her head. "That's why I mentioned them—you asked about strange goings on—Tarik shouldn't have been here."

"Foster must have gotten the cyanide from the apricot pits, though," I murmured to Quinn.

"Oh!" Winters perked up. "If it's cyanide you want, it would be much less trouble to get it from the pellets we use for the beetle infestations in the Glasshouse."

I stared at him. "There are cyanide pellets. On the property."

"Naturally. Much more efficient than grinding apricot pits like some medieval alchemist," Winters replied with the matter-of-fact tone of someone discussing tea preferences. "We keep them locked in the gardening shed behind the main house.

Though I don't recall mentioning those to Mr. Foster during his gardening inquiries."

"Also, about Dr. Thorne's ceremonial cup," I continued, trying to sound professionally detached rather than like a bloodhound who'd caught a promising scent, "we understand it was quite distinctive. Did he ask the staff to place it on the table before setting the dinner?"

Freddie's face brightened with the eagerness of someone finally getting to share useful information. "Oh yes, that lovely greenish thing! Dr. Thorne brought it down to the dining room himself, round about teatime. Said he wanted to make sure it was properly positioned for his toast."

Quinn leaned forward slightly, his attention sharpening. "And after he placed it?"

"Well, Mr. Foster took a keen interest while we were finishing the preparations," Laila offered, her needle pausing in its steady rhythm. "Said he was fascinated by ancient glazing techniques. Kept turning it this way and that, examining every inch."

Excitement swept me. "Foster handled the cup directly?"

"Oh yes," Freddie confirmed cheerfully. "For a good few minutes, I'd say. Very thorough examination. Talking all sorts of information about the firing process and such. Seemed to know quite a bit about pottery, actually."

Or quite a bit about how to crush cyanide pellets and add them into a waiting cup.

While Quinn and I cataloged evidence of Foster's murderous pottery appreciation, I couldn't help but notice how Annie had somehow migrated to the wooden stool directly beside Freddie's workstation. Their conversation had developed its own gravitational pull.

"London wasn't kind to me, miss," Freddie was saying, his usual nervous energy replaced by something quieter, more vulnerable. "Got accused of pinchin' silver from me employer's house. Wasn't true, of course, but when you're just hired help and the master's nephew needs someone to blame for his gambling debts..."

Annie's expression softened with genuine sympathy. "How perfectly dreadful. No wonder you were grateful for Lady Blackwood's offer."

"Gave me a fresh start when no one else would," Freddie nodded, his voice carrying a fervent loyalty. "Don't care what anyone says about her collection or her methods—she saw past the accusations to the man underneath."

The faith in his voice was touching. He'd been falsely accused once, and now was working in a household where murder had made everyone suspicious of everyone else.

Quinn moved closer, ostensibly to examine Winters' ledgers but somehow ending up near enough that I could feel his warmth radiating through the cool morning air. "Loyalty is admirable," he murmured, just loud enough for me to hear, "though it sometimes blinds people to uncomfortable truths."

I glanced first at Annie's protective posture toward Freddie, and then at Quinn himself, wondering if we were all guilty of the same selective blindness when it came to people we'd grown fond of.

"Right then," I announced. "Let's reconstruct Mr. Foster's itinerary for Monday, shall we?"

I began pacing the length of the servants' common room, my morning dress swishing against the stone floors as my mind organized the evidence.

"Winters, you mentioned Foster arrived early and spent considerable time surveying the architecture?"

"Indeed. Before noon, I'd say. Wandering the grounds with the dedication of a man conducting a property assessment." Winters adjusted his spectacles. "Though his questions about the estate's... practical arrangements seemed oddly specific."

"The gardening consultation with you, Freddie, happened around teatime?"

"Aye, just after I'd finished with the silver service." Freddie nodded eagerly, apparently thrilled to contribute to our timeline reconstruction. "Went on for ages about traditional pest control methods and storage procedures."

"But you said the cyanide is kept locked in the shed."

Freddie ducked his head, then glanced at a ring of keys on the wall. "I might have mentioned..."

"I see. And the ceremonial cup examination occurred immediately after Dr. Thorne positioned it in the dining room." I turned to Quinn. "Multiple opportunities for reconnaissance, poison acquisition, and direct access to the murder weapon."

Laila looked up from her needlework with wide eyes. "You really think Mr. Foster...?"

"I think Mr. Foster conducted himself with the efficiency of someone following a very detailed plan." A coil of understanding wound itself low inside me. A man capable of such methodical preparation wouldn't hesitate to eliminate witnesses—or nosy archaeologists who'd gotten too close to the truth.

Quinn's hand found the small of my back, his touch both steadying and charged with unspoken meaning. "The question now is whether he knows we've figured it out."

The servants' common room suddenly felt smaller. Foster wasn't just a murderer—he was a murderer who'd successfully plotted an elaborate killing under the noses of a houseful of witnesses.

"We need to search his room," I announced, though my voice carried less confidence than I'd intended. "Physical evidence, traces of the cyanide preparation, anything that connects him definitively to—"

"Absolutely not." Quinn's interruption was swift and final. "Foster's dangerous enough without cornering him in a private space."

I bristled at his protective tone. "I wasn't planning on 'cornering' anyone."

"The suspect has already killed once." Quinn's jaw tightened with what I was learning to recognize as his intelligence officer demeanor. "We involve Hassan immediately."

"With what? Circumstantial evidence and some odd conversations with staff?" I gestured toward our assembled witnesses, who were watching this exchange with the fascination of audience members at a dramatic play. "Hassan needs irrefutable proof, not theories about pottery appreciation."

Freddie cleared his throat. "Beggin' your pardon, but I could help with that searching business. Know every inch of this place, I do. And Mr. Foster's got no reason to suspect the help."

Annie's protective instincts flared immediately. "No, Freddie. It's far too dangerous."

The tender concern in her voice made something twist in my chest—part maternal pride, part terrified recognition that we were all now potential targets.

Quinn moved closer. "Some battles require strategic patience rather than brilliant frontal assault, Dr. Bell."

The way he said my name sent a shiver down my spine, even as I wanted to throttle him for his infuriating reasonableness.

"Fine," I conceded with as much dignity as I could muster. "But we're not letting Foster slip away while we debate investigative methodology."

CHAPTER NINETEEN

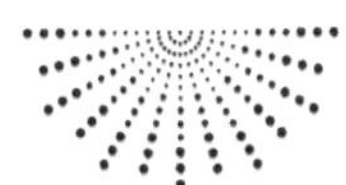

$\mathcal{L}$ady Blackwood foiled my immediate plans to search Foster's belongings by insisting we all gather for breakfast in the Dining Room once again. She'd designed another buffet along the mahogany sideboard—this one notably simpler than previous meals, featuring modest offerings of flatbread, honey, fresh dates, and Turkish coffee that filled the air with rich, comforting aromas.

The formal dining table had been pushed against the far wall and covered with a pristine white cloth, and fresh jasmine from the garden filled crystal vases in what seemed like a deliberate attempt to mask the room's association with death through the aggressive application of natural beauty.

I surveyed the assembled breakfast party with growing unease. Richard sat hunched over his Turkish coffee like a man contemplating his mortality, while Yasmin picked at her flatbread, and Whitmore maintained his fake-scholarly composure.

Hassan was still a member of our house party, insisting on filling the gap left by the local police.

Harrison Foster was notably absent.

"Inspector Hassan," I began, approaching him near the French doors, "Mr. Foster claims to have documentary evidence proving Professor Whitmore threatened Dr. Thorne. However, I suspect this 'evidence' is as authentic as a tourist's papyrus scroll. Has he shown it to you?"

Quinn materialized at my shoulder. "The timing is suspicious. False evidence planted to redirect suspicion while he covered his tracks."

Hassan's eyes sharpened with interest. "You believe Foster—"

"I believe Foster has been manipulating this entire investigation from the moment Thorne collapsed. His revelation about Whitmore was designed to send us chasing shadows while he arranged his escape."

Lady Blackwood looked up from her delicate breakfast preparations with alarm. "Escape? But surely Harrison wouldn't simply... leave? Without proper farewells?"

"Has anyone seen him this morning?" I asked, though I already suspected the answer.

A chorus of head shakes confirmed my fears.

Quinn gave an exasperated snort. "He can't have gone far, not without arranging a car, which Lady Blackwood would have heard about."

Lady Blackwood shook her head in silent answer to the unspoken question.

Hassan straightened with renewed authority. "I will contact the local police immediately. But first, this supposed evidence against Whitmore—"

"Doesn't exist. A delay tactic, most assuredly."

"Excuse me, my lady—" The housemaid Laila was murmuring to Lady Blackwood. "You should know, Mr. Foster sent for an early coffee, as he was feeling unwell."

"Right then," I announced with more confidence than I felt, "time to confront the elusive Mr. Foster properly, if he can be found. We should get him in a confined location. Let's say the Glasshouse."

Lady Blackwood sighed. "Laila, please go to Mr. Foster's room with a message. Tell him... tell him we've made an important discovery about the murder weapon. And that his presence is requested in the Glasshouse."

The lie rolled off her tongue with admirable smoothness for someone who claimed to value proper social etiquette above all else.

Hassan agreed to keep his distance while I worked my plan.

I sent a message to Winters through Freddie, then led Quinn across the estate grounds, following a gravel path that wound between date palms and flowering shrubs toward Lady Blackwood's pride and joy—the Victorian glasshouse that gleamed in the early sun like a crystal palace dropped into the Egyptian desert.

"Remind me," Quinn murmured as we approached the structure, "exactly how we're planning to trick a murderer into confessing? Because my experience suggests such men don't typically crumble under pressure from amateur investigators, however brilliant."

I did love it when he called me brilliant.

"Easy. Winters is bringing us the cyanide pellets from the gardening shed. We convince Foster that we've stumbled onto his poison source but don't understand how dangerous it is." I tried to ignore how his sleeve kept brushing my arm as we walked. "When he believes we're about to contaminate the Glasshouse accidentally, he'll be forced to intervene, revealing his knowledge of the murder weapon."

"Hmm." Quinn seemed unconvinced.

The Glasshouse loomed before us, its tropical foliage visible through condensation-clouded panes.

Quinn stopped so abruptly that I nearly collided with his back, his hand shooting out to catch my arm with iron-tight fingers. "Don't move."

"What are you—" I began, then saw his face.

"Look." He jutted his chin toward the Glasshouse.

I peered through the condensation, to the foliage within.

And to a figure on the floor.

Harrison Foster lay sprawled among the exotic ferns like a

discarded mannequin, his limbs arranged in the unnatural angles of death.

"Looks like our trap just became a crime scene."

I crept closer. "The same telltale signs," I whispered, cataloging the physical evidence even as my hands shook. "Same red complexion, the foam around his lips. Exactly like Thorne."

Quinn produced a handkerchief from his jacket, pressing it over his nose and mouth before approaching the glass doors like he was navigating a minefield.

I followed at a distance, careful steps tamping down the urge to bolt. "Be careful—"

But he was only pulling open the door, then stepping back to release any toxic gases that may have built up inside.

Quinn glanced at me and I nodded. "I can smell it. Someone must have used those pellets. In the air this time."

I ran a hand through my hair. "This changes everything."

Indeed, it did. We'd been catastrophically wrong about Foster's guilt and been too late in the realization to save him.

"Hassan needs to see this immediately," I said, though my voice sounded distant to my own ears. "And we need to accept that our brilliant deductive reasoning just took a rather dramatic turn."

Quinn's hand found mine, anchoring me as the scope of our mistake became clear. "Foster wasn't our killer. He was simply another victim—one who happened to be convenient for someone else's purposes."

The morning sun gleamed off the glass structure, indifferent to the human tragedy contained within. Somewhere in Lady Blackwood's estate, a murderer who'd eliminated two people walked free, probably laughing at our amateur detective work.

"Back to the drawing board then," I managed, squeezing Quinn's fingers as much for my own comfort as his. "Though next time," I said, staring at Foster's corpse through the gleaming glass, "I'm requiring all suspects to check in hourly."

Quinn's dark chuckle held no humor. "At this rate, we'll

solve the case through process of elimination—literally. Though I do hope we identify our killer before we run out of house guests entirely."

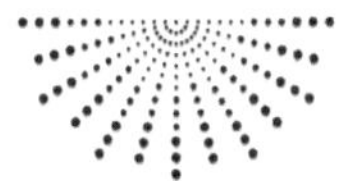

The morning air hung still around the glasshouse, crystalline in its deceptive tranquility. Through the condensation-clouded glass, Harrison Foster's body remained grotesquely visible among the exotic ferns, a macabre centerpiece in Lady Blackwood's botanical pride.

Freddie came running across the gravel path, drawn by some servant's intuition that catastrophe had struck again.

Quinn moved with the efficiency of someone trained for crisis management, positioning himself between the glasshouse and the main house to intercept the inevitable rush of curious guests and panicked servants.

"Stay back," Quinn called sharply. "The air around the structure may still be dangerous."

Lady Blackwood appeared on the path, her morning dress billowing as she hurried toward us with Professor Montague close behind. The moment she glimpsed Foster's prone form through the glass, her face drained of all color.

"Not again," she whispered, clutching Montague's arm for support. "Not in my home, not on my property."

Her distress was genuine, but I caught the undertone of social mortification beneath the horror. Two murders at a respectable estate gathering would destroy her reputation permanently—assuming any of us survived long enough for social consequences to matter.

"Eleanor, sit down before you faint," Montague urged gently, guiding her to a wrought-iron garden bench positioned at a safe distance from the glasshouse. His protective tenderness was touching, though his own face had gone gray with shock.

Richard materialized from the direction of the house, his morning jacket pristinely pressed despite the early hour. "Good God, what's happened now?"

His question carried more exasperation than surprise, as though murders were becoming a tiresome social inconvenience.

"Foster," I managed, pointing toward the glass structure. "Same method as Thorne."

Quinn continued directing traffic with quiet authority, keeping everyone away while we waited for Hassan. I noticed how naturally he'd assumed command of the scene—another reminder of his professional training that I'd been too naive to recognize earlier.

Hassan's arrival could be heard long before he appeared— boots striking gravel, his voice cutting through the morning air like a scimitar through satin.

"Where is he?" The inspector rounded the corner of the main house at a near-run, his usually impeccable composure replaced by barely contained fury.

When he spotted our little tableau—Foster's body visible through the glass, Lady Blackwood sobbing on her garden bench, the rest of us clustered at what we hoped was a safe distance—his expression darkened to something positively murderous.

"Two deaths," he snarled, his gaze fixing on me with laser intensity. "Two murders while you've been playing detective games with this investigation!"

The accusation hit like a slap. "Inspector Hassan, we were attempting to—"

"You were attempting to interfere with official police business!" His voice rose with each word. "And now a second man is dead because amateur investigators thought they could outsmart a killer!"

Quinn stepped protectively closer to me, his composure honed to a blade's edge. "Inspector, Dr. Bell's analysis has been instrumental in identifying—"

"Instrumental in identifying nothing!" Hassan's fury encompassed us both now. "Foster was your primary suspect, wasn't he? The man you were so certain had murdered Thorne?"

My mouth opened then closed soundlessly.

"Yes," I finally sighed. The admission tasted like ashes. "We believed Foster was guilty."

"And while you were constructing your brilliant theories about his guilt, the real killer was planning his next move." Hassan's contempt was palpable. "How many more people will die while you indulge your detective fantasies?"

Lady Blackwood's sobs provided a heartbreaking soundtrack to my professional humiliation. Every tear felt like an indictment of my arrogant assumption that archaeological methodology could solve modern murders.

"Inspector," Montague ventured cautiously, "surely civilian assistance, however misguided, doesn't negate the police's primary responsibility—"

Hassan's glare could have melted the sphinx. "The police responsibility is to conduct proper investigations without interference from well-meaning amateurs who watch too many stage productions."

The reference to theatrical productions made me wince. Had my approach really been that dramatic? That obviously inadequate?

I refrained from pointing out that Hasssan was *not* the police, and the actual authorities seemed disinterested at best.

"I should have both of you removed from this property immediately," Hassan continued, his voice dropping to deadly quiet. "Clearly, your presence is compromising the safety of everyone here."

Richard stepped forward with surprising authority. "Now

see here, Inspector. These people are guests, not criminals. You can't simply—"

"Can't I?" Hassan smirked. "Mr. Sullivan, your own presence here remains highly suspect. I suggest you avoid drawing additional attention to your... questionable activities."

The threat hung in the air. Richard's face flushed, but he retreated without further argument.

Quinn's hand found mine once more, a small, deliberate pressure.

Two people were dead, and I'd been completely, catastrophically wrong about everything.

Hassan approached the Glasshouse.

"Nobody else comes within fifty feet," he commanded, producing a handkerchief to cover his nose and mouth. "The air may still contain traces of hydrogen cyanide."

I watched helplessly as he circled the glass structure, examining the scene from multiple angles before venturing closer to the partially open doors.

"Victim is Harrison Foster," Hassan called out, his voice muffled by the handkerchief. "Same physical symptoms as Dr. Thorne—red complexion, white foam around the mouth, distinctive positioning suggesting rapid death."

Speaking of performances... Whom did Hassan consider his audience?

"Time of death?" Quinn asked.

Something told me the Antiquities Service Director was not remotely qualified to answer this question.

"Difficult to determine precisely in this heat."

Freddie cleared his throat nervously. "Beggin' your pardon, Inspector, but Laila served Mr. Foster his morning coffee in his room 'round seven o'clock. Said he was feeling poorly."

Hassan nodded grimly. "So, between seven this morning and now—approximately two hours for the killer to plan and execute this murder."

My mind raced through the implications. Had someone known we suspected Foster, perhaps even encouraged that suspicion, then eliminated him before he could defend himself or reveal what he knew?

"The Glasshouse doors are unlocked," Hassan observed. "Why did he not simply leave?"

Quinn raised his hand. "That was me. I pulled out the pin that had been used to secure the doors." He pointed to the piece of metal on the ground. "I used a cloth to cover my hand."

Hassan shook his head, then pointed. "See these scratch marks around the exterior latch? This was secured from the outside after Foster entered."

The methodical nature of the murder made my blood run cold. Someone had lured Foster inside, activated the cyanide, then trapped him there to die.

"Sodium cyanide pellets dissolved in that water dish," Hassan continued, pointing toward a ceramic vessel nestled among the tropical plants. "Same source as the Thorne murder —no doubt from your own estate supplies, Lady Blackwood."

She looked up from her handkerchief with fresh horror. "My supplies? But I don't understand—"

"Pellets likely used for pest control," Hassan explained with diminishing patience. "Someone with detailed knowledge of your household management has been accessing your chemical stores."

I glanced at Quinn. We'd been so focused on Foster's suspicious behavior that we'd missed the obvious—someone with intimate access to the estate could have planned these murders.

"Can you determine how the cyanide was activated?" I asked, though my voice carried none of its earlier confidence.

Hassan's look suggested I'd forfeited the right to ask investigative questions. "Water and enclosed space, Dr. Bell. The killer simply needed Foster inside with the doors secured."

The simplicity was terrifying. No elaborate poisoning schemes, no complex timing mechanisms—just a man trapped in a glass box with deadly chemistry.

I forced myself to catalog the evidence, though my hands trembled slightly as I filed each observation. Foster's body lay approximately six feet from the water dish, suggesting he'd realized the danger and tried to reach the door. His face was turned toward the glass panels, mouth open as though he'd been calling for help that never came.

The positioning told a story I didn't want to read—of growing awareness, desperate struggle, inevitable failure. This wasn't the quick death of Thorne's poisoned cup. This was prolonged, terrifying, deliberate.

"Professional execution," Hassan concluded grimly. "The killer understood exactly how long the process would take, how to ensure complete success, how to minimize their own risk."

Professional execution. The phrase echoed in my mind with horrible resonance. We weren't dealing with a crime of passion or opportunistic murder. This was an elimination carried out with cold-heartedness.

The walk back to the main house felt like a funeral procession, each step heavy with the weight of my spectacular failure. Quinn remained beside me, though his protective presence now felt more like pity than partnership.

My brilliant deductive reasoning had been not just wrong, but catastrophically, fatally wrong. While I'd been constructing elaborate theories about Foster's guilt, someone else had been planning his death—possibly encouraged by my very public accusations.

"I killed him," I said quietly, the words tasting like poison themselves. "My investigation got Harrison Foster murdered."

"Clarissa—" Quinn began, but I cut him off.

"No, don't." I stopped on the gravel path, forcing myself to face the brutal truth. "Think about it. Someone wanted Foster dead, but they needed to distract us from the truth. What better than having the amateur detective build a case against someone publicly?"

The horrible logic of it made my breath catch. Every piece of evidence we'd found, every suspicious behavior we'd cataloged—what if it had all been concocted? What if the real killer had been feeding us information, guiding our investigation toward the conclusion they wanted?

"Foster's reconnaissance of the property," I continued, my voice gaining the manic edge of someone whose worldview was crumbling in real time. "His questions about Thorne's cup and the poison sources. His revelation of evidence against Whitmore. What if none of it was criminal behavior? What if it was legitimate investigation?"

Quinn's expression grew increasingly troubled as he followed my reasoning. "You think Foster was investigating the same conspiracy we were?"

"Maybe Foster knew exactly what was happening and was trying to stop it." The admission felt like swallowing broken glass. "His secret relationship with Yasmin, his knowledge of artifact smuggling networks—what if he came here to expose the killer, not to commit murder?"

The desert wind stirred the palm fronds overhead, creating shifting patterns of shadow that seemed to mock my earlier confidence. I'd been so proud of my analytical methods, so certain that archaeological training qualified me for criminal investigation.

Instead, I'd been played like a novice handling her first pottery sherd—clumsy, overconfident, completely missing the obvious.

"The evidence against him was too perfect," I realized, my voice barely above a whisper. "Too neatly laid out, too obviously suspicious. Someone wanted us to find it."

Quinn moved closer, his hand settling on my shoulder with gentle firmness. "Even if that's true, you couldn't have known—"

"Couldn't I?" I pulled away from his comfort, needing the sharp edges of self-recrimination. "I solved Dr. Sutherland's murder through observation and analysis. But this time, I let my ego override my methodology. I wanted to be brilliant, wanted to impress Hassan and prove myself capable. 'Pride goeth before destruction,'" I murmured, "'and a haughty spirit before a fall.'"

"I just can't buy it. Such specific questions. How could Foster know what the killer had planned?"

We found ourselves in the Salon again, though the room felt different now—less like a gathering space and more like a holding pen for suspects. The morning sun streaming through the tall windows seemed harsh rather than welcoming, illuminating every crack in Lady Blackwood's decorative scheme.

The servants brought coffee into the Salon, though the bitter aroma made my stomach churn. I stared at the delicate porcelain cup in my hands—another blue-glazed artifact that suddenly seemed ominous rather than beautiful—and cataloged the magnitude of my failure.

Every piece of evidence that had convinced me of Foster's guilt now demanded reexamination.

"I was so proud of my deductive methods," I murmured, setting down the coffee cup before my trembling hands could betray me further. "I thought my training made me qualified to solve murders."

Quinn attempted reassurance from his position near the window. "Your analysis of the physical evidence was brilliant, Clarissa. The ceramic fragments, the poison delivery method, the timeline reconstruction—"

"All worthless," I interrupted, "because I misidentified the killer. I built an elaborate case against an innocent man while the real murderer watched and planned their next move. My father always warned me about academic arrogance," I whispered. "He said scholars who ventured outside their expertise usually embarrassed themselves publicly."

The reference to Father's warnings carried bitter irony, given his own criminal activities in the antiquities trade. Perhaps failure ran in the Bell family—we were all capable of spectacular misjudgment when our egos overrode our better sense.

Quinn attempted another approach. "Even experienced investigators make mistakes, Clarissa. The important thing is learning from—"

"Two people are dead," I cut him off sharply. "This isn't a scholarly debate where incorrect theories can be revised in the next journal article."

Professor Whitmore seemed to decide the Salon was not a good place to pass the time. He paused in the door on his way out. "Dr. Bell, you mustn't blame yourself. We all believed Foster's behavior was suspicious."

His attempted kindness only made the failure sting worse. Even if others had shared my suspicions, I'd been the one building the case, confidently presenting evidence, convincing Hassan and Quinn that Foster represented the primary threat.

"Let's review everything we thought we knew about Foster's guilt," I said when Whitmore had left, forcing myself to approach this like a proper archaeological reassessment. When you discover that your dating methods have been wrong, you don't abandon the site—you reexamine every artifact with new methodology."

Quinn settled into the chair beside mine, his notebook appearing with practiced efficiency.

We talked through each point of suspicion.

"Perhaps someone played us perfectly." The admission left my mouth dry. "They fed us just enough genuine information mixed with strategic misdirection to guide our investigation exactly where they wanted it to go."

Quinn closed his notebook with decisive finality. "Which means we need to completely restart our analysis. Everything we believed about motives, opportunities, and capabilities requires reexamination."

The prospect felt overwhelming. How could I trust any conclusion when I'd been so spectacularly wrong about everything? How could I identify truth when I'd proven so susceptible to manipulation?

"What if Foster wasn't just investigating the same conspiracy we were," I said slowly, the realization crystallizing. "What if he was ahead of us. He'd already identified the real killer. And that's why he had to die." My voice grew stronger as the logic became inescapable. "Not because he was guilty, but because he knew who was. Maybe his elimination wasn't covering up past crimes, It was preventing future exposure."

CHAPTER TWENTY-ONE

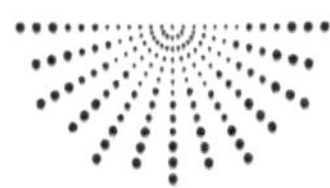

The late-morning sun cast long shadows across the courtyard as I descended the main staircase with my field satchel slung over my shoulder and an admittedly reckless determination settling in my gut. Three days of murders, deceptions, and mounting evidence had crystallized into a single determination: I needed to see Karnak Temple for myself.

The Salon held its usual collection of suspects attempting normalcy over coffee—a performance that might have been more convincing if we weren't all avoiding eye contact and jumping at sudden movements.

"I'm going to examine the site where Dr. Thorne planned his demonstration," I announced, my voice carrying more confidence than I felt. "The astronomical alignment he was investigating may hold clues about why someone was willing to commit murder over a stone sphere." Or disc. Whatever.

Inspector Hassan immediately straightened in his chair, his coffee cup clattering against its saucer with the decisive ring of masculine authority. "Dr. Bell, I must strongly advise against leaving the estate while the investigation remains active. The murders—"

"Cannot be solved by sitting here rehashing the same

conversations while drinking increasingly bitter tea." I shouldered my satchel more firmly, channeling every ounce of Oxford-trained determination into my posture. "I'm an archaeologist, Inspector. I examine sites, not just theories."

Hassan's dark eyes flashed with what I was beginning to recognize as his brand of irritation—the look of a man who'd discovered that foreign women with advanced degrees were more difficult to manage than his superiors had led him to believe.

"Very well." His tone was clipped. "I cannot officially prevent you from visiting Karnak Temple, but I will be accompanying you. I must ensure that you don't do anything that would harm Egypt's interests or compromise evidence at the site."

I bristled at the implication that my professional examination might somehow damage—well perhaps his concern wasn't entirely unreasonable. Still, principles demanded objection.

"I hardly think my methodical survey would—"

"I'm coming with you as well." Richard rose from his seat with the decisive movement of a man who'd just remembered he was supposed to be playing the protective suitor. "For your protection, of course. These murders prove how dangerous this entire situation has become."

Quinn's voice cut through the mounting testosterone with deceptive calm. "How touching that you're so concerned about Clarissa's safety." He set down his coffee cup. "I'm not letting her out of my sight."

The possessive undertone in Quinn's statement caused both attraction and fury to rise in me, like a tide meeting a contrary wind.

"Gentlemen." I employed my best lecturing voice. "I am an educated and experienced archaeologist. I neither need nor want three escorts treating me like a helpless debutante who might swoon at the sight of ancient stones."

Richard's face flushed. "Clarissa, be reasonable. Two people are dead—"

"Which is precisely why I need to examine the evidence,

not cower behind masculine protection while perfectly good data sits waiting to be analyzed." I turned toward the door with what I hoped looked like confident purpose rather than stubborn recklessness. "Besides, Inspector Hassan is officially accompanying me, which means the rest of you can stay here and practice not murdering each other for approximately three hours."

The silence that followed carried the weight of offended male egos.

"Though I suppose, if you're all determined to tromp through Karnak disrupting my survey, I can't physically prevent you. Just try not to step on my toes."

Hassan rose with the dignity of someone whose authority had been acknowledged, even if somewhat grudgingly. "I will arrange transportation."

"I'll arrange better transportation," Richard countered immediately. "I can hire a private automobile. Much more comfortable than whatever the Inspector would manage."

The competitive undercurrent was becoming ridiculous. If they started measuring satchels next, I was walking to Karnak.

"Fine." I moved toward the door. "Hassan arranges transportation. Richard provides contingency automobile if Hassan's arrangements prove inadequate. Quinn stops looking smug. Everyone meets in the courtyard in thirty minutes wearing sensible shoes and attitudes adjusted for actual productive work."

I escaped before anyone could argue further, though I heard Richard's protest ("Clarissa, really—") cut short by what sounded suspiciously like Quinn's low chuckle.

Annie materialized in my bedroom. "Going to the temple, I hear, miss?"

"Apparently with an entire entourage." I began checking my field kit with more vigor than necessary.

"Mr. Quinn seems particularly determined to accompany you."

The knowing tone in her voice stilled my hands on my

notebook. "Mr. Quinn is professionally interested in the arti-facts. That's all."

"Of course, miss." Annie's expression remained perfectly neutral.

I shot her what I hoped was a disapproving look. "We're investigating murders, Annie. Not conducting romantic field studies."

"Yes, miss. Though I suppose there's no reason you can't do both efficiently."

Before I could formulate a response, a knock sounded at my door. I opened it to find Quinn leaning against the door-frame with that insufferable half-smile that made rational thought more difficult than it should be.

"Ready for your expedition?" His eyes tracked over my field attire with appreciation that felt distinctly unprofessional. "Though I feel compelled to mention that inviting both Hassan and Sullivan seems strategically questionable."

"I didn't invite anyone." I stepped into the corridor, aware of his proximity. "You all invited yourselves."

"Fair point." He fell into step beside me, his hand settling briefly at my elbow to guide me around a servant carrying linens. The touch lasted perhaps two seconds and yet managed to scramble my thoughts entirely. "Though I should warn you —Sullivan spent breakfast asking the staff pointed questions about my business dealings."

My stomach clenched. "What kind of questions?"

"The kind that suggest he's either genuinely concerned about your welfare or gathering information for his own purposes." Quinn's voice dropped lower as we descended the stairs. "Just promise me you'll be careful. Karnak Temple is isolated, the suspects are desperate, and Hassan's protective instincts may not extend to preventing harm from respectable American gentlemen."

The concern in his voice made my eyes tingle. "I can handle Richard."

"I know you can." His smile held gentleness. "But you shouldn't have to handle him alone."

Minutes later, I found myself wedged between competing masculine energies in what felt less like transportation and more like strategic entrapment—Richard's anxious protectiveness radiating from my left, Quinn's dangerous magnetism occupying my right peripheral vision, and Hassan's authority filling the front seat with official disapproval. Each man seemed convinced he knew what was best for me, and their silent competition filled the motorcar with suffocating tension.

Specimen: Male Protective Instinct (Collective), Notable Characteristics: Inversely proportional to actual helpfulness.

When Karnak Temple first came into view, my irritation dissolved into breathless wonder that no amount of training could diminish. The massive columns rose like a forest of stone giants, their surfaces carved with hieroglyphs that caught and held the morning light in ways that made my scholar's heart ache. The sheer scale dwarfed human concerns—murders, romantic complications, career anxieties—all rendered temporarily insignificant before monuments built for eternity.

"My word," I whispered, momentarily forgetting my escorts entirely. "What a marvel!"

We tumbled out of the automobile, and I moved through the temple complex with growing absorption, following Thorne's notebooks to locate the specific alignment he'd been studying. My companions fell into step behind me—Hassan providing historical context, Quinn scanning sight lines with professional paranoia, and Richard fumbling with a leather-bound guidebook that he clearly hoped would render him useful.

The area was relatively secluded, tucked away from the main tourist routes where morning sunlight would strike a particular angle of carved symbols at precisely the right moment. The perfect spot for someone to position the Astral Sphere at dawn and observe whatever astronomical phenomenon Thorne had predicted.

"This temple represents over two thousand years of continuous construction," Hassan explained, his professional pride apparently overcoming his official displeasure with my entire existence. "Each pharaoh added to its glory, creating the largest religious complex ever built."

I traced my fingers over hieroglyphs worn smooth by centuries of sun and sand, my mind cataloging construction phases and architectural evolution. Somewhere in this vast complex lay evidence explaining why two men had died over astronomical alignments and a blue stone artifact.

Quinn surveyed the surrounding areas with calculating eyes that had nothing to do with archaeology. "Excellent sight lines from multiple positions. Someone could observe from considerable distance without being detected."

The tactical observation sent a chill down my spine despite the Egyptian heat. He was right, of course. Anyone positioned on the surrounding structures could have watched Thorne prepare his demonstration, identified the Sphere's location, and planned... whatever they were planning.

Richard fumbled with his guidebook, clearly attempting to contribute something beyond expensive transportation. "Yes, well, according to this, the temple was dedicated to Amun-Ra and... er... features excellent examples of New Kingdom architecture."

His shallow understanding was painfully obvious beside Hassan's expertise and Quinn's tactical observations. I felt an unwelcome pang of sympathy—Richard was genuinely trying, even if his efforts only highlighted how fundamentally unsuited we'd always been.

"What will we see when we return for the Winter Solstice in two days?" Quinn asked.

Two days. Forty-eight hours to solve two murders, recover a missing artifact, and prevent the conspiracy that had killed two men from succeeding.

Richard shifted uncomfortably beside me. "Yes, you should know, Clarissa, I've arranged my departure for Saturday morning. After the ceremony, of course. Business obligations in Cairo, you understand."

"Hmm." Quinn's voice held amusement. "We shall miss

you. Professor Whitmore mentioned he and Dr. Mujahid are also departing Saturday."

Hassan's expression grew grim. "And I must return to Cairo by Monday with or without the Astral Sphere. The Ministry will not tolerate further delays."

So, in less than forty-eight hours, every suspect would scatter to different corners of the globe, likely taking the artifact and its secrets with them. The Operation Indigo conspiracy, if it were connected, would go cold again, and the murders would remain forever unsolved.

Hassan studied Richard with sharp attention. "Mr. Sullivan, your employer's business dealings remain under considerable scrutiny. Perhaps it would be best for you to delay your departure."

Richard went pale. "I'm sure I don't know what you mean, Inspector."

Hassan's smile held no warmth. "Clearly you are aware that Armand Bell's acquisition methods have attracted... official interest."

"Now see here—" Richard began desperately.

"The murders may well be connected to these illegal exports," Hassan continued. "Someone who felt threatened by exposure, perhaps. Someone with significant financial interests in maintaining certain... arrangements."

A soft footstep on stone made us all turn with varying degrees of alarm.

A lean man in a white linen suit emerged from behind one of the massive columns, a leather notebook clutched in his hand like a weapon. He'd clearly been eavesdropping, and from his expression of satisfied intensity, he'd heard everything he needed.

"Gentlemen, Dr. Bell," he said in accented English, offering a slight bow that managed to convey both courtesy and contempt. "Permit me to introduce myself. I am Mahmoud Farid, correspondent for *Al-Shura* newspaper. I have been following this most fascinating story."

Hassan's face darkened like a thundercloud. "What story would that be, Mr. Farid?"

"Murder and antiquities smuggling among the British colonial community." Farid's smile was sharp as a blade and twice as dangerous. "Two deaths at Lady Blackwood's estate, a missing artifact of considerable value, and connections to illegal export operations spanning three countries."

Richard stepped forward, his voice strained with barely controlled panic. "I'm sure you're mistaken about—"

"Am I?" Farid consulted his notebook. "Dr. Jasper Thorne, poisoned with cyanide Monday evening. Harrison Foster, found dead this morning using the same method. Both men connected to a mysterious artifact called the Astral Sphere, now missing."

Ice formed in my stomach, crystallizing around the terrible realization that our investigation had been observed, documented, and was about to become very public entertainment.

"How can you possibly know these details, and so quickly?" My voice came out steadier than I felt.

"I have excellent sources, Dr. Bell. Including information about your family's involvement in cultural theft." Farid's eyes glittered with journalistic hunger—the look of someone who'd discovered a story that could make careers. "American millionaire Armand Bell has been acquiring Egyptian artifacts through questionable channels for years. This story will run in Sunday's edition."

"You cannot prove—" Richard began.

"Can I not?" Farid flipped through his notes with confidence. "I have transactions, shipping records, and witness testimonies connecting the Bell family to illegal antiquities exports. And your presence here, Mr. Sullivan."

Richard's face had gone ashen. "Name your price."

The words hung in the desert air like an admission of guilt —like confirmation of every terrible suspicion I'd been trying not to acknowledge.

Hassan's expression shifted from official displeasure to active suspicion, while Quinn watched with cat-like stillness.

"You cannot bribe the Egyptian press, Mr. Sullivan," Farid said with cold satisfaction. "Your assumptions about purchasing silence will not work here. This story represents justice for decades of cultural theft."

"If you publish lies about my father—" I started, though my voice lacked conviction because they probably weren't lies at all.

"Not lies, Dr. Bell. Truth." Farid's gaze held something almost like pity beneath the professional determination. "My sources include someone very close to this investigation," Farid continued smoothly. "Dr. Yasmin Mujahid has been quite helpful in documenting the colonial archaeological community's... excesses, but I was hoping for another quote, from one of you."

My mind reeled. Yasmin, feeding information to the press? The Egyptian archaeologist had seemed committed to scholarly integrity, but perhaps her nationalist feelings ran deeper than professional courtesy. Or perhaps she simply understood that preserving Egypt's heritage required exposing the networks that plundered it.

"Sunday's edition will detail the entire network," Farid announced with the finality of an execution date. "The deaths, the missing artifact, the international smuggling operation, and the prominent families who built their reputations on stolen Egyptian heritage. The world will know the truth about these murders and the cultural crimes they were meant to conceal."

"Well, you're not getting any quote here, man." Quinn took a few aggressive steps toward the journalist.

The man got the hint and backed off quickly.

The carriage ride back to Lady Blackwood's estate passed in tense silence, each passenger lost in private calculations of disaster. I stared at the passing landscape—palm trees and fields giving way to the estate's manicured grounds—while my mind raced with terrible mathematics: less than forty-eight hours before suspects scattered globally, less than seventy-two hours before newspapers destroyed Father's reputation.

Richard finally broke the silence, his voice hollow with

desperation. "Clarissa, we have to leave. Tonight. I can have us on a steamer to Alexandria by morning, then passage to New York before this scandal breaks."

"Running away proves guilt," Hassan observed grimly from the front seat.

"Staying proves nothing if we're destroyed by false accusations," Richard shot back. "Once the newspapers print those stories, Egyptian authorities will show no mercy to foreign nationals. They'll make examples of us to demonstrate their independence."

Quinn spoke for the first time since leaving Karnak, his voice carrying the weight of someone who understood exactly how nationalist movements weaponized scandal. "He's not wrong about official response. Nationalist sentiment is running high, and a good scandal involving British and American criminals would play very well with the public."

I closed my eyes, feeling walls closing in from every direction. The murders unsolved, the artifact missing, Father's reputation in mortal peril, and suspects preparing to vanish beyond reach.

"I won't abandon the investigation," I said quietly, though my conviction felt fragile. "Not when we're this close to the truth."

"Close to the truth?" Richard laughed bitterly. "We're close to imprisonment or worse. Whatever you think you can discover in the next two days—"

"Will have to be enough," I finished firmly, channeling every ounce of stubborn determination that had gotten me through Oxford and Giza and every other disaster my academic ambitions had generated.

CHAPTER TWENTY-TWO

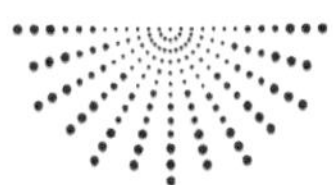

I found Dr. Yasmin Mujahid on the private balcony of her guest room, seated at a small wrought-iron table with papers spread before her like tarot cards predicting doom. The late afternoon sun cast golden light across the scene, transforming the Valley of the Kings in the distance into a romantic watercolor while leaving shadows pooling beneath her dark eyes.

"Dr. Mujahid," I began, stepping onto the balcony. "May I join you?"

She gestured to the empty chair across from her without looking up from her documents. "Dr. Bell. I wondered when you would come." Her voice carried weary resignation rather than surprise. "Though I expected Mr. Quinn as well, given how inseparable you two have become."

"This conversation is between colleagues," I replied, settling into the chair and noting how her papers were positioned to prevent casual observation. My earlier catastrophic misjudgments with Foster had taught me the value of careful approach over dramatic accusations.

Yasmin finally raised her gaze, and I caught the flash of social obligation beneath her scholarly composure. "Colleagues trapped together by Lady Blackwood's hospitality and official suspicion."

The edge in her voice spoke to deeper frustrations than mere travel delays.

"The journalist, Mahmoud Farid," I said directly, abandoning diplomatic circumnavigation for honest confrontation. "He claimed to have excellent sources about the murders, including someone close to the investigation. He mentioned you specifically."

Yasmin's expression hardened into something approaching stone. "And you assume I've been feeding scandal to the press for what—nationalist revenge? Cultural vendetta against colonial archaeologists?"

"I assume you've been protecting Egyptian interests," I corrected. "The question is whether that protection extends to eliminating threats to cultural heritage."

She laughed, though the sound held no humor. "Eliminating threats. How dramatically you phrase it, Dr. Bell." Her fingers drummed against the table's iron surface. "Yes, I spoke with Farid. Yes, I provided information about the looting networks operating through legitimate channels. But murder details?" She shook her head decisively. "Those came from other sources."

"What other sources?"

"Ask yourself who benefits from having this scandal published immediately," Yasmin replied. "Who needs the investigation concluded quickly, before deeper examination reveals uncomfortable truths?"

The implication hung between us. Someone wanted the newspaper story to force rapid resolution, to create pressure that would drive away investigations before they uncovered more dangerous secrets.

"Your father's business dealings make convenient targets," Yasmin continued, her voice softening slightly. "Wealthy American collector, questionable acquisition methods, daughter whose expertise facilitates authentication—it's a perfect story for nationalist newspapers. But it's also a perfect distraction from more immediate criminal activities."

I felt the heat rising. "My family's reputation—"

"Will survive, assuming you can prove the murders aren't connected to antiquities smuggling." Her dark eyes held steady on mine. "Can you prove that, Dr. Bell?"

Before I could formulate a response, she shifted in her chair, the movement causing afternoon light to strike her classical profile. "But you didn't come here to discuss press relations. You came about my argument with Harrison."

The direct statement caught me off-guard. I'd prepared for defensive maneuvering, not voluntary revelation. "I overheard raised voices in the garden. It seemed... significant given subsequent events."

"Significant because you assumed criminal conspiracy rather than personal conflict." Yasmin's tone carried gentle mockery. "Your training serves you well with artifacts, Dr. Bell, but human motivations are more complex than ceramic typologies."

She stood, moving to the balcony's edge where evening breeze stirred the papers on her table. "Harrison Foster and I had a relationship several years ago in Cairo. Brief, intense, ultimately impossible given our different approaches to cultural preservation."

I waited, as she chose words to reveal truth while protecting privacy.

"He believed in working within the colonial system—charming British patrons, accommodating American collectors, achieving gradual reform through diplomatic compromise." Her voice carried old frustration. "I believed such accommodation was complicity with theft."

"The argument I overheard?"

"Harrison wanted to resume our relationship. He claimed his recent activities proved his commitment to genuine cultural protection rather than merely profitable accommodation." She turned back toward me, her expression mixing sadness with exasperation. "He was wrong about both the relationship and his activities."

The revelation recontextualized everything I'd observed. Foster's agitation around Yasmin, his attempts to speak privately with her, even his defensive behavior when questioned—none of it had been criminal conspiracy. It had been unwanted romantic pursuit combined with professional disagreement.

"He thought investigating the smuggling network would impress you?"

"He thought many things that weren't particularly intelligent," Yasmin replied dryly. "Harrison always believed charm and good intentions could overcome fundamental philosophical differences. Our argument was my attempt to explain, once again, why romantic reconciliation was impossible."

"You must think me very naive," I said quietly.

"I think you've been thrust into a situation requiring skills your training never provided," she replied with unexpected kindness. "Detecting human deception is quite different from authenticating artifacts. Though both require careful observation and healthy skepticism about obvious conclusions."

The comparison stung because it was accurate. I'd approached criminal investigation like excavation. But artifacts couldn't lie, couldn't manipulate evidence, couldn't devise elaborate deceptions to frame innocent parties.

"Harrison wasn't particularly likeable," Yasmin continued, settling back into her chair. "His methods were questionable, his ego insufferable, and his romantic persistence bordered on harassment. But he wasn't a murderer, Dr. Bell. He was simply a man whose ambitions exceeded his capabilities."

"The timing of his death troubles me," I admitted. "Someone eliminated him precisely when we'd identified him as the primary suspect."

Yasmin nodded grimly. "The question becomes: who possessed both the knowledge to manipulate amateur detectives and the access to commit the murders themselves?" Yasmin's fingers steepled thoughtfully. "Someone who understood exactly how you would respond to specific types of evidence."

I leaned forward. "The morning Foster died—can you remember what time you came downstairs?"

"Quite early," she replied, though uncertainty clouded her expression. "The sun was just beginning to touch the eastern walls of the courtyard. Perhaps six-thirty? Seven at the latest."

"Did you see anyone else moving about the estate?"

Her brow furrowed in concentration. "I passed Laila on the main staircase. She was carrying a coffee service upstairs—to Foster's room, I assumed, given the timing. Poor girl looked half-asleep, but she managed a polite greeting."

A jolt of realization snapped through me. "You're certain it was Foster's coffee service?"

"Laila could confirm the exact time if you need precision," Yasmin offered. "She seems quite methodical about the morning routines, unlike some of the other servants who appear perpetually flustered."

I was already calculating timelines. If Laila was serving Foster coffee when Yasmin encountered her on the stairs, then Foster was alive when Yasmin came downstairs. The timing would establish her alibi definitively—assuming she was telling the truth about the encounter. I'd check with Laila.

"After you came downstairs, did you see any of the other guests?"

"Professor Montague was in the Library, reading by the window light. Quite devoted to his scholarly routines, that one." She paused, consulting her memory. "Professor Whitmore was examining something in the Salon—papers, I think. He looked up when I passed but didn't speak."

"What about Mr. Sullivan?"

"Your former fiancé was pacing the terrace, already smoking cigarettes with nervous energy. He nodded when he saw me but seemed preoccupied with his own troubles." Her tone carried subtle sympathy. "Romantic entanglements at crime scenes create such complications, don't they?"

I ignored the personal observation, my mind racing

through implications. "All three men were visible and accounted for during the critical timeframe. We all saw them at breakfast after that."

"Unless one of them committed murder with supernatural speed, yes." Yasmin's expression grew thoughtful. "Which leaves an interesting question about who wasn't visible during those crucial morning hours."

The terrible mathematics were becoming inescapable. Quinn had been with me when we discovered Foster's body. The servants could no doubt be verified through kitchen routines and household duties. Every guest could be placed somewhere visible during the timeframe when Foster was walking to his death.

"Lady Blackwood," I whispered, the name feeling like poison in my mouth.

"The gracious hostess who directed this entire gathering," Yasmin sighed. "Who had intimate knowledge of every guest's routine, complete access to household supplies, and the authority to move about the estate without question or suspicion."

My world tilted as the implications cascaded. Eleanor Blackwood, with her enthusiasm for Thorne's theories and her perfectly timed expressions of horror at each murder. The woman who'd positioned herself as the innocent victim of circumstances, watching with apparent dismay as her house party deteriorated into murder.

"She knew exactly how we would respond to Foster's suspicious behavior," I realized, my voice growing stronger as the logic crystallized. "She fed us just enough genuine information to guide our suspicions precisely where she wanted them."

"And when Foster threatened to expose her real activities, she eliminated him using your amateur detective work as perfect justification." Yasmin's dark eyes held something approaching respect. "Quite sophisticated planning, really. Using the investigators themselves as cover for murder."

The desert breeze again stirred the papers on her table, and I caught glimpses of her documentation—not criminal plans, but scholarly research about cultural preservation. She'd been exactly what she appeared to be: a passionate advocate for protecting her country's treasures.

"I need to verify the timeline with Annie and the servants," I said, rising from my chair with sudden urgency. "If Laila confirms your encounter on the stairs—"

"She will," Yasmin interrupted confidently. "The girl has an excellent memory for household routines. But Dr. Bell—" She caught my arm as I moved toward the door. "Be very careful who you trust with this revelation. Lady Blackwood has demonstrated considerable skill at eliminating threats to her operations."

The warning sent ice through my veins. Somewhere in this elegant estate, surrounded by tacky decorations and gracious hospitality, walked a killer who'd already proven capable of murder.

And I was about to expose her with nothing but circumstantial evidence and amateur deductive reasoning that had already proven catastrophically wrong once before.

CHAPTER TWENTY-THREE

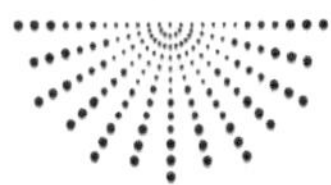

*L*ady Blackwood made her announcement at breakfast the next morning with the flair of someone unveiling a particularly dramatic piece of statuary. "A morale-boosting expedition!" she declared, her hands fluttering like enthusiastic doves. "We shall visit Mr. Carter's marvelous work at Tutankhamun's tomb. Everyone needs a respite."

I translated this mentally as: *Let's all pretend two men haven't been murdered under this roof and distract ourselves with dead pharaohs instead.*

I'd verified Yasmin's details about her whereabouts yesterday morning. She was indeed downstairs before Foster even left his bedroom, and had been in plain sight all morning, along with the rest of the men.

"I've arranged special permits through my connections," Lady Blackwood continued, which I noted was the second time in two days she'd reminded us of her extensive network. One might almost think she wanted us to remember how many influential people owed her favors.

The gathered suspects—I mean guests—responded with varying degrees of enthusiasm. Richard perked up immediately, no doubt envisioning himself posed heroically against ancient ruins for some future memoir. Yasmin's expression suggested polite interest masking deeper calculation. Professor Montague beamed at Lady Blackwood with the devotion of a particularly loyal terrier.

Quinn caught my eye across the breakfast table, one eyebrow rising in silent question. I gave the tiniest shrug that translated roughly to: *This is either monumentally tone-deaf or strategically brilliant, and I haven't decided which yet.*

"How delightful," I said aloud, because one must maintain proper social conventions even when cataloging murder suspects. "I've been meaning to see Carter's progress."

"Excellent!" Lady Blackwood's smile brightened the room. "We leave within the hour. Do dress appropriately. The Valley can be quite... unforgiving."

Like your methods of pest control.

Not enough motorcars for us all, so carriages were arranged and brought. Multiple vehicles also meant opportunities for private conversations, which I suspected was either Lady Blackwood's intention or a happy accident I intended to exploit ruthlessly.

I positioned myself with deliberation, managing to secure a seat beside Lady Blackwood herself while Professor Montague settled opposite us. The other carriages sorted themselves into their natural hierarchies—Quinn with Hassan, Richard with various servants, Yasmin with Whitmore.

As we lurched into motion, Lady Blackwood deployed her fan. The morning heat was already gathering strength, transforming the landscape into something shimmering and otherworldly.

"Such a relief to escape the estate," she sighed. "The atmosphere has become quite oppressive."

"Murder does have that effect," I agreed pleasantly. "Along with attracting flies."

Montague coughed into his handkerchief.

Lady Blackwood's fan paused mid-flutter before resuming its rhythm.

"You Americans," she said with forced lightness. "So refreshingly direct."

I filed this under: *British euphemisms for 'tactlessly boorish.'*

The road toward the Valley wound through desolated terrain. Limestone cliffs rose like ancient stage sets, their surfaces carved by time and wind into shapes that suggested forgotten temples.

I began my probing with attempted subtlety. "Lady Blackwood, I've been curious about estate management. Particularly the chemical supplies used for pest control?"

Her fan maintained its steady tempo. "Oh, yes, you must mean the cyanide. Dangerous, obviously. But one must be vigilant against insects in this climate."

"I've heard some sites use quite sophisticated methods. Fumigation chambers, specialized compounds..."

"Indeed." Her eyes flickered with something I couldn't quite identify—pride? Wariness? "Charles always insisted on the most effective solutions. He couldn't abide anything that might damage his artifacts."

"Of course," Montague interjected loyally. "Lord Blackwood was meticulous about preservation. I recall him explaining the proper cubic footage calculations for fumigation —terribly complex mathematics."

I made a mental note: *Montague knows about the measurements. Filing under: suspicious or merely well-informed colleague?*

The conversation drifted to safer topics—the weather, Carter's astonishing luck, the international sensation surrounding the tomb's discovery. But I noticed Lady Blackwood's composure had acquired a brittle quality.

As our carriage crested a rise, the Valley of the Kings revealed itself with dramatic timing. The landscape shifted from merely impressive to genuinely otherworldly—a amphitheater of cliffs surrounding a desolate valley floor where the ancient Egyptians had hidden their most precious dead.

And where, apparently, modern Egyptians were excavating them with considerable enthusiasm and international press coverage.

The scene below was chaos: Carter's excavation site

swarmed with workers, officials, journalists, and various Europeans in increasingly wilted formal wear. The contrast between timeless antiquity and contemporary spectacle created a cognitive dissonance that made my head ache.

Or possibly that was just dehydration.

"Magnificent, isn't it?" Lady Blackwood's voice held genuine reverence. "To think we're among the first to witness such treasures."

"Charles would have loved this," Montague added softly.

Lady Blackwood's expression flickered—grief or calculation, I couldn't determine. "Yes. Though he might have preferred acquiring the artifacts to merely observing them."

I filed this under: *Interesting choice of words from a widow.*

As our carriages discharged their contents, Howard Carter himself appeared to greet us. He wore the expression of a man caught between passion and obligation—enthusiasm warring with exhaustion in the lines around his eyes.

"Lady Blackwood?" The voice came from the sensible center of the chaos. Carter wore fatigue like a well-cut suit: crisp collar, dust in the seams, eyes fatigued but alert. He took in our permits with a glance, our faces with another, and kept the work moving with small nods that could have marshaled cavalry.

"Your timing is excellent. We're just beginning to bring out a new section of pieces." He said this with admirable courtesy, given he was probably desperate to return to his excavation.

Lady Blackwood made introductions, and we were invited to follow Carter down into the most famous tomb in the world.

The tour that followed defied adequate description. Carter guided us through chambers where three thousand years compressed into immediate presence—golden shrines gleaming in lamplight, painted walls depicting the pharaoh's journey through the underworld, artifacts in such profusion that cataloging them would require years.

"Mr. Carter," I said, trying not to sound twelve. "Your

cataloguing system is—" I searched for a word that didn't sound like worship. "Exemplary."

He offered a wry half-smile. "It needs to be. The world's eyes are unkind and very numerous. We've had to assign guards to everything, if you take my meaning. Locks on locks. Inventories of inventories." His gaze slid to the entrance where a knot of officials, soldiers, and opportunists vibrated like bees. "It isn't the past that worries me most. It's the present."

"My constant complaint," I said, and his smile deepened, just a fraction.

Then his head cocked, birdlike. "Have we met? No—wait. You remind me of Miss Aldridge—worked with us last season. Sharp mind, excellent hands. A charming woman." He smiled. "We need more of you."

I accepted the compliment like a fragile figurine and set it on a high shelf. Being seen for one's work rather than one's money was a novelty I intended to savor later, when no one was dead.

I found myself standing before a gilded shrine, studying the hieroglyphs with professional fascination, when Lady Blackwood materialized at my elbow.

"Extraordinary craftsmanship," she murmured. "One can understand why collectors become... passionate about acquisition."

"Even when acquisition methods are questionable?" I asked, keeping my tone academic.

Her fan snapped open with a click. "Not you, too, Dr. Bell? Harrison Foster seemed to think he could threaten me with exposure of perfectly legitimate transactions." The words emerged with cocktail-party casualness. "The man had no appreciation for the risks Charles took to preserve these artifacts from political instability."

I continued examining the hieroglyphs while excitement sharpened my focus. She'd just admitted Foster threatened her. *Motive: delivered with remarkably poor judgment.*

"Foster struck me as rather presumptuous," I offered neutrally.

"Insufferably so." Lady Blackwood's voice sharpened. "He seemed to think he'd discovered some irregularity in Charles's acquisition methods. He couldn't possibly understand the complexities involved. But we shouldn't speak ill of the dead, now should we?"

Two statements. Both revealing. Both suggesting Foster had leverage over Lady Blackwood regarding her late husband's potentially illegal antiquities trading.

Also: she seemed remarkably unbothered by his death.

"The heat must be affecting me," she said suddenly, her fan accelerating. "I'm talking far too freely."

Yes, I thought. *You certainly are.*

Montague appeared with the timing of someone who'd been hovering nearby, possibly eavesdropping. Was his concern for Lady Blackwood's self-incrimination or his own exposure by association?

"Shall we view some of the other tombs?" he suggested with forced brightness. "The painted reliefs are particularly fine."

The afternoon heat transformed the Valley into something approaching purgatory. Even the shadows seemed to radiate warmth. Our party began dispersing like water seeking lower ground—some retreating to shaded areas, others examining artifacts with varying degrees of genuine interest.

I found myself studying a display of canopic jars when Lady Blackwood rejoined me, apparently recovered from her earlier indiscretion.

"Dr. Bell," she began with renewed composure. "I hope you won't place too much importance on idle conversation. The stress of recent events has left me quite scattered."

"Of course," I replied, which we both understood meant: *Too late, I've already cataloged everything you said.*

"Foster's death, while tragic, was clearly the work of someone unstable." Her voice carried the firmness of someone constructing official narrative. "No doubt the same person who killed poor Jasper. A madman, certainly."

"Or a very calculating individual," I suggested.

Her fan paused. "One mustn't see conspiracy where it doesn't exist."

Before I could respond—probably with something *refreshingly direct*—Montague materialized.

"Ladies," he said with excessive cheer. "The light is becoming quite harsh. Perhaps we should begin our return journey?"

But he lingered as Lady Blackwood drifted toward other guests, and his expression shifted into something more calculated.

"Dr. Bell, I must apologize for Lady Blackwood's... frankness." His voice dropped to confidential levels. "She's been under tremendous strain. I do hope you won't read too much into emotional statements."

"I make it a practice to read exactly as much as statements warrant."

Montague's smile acquired edges. "Then perhaps you should direct your reading toward more productive subjects. Professor Whitmore, for instance."

My interest sharpened. "What about Professor Whitmore?"

"Simply that if one is looking for someone with genuine motive to murder Foster..." He let the sentence dangle like bait. "Whitmore has been asking pointed questions about shipping manifests and acquisition records. Almost as if he had official interest in such matters."

Deflection, possibly protective, definitely suspicious.

"How observant of you."

"Whitmore is the one to watch," Montague continued with studied casualness. "If you're looking for someone with reason to murder Foster, that is. The man's been asking too many questions, and is far too interested in Charles's business dealings."

The irony of this statement, delivered while defending Lady Blackwood—who'd just admitted Foster threatened to expose those very dealings—was not lost on me.

"Oh?" I tried to sound noncommittal, but curious.

Montague cleared his throat. "I hate to cast aspersions. But in this case, I'm not wrong. The man travels first-class, stays at the best hotels, never refuses a decent claret, and would have you believe he lives on a professor's wages. I've never met a stipend that generous."

"And you've seen him question people," I prompted.

"Endlessly. Everyone's background, everyone's movements. He needles Eleanor about Charles's business with an indecency I find... unseemly." His jaw tightened. "A gentleman doesn't press a grieving lady about her late husband's accounts. It smacks of predation."

I made a small sound, possibly of agreement or perhaps sympathy.

He leaned in. "You must understand. Eleanor is... fragile. Brave! But fragile. People like Whitmore—men who make a profession of prying—don't understand the harm they do."

With that, he led me back toward Tutankhamun's hive of activity, where Howard Carter was holding court for the tourists.

"People imagine that treasure is resilient," he was saying. "It is not. It is just very expensive dust trying not to happen."

The crowd chuckled obligingly.

"Everyone wants to be photographed with a pharaoh, but no one wants to pay for the storage crates. We've guards at the entrance, guards at the guards, and a watch kept on the guards' cousins if they sell cigarettes. Meanwhile, scholars quarrel over provenance like bishops over relics."

"While tomb robbers of the modern variety have business cards," I murmured.

He didn't smile. "There is more money in theft now than ever there was in excavation. And more excuses."

Lady Blackwood slipped beside me, bumping my shoulder.

"I must apologize for Nigel," she began, fan furling with surgical neatness. "He has the soul of a Boy Scout and the discretion of a fountain. One hates to see a grieving lady gossiped about by overzealous protectors."

I arranged my mouth into sympathy. "Protectors do tend to interpret 'help' broadly."

"And to misdirect, however well intentioned." The fan ticked once against her glove. "I do hope you won't let his... embroidery influence your investigation, my dear. It would be terribly unfortunate if you focused your attention in the wrong direction."

A pause, heavy with implication.

"Again," she added, like silk laid over a blade. And then moved away.

Quinn materialized, as he does, without tripping a single wire. "She invite you to tea," he asked, "or to your funeral?"

"Both," I said. "Possibly at the same time. The cakes will be cyanide, but the napkins will be monogrammed."

He didn't laugh. "You're pale."

"Compliments will get you nowhere."

"You staying alive would," he said softly.

Which would have qualified as romantic tension if the Valley hadn't been full of death. As it was, it felt like a comforting hand on a shoulder you hadn't realized you were carrying too high. I breathed, once, and let it out in an orderly fashion. "Noted. I shall endeavor to schedule my murder for after luncheon."

"Do not schedule anything without me," he said, and was gone to intercept Hassan before the inspector's impatience murdered a site official.

CHAPTER TWENTY-FOUR

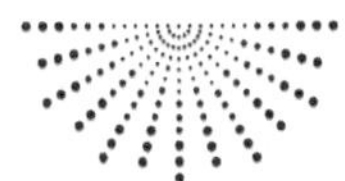

As our party gathered for Carter's final words and then began drifting toward the parking area, I let my bootlace develop a sudden fascination with its own existence, then discovered my notebook possessed depths of intellectual urgency that simply couldn't be ignored while walking.

The party thinned around me. By the time I'd finished my display of academic absorption, the chattering herd had wandered far enough ahead that their conversation became a pleasant hum of meaningless syllables.

Whitmore, bless his observant soul, noticed the gap and drifted back with the sort of well-bred casualness that suggested either excellent manners or professional training. Possibly both.

"There's a view," I announced, which was roughly as informative as declaring that Egypt contained sand. I steered us toward a promising seam in the limestone where the cliff had carved itself a pocket of shade and the wind possessed enough discretion to keep our secrets to itself.

"Professor," I began, arranging my voice in its most innocent register, "Montague tells me you rifle through desks for sport, subsist entirely on claret and mysteriously generous stipends, and interrogate widows about their shipping receipts.

But of course, he is unaware of your true profession. If that's all it is."

He didn't bother with the surprise I'd been expecting. Instead, his mouth performed a small, dry movement that might have been humor if he'd been that sort of man.

"Montague enjoys constructing theories," he said. "I prefer working with data. When a ledger needs examining, I examine it. As for my apparent prosperity—appearances matter considerably in this work. There are doors that swing open for men with decent tailoring that remain permanently sealed against men who perspire on third-class railway benches."

"Yes, Quinn shared that it's not merely professorial wages funding your wardrobe."

"And Benedict Quinn has also vouched for you." He gave me another of those reluctant smiles.

"My actual work," he said, lowering his voice to something that wouldn't carry beyond our limestone alcove, "occupies the intersection between archaeology and subjects that governments prefer not to see committed to official memoranda. The networks that facilitate antiquities smuggling also transport information. During the war, they moved people. Since the Armistice, they've been moving money, influence, and political leverage with equal efficiency. My assignment is to map these networks comprehensively. Cartography requires proximity, which necessitates... certain comforts. It also demands asking uncomfortable questions about shipping manifests, regardless of their effect on widows' sensibilities."

"And Lady Blackwood knows none of this, I take it?"

He acknowledged this with the smallest possible nod. "I managed to get myself invited to Thorne's demonstration. But Jasper Thorne represented a problem precisely because his naiveté made him valuable to people who possessed none. That situation is concluded. The more pressing concern wears superior perfume."

"Eleanor," I said, because we'd all apparently graduated to using first names when discussing murder suspects.

Another slight inclination of his head confirmed my

deduction. "Lord Blackwood operated an unofficial syndicate, encouraging respectable British families to 'invest' in priceless Egyptian cultural artifacts, under the radar of any governmental control. The *pricelessness* was entirely fictional. The money, however, moved quite efficiently. What he'd constructed was an elaborate scheme exploiting Westerner's insatiable appetite for all things Egyptian—laundering romantic notions about antiquities into negotiable securities."

"And then died with convenient timing," I observed, since we'd also become comfortable with rudeness this week.

"Before exposure became inevitable," Whitmore agreed. "He bequeathed his widow a house, an impeccable reputation, and a strongbox full of documentation that could embarrass not merely herself but a dozen families who still host government ministers at dinner parties."

"Ledgers, correspondence, bearer bonds," I said, unable to resist organizing the components. "Initials, signatures, keys to everything."

He glanced at me with the expression of someone recalibrating his assessment of the pigment specialist's organizational capabilities. "Precisely. Lady Blackwood discovered more than the usual widow's financial obligations. She'd inherited functioning criminal machinery. I believe she's been attempting to prevent it from grinding her to powder ever since."

"And Foster's role?"

"Foster," he said with a sort of practiced boredom, "specialized in locating sellers for clients. While investigating potential suppliers, he employed his standard methodology—pulling at any thread that resembled financial opportunity. The Blackwood finances constitute a complex tapestry. He located the critical knots. He realized the widow was sitting on stolen funds and enough social dynamite to level half of Cairo's European quarter. Naturally, he presented himself as a solution."

"Blackmail as boutique service," I summarized. "Discretion tied with ribbons."

"He offered 'protection,'" Whitmore said. "In exchange for

mutually beneficial arrangements. She paid inflated prices for pieces he 'located'—some of which he undoubtedly located in her own storage rooms—while allowing him to acquire selected objects from her collection at terms that would insult a pawnbroker's professional standards. The money flowed toward him in both directions. So did access to increasingly valuable inventory."

"Pay too much when buying, accept too little when selling. You must appreciate the mathematical elegance."

He inclined his head. "Entirely deniable for anyone choosing blindness. Not quite deniable enough for household staff with functioning consciences. The financial drain has been visible in the estate's accounts for months. If you've observed Winters counting candles as if they might develop legs and abscond, you understand the economic pressures that followed."

"Her motive," I said, declining to soften the accusation. "Protect the family name, the estate, the donors' dinner invitations. Prevent the inevitable cascade of scandal."

"Protect herself," he added. "Because legal innocence expires at the moment one begins spending money one knows shouldn't exist. When police arrive with ledgers asking why the widow paid the same man twice for identical scarabs, nobody applauds her devotion to cultural preservation."

"And maintaining perfect politeness," I observed, "is apparently a very expensive sport."

"I think she invited Foster to the house," Whitmore continued, the limestone obligingly providing enough echo to lend his words official weight, "not because she enjoyed his conversation but because she preferred observing the knife's approach. It's easier to monitor a wolf if it shares your parlor furniture."

"Also easier," I noted dryly, "to set traps with precision."

He didn't flinch from the implication. "I'm sharing this information now because your investigation has intersected with mine, and because—since yesterday's discovery—I can see

I'm not the only person monitoring which guests might be useful, and for what purposes."

"Since yesterday," I repeated, hearing the Glasshouse door click in memory like a metronome. "You believe she used me."

"I believe," he said, and for the first time something resembling actual emotion penetrated his professional varnish, "that you publicly suspected a man who richly deserved suspicion, and someone exploited that noise to mask the sound of different activities entirely. I don't assign those activities to Lady Blackwood casually. I also don't exempt her by virtue of superior credentials."

"Why inform me at all?" I asked. "Isn't this precisely the sort of intelligence one reports for men with rubber stamps?"

He looked past me toward the main path, where Quinn's silhouette had arranged itself in an "I'm-not-eavesdropping" angle, with Hassan's granite patience visible in the middle distance. "Because Foster's death represents escalation. If I channel everything through official procedures, it will be next week—or maybe next month—before anyone with actual authority remembers that two men have died and an extremely valuable artifact has disappeared. An Englishwoman is more likely to receive tea invitations than an arrest warrant, and *my lady* conducts her finest work over tea service."

"And because," I added, "when an English citizen commits murder in Egypt, it transcends simple crime. It becomes a telegram. Twenty telegrams."

"It becomes an international incident," he agreed with limestone bleakness. "Incidents generate headlines, headlines inspire parliamentary speeches, speeches become policies that destroy people who had nothing whatsoever to do with the original problem. My assignment is incident prevention. It has not proceeded successfully."

His composure was impeccable. But underneath, I suspected, were bruises shaped like government memoranda and bureaucratic disappointment.

"So," I said, organizing the components, "Lord Blackwood

looted and profited, Foster extorted, Eleanor paid, and now someone has graduated from arithmetic to applied chemistry."

"Possibly," he said. "But if you intend to confront her, don't rely on moral indignation and colorful adjectives. You'd better have proof. She is fundamentally a woman of paperwork."

Behind us, laughter drifted from the main path.

"Thank you," I said, which translated roughly to: *Message received and understood; investigation continuing.*

He gave another quick nod, and for one moment the intelligence operative and the archaeologist shared minimal professional respect founded on mutual recognition.

We hurried ahead to join the others at the carriages, and I found myself cataloging revelations:

One: Lady Blackwood admitted Foster threatened her regarding Charles's "legitimate" transactions.

Two: She revealed Foster discovered "irregularities" in acquisition methods.

Three: She displayed no genuine grief over Foster's death.

Four: Montague was actively protecting her by deflecting toward Whitmore.

Five: Multiple people seemed invested in managing Lady Blackwood's narrative.

We circled for the return journey, and Lady Blackwood smiled benevolently on us all. "Such a stimulating expedition," she trilled, as if we'd been hat shopping. "How extraordinarily fortunate we are."

"'Fortunate' is certainly one word," I agreed. "Especially since none of us are dead.'"

For one moment the smile slipped and something slightly vicious seemed to peer out from behind the social conditioning. Then the fan reappeared, and the beast retreated into its cage of good breeding.

I deliberately chose a different carriage for our return, and settled beside Quinn, who'd been conducting his own observations. None of our party joined us.

"Productive excursion?" he murmured as the carriage lurched into motion.

"Lady Blackwood confessed to being threatened by Foster. Montague tried to redirect suspicion toward Whitmore. And I'm increasingly certain we're dealing with either a very obvious murderer or a very sophisticated one pretending to be obvious."

The "morale-boosting expedition" had certainly boosted something—primarily my certainty that Lady Blackwood was either remarkably indiscreet or remarkably confident. Possibly both.

The question was: confident about what? Her innocence? Or her ability to manage the consequences of guilt?

The answer, I suspected, waited back at the estate. Along with two bodies, one missing sphere, and a killer who'd demonstrated considerable skill at arranging deaths.

I squared my shoulders—which one does in lieu of actual confidence sometimes—and prepared to transform observation into criminal detection.

As we headed for the estate, the Nile gleaming copper in the afternoon light, I mentally prepared my next steps. Examine Lady Blackwood's ledgers. Reconstruct Foster's final morning with mathematical clarity.

And perhaps, if time permitted, determine whether Montague was genuinely protecting Lady Blackwood or participating in conspiracy.

Simple tasks, really. For someone who wasn't investigating murder while managing romantic complications, family scandal, and the growing certainty that I was playing a game whose rules kept changing.

As it turned out, our return to the estate was postponed.

The carriages slowed to a stop on the *Corniche el Nil*, the scenic road that ran alongside the Nile's banks.

Ahead, Montague helped Lady Blackwood to the street, and the rest of us followed suit.

"Now what?" Quinn murmured.

Lady Blackwood approached. "I absolutely insist you all

enjoy the rest of the day thoroughly. In fact—what could prove more restorative than evening breezes? I've arranged a sunset cruise for the young people."

She delivered this like a papal blessing and a bookkeeping entry simultaneously.

"Young people?" Quinn's voice held amusement.

"Yasmin, naturally. Dear Clarissa. Mr. Sullivan. And you, Mr. Quinn."

Richard brightened as if someone had wound his internal spring. "How delightful."

Yasmin achieved a smile that masked something sharper. "Extraordinarily thoughtful."

Quinn refrained from rolling his eyes. "Such kindness. We're overwhelmed."

"Then it's settled," Eleanor announced, meaning it always had been. "Captain Haroun awaits at the quay. You'll return by dinner. I'll entertain Inspector Hassan, Professor Whitmore and Nigel at the estate. I'll be rather dull company for such a lovely evening, of course."

Translation: watchdogs remain ashore; puppies go sailing.

I smiled. "How perfectly arranged."

The fan fluttered with satisfaction. "I do try."

CHAPTER TWENTY-FIVE

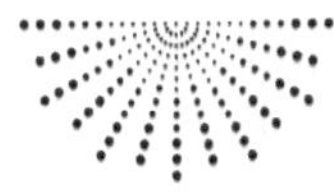

The felucca bobbed at the dock like a cork in champagne, and I suspected the evening ahead would be equally effervescent—and likely to give me a headache, mostly due to the delay to my investigation.

"Allow me," Richard declared, extending his hand toward the boat with gallantry. His palm was already damp with perspiration, though whether from the evening heat or mounting panic over the open water remained unclear.

Quinn, meanwhile, had efficiently assessed the boat's rigging and was discussing wind conditions with the captain in perfectly serviceable Arabic. The contrast was rather like watching a peacock preen while a hawk simply flew.

Yasmin settled herself gracefully in the stern. "Nothing quite like a pleasure cruise while investigating multiple murders. Very British approach to crisis management."

I accepted Quinn's steadier hand into the boat, noting that Richard had turned an interesting shade of gray before we'd even left the dock. "Are you quite well, Richard?"

"Perfectly fine," he managed, though his grip on the boat's edge suggested otherwise. "Just... taking in the ambiance."

The felucca pushed off with a gentle lurch that sent

Richard grabbing for the nearest solid object—which happened to be my arm.

Quinn raised an eyebrow, to which I shrugged.

As the sail caught the evening breeze and we glided into the Nile's current, Richard attempted what I could only assume was meant to be romantic reminiscence. "This reminds me of our riverside picnics in Newport, Clarissa. Remember that lovely evening when—"

"When you lectured me about proper ladies not studying decomposed pigments?" I supplied helpfully. "Charming memory."

He flushed. "That's not... what I meant was the sunset, the water..." His voice took on an edge of desperation. "We should do that again. Soon. Very soon, actually. Perhaps you could leave with me for Alexandria tomorrow morning?"

Quinn's head turned sharply. "Tomorrow? Rather sudden, isn't it?"

"Sudden? We've already had two murders. What more incentive do we need?" Richard's laugh had all the naturalness of a museum display. "Before things get worse."

"Worse how, exactly?" Quinn's diplomatic tone didn't quite mask his irritation.

Richard fumbled with his collar, which seemed to be strangling him despite the evening breeze. "Just... complications. Legal complications. The sort that become rather public rather quickly."

I studied his face. "You mean the Sunday newspaper story."

His complexion now matched the limestone cliffs in the fading light.

"Now see here," Richard began, attempting to rally some dignity while gripping the boat's side like a life preserver. "Armand Bell is a respected patron of the arts."

Quinn leaned forward with interest. "And what exactly constitutes 'completely legitimate' in Egyptian antiquities these days?"

"Proper documentation, fair market prices, willing sellers—"

"Willing sellers?" Yasmin's voice sharpened. "How delightfully naive. Tell me, Mr. Sullivan, what constitutes 'willing' when families are selling their heritage to buy bread?"

Richard's attempt to respond was interrupted by a distinctly green expression as the boat hit a small wake. He pressed his handkerchief to his mouth.

The silence that followed was broken only by the gentle slap of water against the boat's hull and Richard's increasingly labored breathing.

Despite his obvious distress, he seemed determined to salvage some vestige of romantic heroism. As the evening air picked up, he began struggling out of his jacket with elaborate care. "You'll catch cold, darling. Allow me—"

"I'm perfectly comfortable, thank you." I watched with fascination as he continued wrestling with the garment like a man fighting a stubborn octopus.

Quinn, observing this display with barely concealed amusement, shifted to offer me his seat in the boat's more sheltered section. "This might be more comfortable for the return journey."

"I'm quite content where I am." Really, it was like being attended by two exceptionally persistent waiters.

When the boat hit a small swell and I shifted my weight naturally to compensate, both men simultaneously reached to steady me—Richard from the left, Quinn from the right. I found myself briefly embraced by four arms and two very different varieties of masculine concern.

"Gentlemen," Yasmin's voice carried the dry amusement of someone watching an absurd performance, "perhaps Dr. Bell is capable of sitting in a boat without requiring a full support staff. She did manage to achieve an advanced university degree and establish herself in Egypt without your assistance."

Richard, now the color of river mud, nonetheless persisted in his gallant attentions, offering commentary on the sunset (*prosaic*), the historical significance of our surroundings (*condescending*), and the superiority of American boatbuilding techniques (*overcompensating*)—the latter delivered while he gripped the Egyptian boat's side with white knuckles.

How did I ever tolerate conversation with him? I began to understand why medieval texts described love as a form of temporary madness.

"At least I've never lied about who I am," he declared, though the effect was somewhat undermined by his voice cracking like an adolescent's.

Quinn's smile held all the warmth of a Cairo winter morning. "No, you just lie about why you're here, what you know, and what your charming employer gets up to in his spare time."

"My credentials are completely transparent—"

"Are they? Because three days ago you claimed to be here for romantic reconciliation only."

I watched this exchange with fascination. "Gentlemen, perhaps we could focus on—"

"I notice you haven't denied the lying part," Richard interrupted, rallying what remained of his dignity. "Tell me, Quinn, exactly how many identities do you maintain? Museum consultant? Murder investigator? What's next, secret pharaoh?"

Quinn's laugh was genuinely amused. "At least my deceptions serve others. Yours seem to serve Armand Bell's bank account."

The two men began an increasingly ridiculous competition over who could demonstrate superior knowledge of river navigation, Egyptian dynastic history, and my personal preferences in everything from tea varieties to archaeological methodology. It was rather like watching two peacocks attempt to out-display each other while one of them was actively molting.

I stopped listening.

The sail sighed as the river shifted from copper to pewter and the sun slid toward the Theban cliffs; in these shortest days of the year dusk drops like a curtain, and by five o'clock the sun vanished cleanly behind the escarpment. A small wind chased a sudden desert chill across the water as we tacked for the landing, lamps pricking to life along the east bank while I drew my wrap tight against the cool.

Yasmin settled back with a rare smile. "How fascinating to observe British masculinity in its natural habitat. All chest-beating and territorial displays, rather like baboons."

"I'm American," Richard protested weakly.

"Ah, well, the American version exhibits identical behaviors," she replied serenely. "But with more volume."

The conversation inevitably turned to Foster's death, and Yasmin's expression grew thoughtful as she watched the sun sink.

"I suppose I should feel more charitable toward the deceased," she began, "but Harrison Foster was not a man who inspired charitable feelings. Particularly not among Egyptian women."

"How so?" I asked, though I suspected I already knew the answer.

"Harrison thought Egyptian women were exotic conquests rather than people. Fascinating specimens to be collected, studied, and eventually discarded." Her voice carried years of accumulated irritation. "He had this infuriating habit of explaining my own country's history to me, usually incorrectly."

Quinn made a sound that might have been sympathetic understanding.

The comparison to Richard was only lost on Richard.

"He collected women like artifacts," Yasmin continued, her scholarly detachment making the words more cutting than anger would have. "Pretty, foreign, and disposable. When I ended things with him, he seemed genuinely surprised—as if my function was decorative rather than intellectual."

Richard, despite his gastrointestinal distress, managed to look uncomfortable. "Surely that's a bit harsh—"

"Is it?" Yasmin's eyebrows rose.

The silence that followed was broken only by Richard's quiet retching over the boat's side.

He recovered quickly from his discussion with the Nile, looking rather like a wilted lily, but apparently decided this was the moment to reassert his masculine credentials. Wiping his mouth with shaking hands, he made what was clearly his final, desperate play.

His seasickness seemed to recede in the face of mounting panic, and he turned to me with the intensity of a drowning man spotting driftwood.

"Clarissa, listen to me carefully. You need to leave Egypt with me. Tonight, if possible. Tomorrow morning at the absolute latest."

The urgency in his voice cut through the evening's gentle beauty like a scalpel. "Richard, what aren't you telling us?"

"Your father sent me specific instructions. If the situation became... compromised... I was to ensure your immediate departure." His words tumbled over each other like stones down a cliff face. "He has influence, connections, resources. He can protect you from all this."

Quinn's expression had gone very still. "Protect her from what, exactly?"

"From being associated with... irregularities. From questions about authentication work that might have been... misunderstood." Richard's voice dropped to an urgent whisper. "Armand has lawyers, political connections, enough influence to ensure this never touches you personally."

"Are you here to save me from a murder investigation? Or to extract me before I realize how deep my family's involvement goes?"

"It's not what you think—"

"Then what is it?" My voice carried the chill of a tomb at midnight.

His silence was answer enough.

Richard made one final, flailing attempt. "The newspaper story will destroy reputations, end careers, possibly result in criminal charges. Armand can weather it—he has resources, legal protection. But Clarissa..." He reached for my hand with desperate intensity. "You could be painted as a knowing accomplice here. Unless you're already safely in New York, beyond extradition treaties, when the story breaks."

The boat seemed to hold its breath around us. Even the evening breeze felt still.

"And if I refuse to run?"

His expression crumpled like papyrus in flame. "Then I can't help you."

The remainder of our river cruise passed in what could charitably be called uncomfortable silence. Richard, having expended his remaining dignity, slumped against the boat's side like a deflated balloon. His seasickness returned with vengeance.

Quinn and I found ourselves sharing meaningful glances over Richard's hunched form—not romantic tension, precisely, but the grim understanding of people who've witnessed something fundamentally ugly.

Yasmin edged closer to me, to comment under her breath. "How fascinating, how crisis reveals character. Like acid applied to uncertain metals—the genuine article remains intact, while the counterfeit simply dissolves." She fixed Richard's green form with clinical assessment. "Desperation, I've noticed, makes men remarkably unattractive. All that clawing and pleading rather destroys the romantic mystique."

When we reached the quay, Richard stumbled off the felucca like a man fleeing a natural disaster.

Quinn helped me ashore with a strong hand. No dramatic gestures or competing attentions—simply competent assistance offered and accepted.

"Well," Yasmin stepped onto the dock with feline grace, "that was more illuminating than most sunset cruises. Though I suspect the view was better from where I was sitting."

Richard, leaning heavily against a mooring post, managed a weak protest. "This isn't over, Clarissa. The offer stands. Safety, protection, a future without... complications."

"You're quite right, Richard. This isn't over. But I'm not running from it—I'm walking directly toward it."

The romantic triangle that had dominated the day's tensions felt suddenly irrelevant, resolved not in Quinn's favor but decisively against Richard's. Some competitions, it seemed, could be lost so thoroughly that victory became impossible to imagine.

Richard had exposed himself completely—not through malice, but through desperation. His fear was genuine. His love might even be genuine, in whatever limited capacity he understood the word.

But I could understand someone's motivations completely and still choose not to trust them with my future. I could feel sympathy for Richard's panic about Father's schemes, acknowledge his genuine concern for my safety, recognize the complicated tangle of emotions driving his behavior—and still firmly refuse his offer.

Perhaps the infuriating complexity that people represented didn't need to paralyze me.

And also...

Romantic Entanglement (Resolved): Outcome satisfactory. Removal recommended.

Within the hour, our carriage wheels crunched on gravel as we arrived back at what I'd begun mentally cataloging as *The Estate of Convenient Deaths.*

I *would* come up with the answers.

Tonight, I would organize my notes, avoid Richard's increasingly desperate marriage proposals, and try not to think about Quinn's presence in the carriage beside me—steady as ballast, impossible to ignore.

One crisis at a time, Clarissa.

Though apparently, I'd chosen a profession—amateur detective—that specialized in multiple simultaneous crises.

Father would be so proud.

Or possibly appalled.

CHAPTER TWENTY-SIX

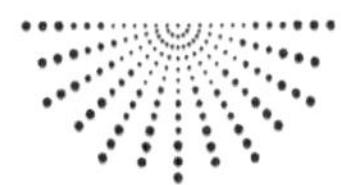

I dragged myself into my room, feeling the weight of a long evening ahead that was also far too short. Sunset on the Nile in December meant that I still had about an hour before our eight o'clock dinner even began. But I had only twelve hours—most of which would be spent asleep—to determine our murderer before everyone left the estate for parts unknown.

Except Lady Blackwood, of course. If she truly was our villain, she wasn't going anywhere. Presumedly.

My faithful companion emerged from the adjoining dressing room, still in her day dress but with her hair unpinned, looking remarkably composed.

I'm sure I looked like someone who had spent the evening unraveling on a felucca while two men fought over her like dogs over a bone.

"Miss Clarissa," she said gently, closing the door behind her. "You look rather... windswept."

I caught sight of myself in the mirror—hair escaping, dress wrinkled from the day's scrambling and evening's nautical adventure, eyes rather wild.

"I look like I've been dragged through the Valley of the

Kings by a camel, then forced onto a boat with two insufferable men while a murderer roams free?"

"That's... remarkably specific, actually."

I began pacing the carpet.

"Annie, I'm completely out of my depth here. I thought I understood murder investigation after our previous adventure, but this case is like trying to read hieroglyphs in a sandstorm while riding a bicycle."

Annie settled herself in the chair by the window, hands folded in that way that somehow always made me feel slightly less likely to spontaneously combust. "Perhaps we should review what you do know, rather than dwelling on what you don't?"

"Right. Yes. Systematic approach. Methodology." I seized upon this lifeline. "First, the suspects."

I swept across to the dressing table and began lining up items. "The blue porcelain vase represents Lady Blackwood. The leather journal is Whitmore. This hand mirror—unfortunately appropriate—represents Richard. The ornate lamp is Montague, and this jewelry box is Yasmin."

Annie watched this performance with the patience of someone who'd grown accustomed to my peculiarities. "Aren't you forgetting someone?"

I surveyed my objects, hands on my hips.

"Mr. Quinn?" She smiled.

"Fine." I grabbed a dented silver cigarette case someone must have left behind on the dresser.

"So, what do we know about each of them?"

"Let's start with the murders themselves." I positioned the items in a rough circle. "Both Thorne and Foster killed with cyanide, but different methods. Thorne via his beloved ceremonial cup during dinner, Foster through a hydrogen cyanide trap in the Glasshouse yesterday morning."

"Different methods suggest what?"

"We have a killer who's adaptable and creative..." I paused, the implications settling like sediment. "And the second murder couldn't have been set up well in advance, like the poisoned cup."

I picked up the blue vase, turning it in my hands. "So, Lady Blackwood. She orchestrated this entire gathering, ostensibly to pressure Thorne into returning the Astral Sphere."

"She does control everything about the estate," Annie murmured. "The supplies, the routines, the servants' schedules."

"Exactly." I set down the vase and picked up the leather journal. "Whitmore—British intelligence, he's finally admitted it. Professional training in elimination techniques. He's mapping postwar networks where antiquities and money flow together, and he claims Eleanor has a trove of incriminating papers from her late husband's sham 'cultural investments.'"

Annie's eyebrows rose slightly. "British intelligence? How many spies does one house party require?"

I nearly choked. I couldn't tell her about Quinn—not yet, not when I was still processing that betrayal myself. She must be referring to me—here to investigate Operation Indigo. "Apparently more than one would think," I managed. "The thing is, Whitmore warned me that Eleanor is 'a woman of paperwork'—that I need to confront her with documentation, not accusations."

Moving to the hand mirror, I grimaced at my own reflection appearing in it. "Richard. Sent by my father with specific instructions to extract me, before I'm linked to anything distasteful. But the timing of Richard's arrival, and that telegram, proved he's here for artifacts, not romance."

"Good riddance to him," Annie said with unusual firmness. "The way he speaks to you—as if you are some wayward child to be collected and managed."

I looked at her in surprise. Quiet, diplomatic Annie rarely expressed such direct opinions about my personal affairs.

She colored slightly but continued. "You're an accomplished archaeologist, Miss Clarissa. You deserve better than a man who treats your expertise as an amusing hobby to be abandoned when inconvenient."

"Thank you, Annie. That... means more than you know." I set down the mirror with more force than necessary. "The lamp represents Montague. Perhaps an academic rivalry with Foster, or at least condescension. Romantic involvement with Lady Blackwood that makes him protective of her interests. He keeps trying to deflect suspicion toward others, but it reads more as chivalrous misdirection than criminal behavior."

Finally, I lifted the jewelry box. "Yasmin. Passionate nationalist who despises colonial archaeology. Had a failed romance with Foster and principled disagreements with his methods. But she's also the one who provided crucial alibi information —she saw nearly everyone during the critical morning window."

Annie tilted her head thoughtfully. "Isn't it interesting that she was so observant? Almost as if she was watching for something specific?"

I froze, the jewelry box halfway to the table. "You mean she was already suspicious? Or..."

"Or she was establishing alibis. Either for herself or for someone she's protecting."

The implications sent a chill down my spine. "Oh, Annie. What if I've been approaching this entirely wrong? What if the killer isn't working alone?"

I handed her the jewelry box and resumed my pacing with renewed agitation. "There are so many layers to this conspiracy. International smuggling networks with my father under investigation. German intelligence using Thorne's research as cover for reconnaissance operations. British counterintelligence with both Whitmore—" I caught myself before revealing Quinn's true nature.

"Both Whitmore—?"

"Both Whitmore and Quinn arguing over politics constantly," I finished lamely.

Annie studied my face with those perceptive eyes that missed very little. "Mr. Quinn has been dishonest with you about something important, hasn't he?"

Trust Annie to see straight to the heart of it. "Rather monumentally dishonest, yes. Though he claims his feelings are genuine, which somehow makes it worse."

"Because genuine feelings entangled with professional deception create impossible moral territory," she said quietly.

"Exactly." I slumped onto the bed. "How am I supposed to trust anything he says when our entire relationship has been built on lies? And yet, when he looks at me..." I shook my head. "This is precisely why I prefer pottery sherds to people. Pottery doesn't have hidden agendas."

"Perhaps," Annie said, "the question isn't whether you can trust him completely, but whether you can trust him in this specific situation. People can be dishonest about their work while being truthful about their feelings."

I stared at her, something shifting inside. "What do you mean?"

Annie set down the jewelry box and faced me directly. "You're trying to make an absolute determination—can I trust Mr. Quinn, yes or no? Like a mathematical proof where the answer must be true or false. But people aren't equations, Miss Clarissa."

"Then what are they?" The question came out more desperate than I'd intended.

"They're..." She paused, searching for words. "They're more like your archaeological sites. You never have complete information about a civilization, do you? You work with fragments, partial evidence, educated guesses based on patterns."

"But I can verify my guesses with additional excavation, cross-referencing, dating analysis—"

"And you can verify Quinn's trustworthiness through his actions over time," Annie interrupted gently. "Not through one grand gesture or perfect honesty about everything, but through consistent behavior in specific situations."

I resumed pacing, her words chasing each other through my mind. "So, you're suggesting... what? That I trust him about some things but not others?"

"I'm suggesting that partial trust is still trust." Annie's voice carried a conviction I rarely heard from her. "Mr. Quinn is vague and complicated when it comes to his profession—that's true. But has he ever lied about protecting you? About valuing your intellect? About believing in your capabilities as an investigator?"

"I... no. Not that I can prove, anyway."

"Then perhaps you can trust him in this investigation, even if you can't trust him to be fully transparent about the rest of his work." She folded her hands in her lap. "You're allowed to trust someone about one thing while maintaining boundaries about another."

The concept felt revolutionary and terrifying in equal measure. "You're saying I don't need certainty before I can trust him?"

"I'm saying you'll never have certainty about another person. Not complete certainty. And if you wait for absolute proof before trusting anyone, you'll spend your whole life alone with your pottery sherds." Her smile softened the words. "Trust isn't about eliminating all risk, Miss Clarissa. It's about deciding which risks are worth taking based on the evidence you do have."

"And what evidence do I have about Quinn?" I asked quietly, genuinely wanting her assessment.

Annie considered this. "He runs into danger to save you. He's validated your investigative instincts even when you were wrong about Foster. He respected your request for professional distance in his letters despite his obvious feelings. He's protected you without trying to control you—which is more than I can say for Mr. Sullivan."

She was right. When I stopped demanding absolute certainty and instead looked at the pattern of Quinn's actions...

She smiled. "So perhaps the question isn't 'Can I trust Mr. Quinn completely?' but rather 'Can I trust Mr. Quinn with this specific situation while maintaining boundaries about his professional secrecy?'"

I stared at her. "When did you become so wise about matters of the heart?"

She smiled and shrugged. "Perhaps I've been having a little adventure of my own."

"Annie! You've been holding out on me." Which was a ridiculous statement, since her infatuation with Freddie was probably visible from the top of the Theban cliffs.

"Well, you've been rather preoccupied with murders and mysterious antiquities dealers and dreadful former fiancés," she said. "But yes, I've learned that people can be many contradictory things simultaneously."

It appeared we were both here to learn the same lesson.

I considered this while absently rearranging my makeshift suspect array. "The most frustrating element is the Operation Indigo connection. Blue-pigmented artifacts keep appearing across multiple cases, the Astral Sphere has unusual blue pigmentation, my father's collections are potentially involved —but I cannot see how ancient pigments connect to modern murders and espionage."

Regarding the sphere-disc controversy, I'd long since surrendered on the matter of nomenclature. Everyone called it the Astral Sphere, even though it was patently not spherical, and at some point one must choose between linguistic accuracy and social survival—though it rankled every time the word "sphere" crossed my lips.

"Maybe they don't connect," Annie suggested. "Maybe the blue pigments are a separate mystery that's coincidentally intersecting with this one."

"Or maybe I'm missing something fundamental about the connection." I picked up the blue vase again, studying it in the lamplight. "Whitmore said Eleanor has incriminating papers. What if the Astral Sphere isn't valuable for its archaeological significance, but for what it represents in these networks? What if the blue pigmentation is some kind of... marker? Identification system?"

"For what?"

"I have no idea. Which brings us back to the immediate problem—I have roughly twelve hours before all suspects scatter to the winds, Hassan returns to Cairo empty-handed, and that journalist turns in an exposé that destroys my family's reputation and possibly my career."

Annie leaned forward. "Then perhaps we should focus on what you *can* solve in that timeframe. If we ignore Operation Indigo, who had the means, opportunity, and specific knowledge to commit both murders?"

I felt my racing thoughts beginning to settle into more methodical channels. "You're right. I've been so overwhelmed by the grand conspiracies that I've lost sight of simple, practical elements. Another version of the 'paperwork' Whitmore talked about."

"Lady Blackwood does seem to control an unusual amount of information about estate operations," Annie observed. "And she's well-informed about everyone's movements and motivations."

"She's definitely been arranging events rather than simply hosting them." I set down the vase with a decisive click. "Annie, I think I've been approaching this backward. Instead of looking for who wanted to commit murder, I should be asking who had the capability to manipulate everyone else—including me—into providing cover for murder."

The mosaic was beginning to shift into a different pattern. "Tonight, I'm going to reconstruct yesterday's timeline in excruciating detail. Every conversation, every movement, every supposed coincidence. And I'm going to start with Laila's memory of carrying coffee to Foster."

"And if you're right about Lady Blackwood?"

I met Annie's concerned gaze with what I hoped was more confidence than I felt. "Then I'll have to prove that a woman who's spent decades managing estates, servants, and social situations is also capable of managing murder. With documentation, not accusations."

"Just... please be careful, Miss Clarissa. If she's as dangerous as you suspect..."

"I know." I reached over and squeezed her hand. "But someone has to stop her before there's a third body. And apparently, that someone is me."

Outside, the desert wind rattled the windows, as if even the landscape sensed this evening would bring revelation—one way or another.

CHAPTER TWENTY-SEVEN

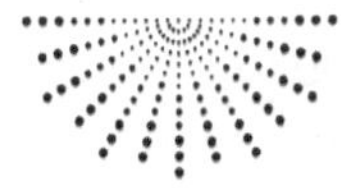

$\mathcal{D}$inner possessed a peculiar atmosphere, like the charged, greenish air before a storm.

"I'll be departing directly from Karnak after tomorrow's ceremony," Yasmin announced, delicately buttering her roll. "No point returning to the estate when my train leaves from Luxor at noon."

Richard immediately brightened. "I've booked passage to Alexandria on the afternoon steamer. Clarissa, the offer stands —we could travel together, perhaps continue to Athens..."

"How persistently optimistic of you." I cut my chicken with excessive concentration. "Though I suspect my father's instructions didn't include a Mediterranean tour."

Quinn's mouth twitched at that, and I felt a surge of satisfaction at having amused him. The man's approval remained dangerously addictive despite everything I'd learned about his professional deceptions.

"Museum duties call to me, I'm afraid," Montague offered. "Though this has been an extraordinary experience. Lady Blackwood, your hospitality during such difficult circumstances has been remarkable."

Our hostess accepted the compliment with gracious

modesty, though I caught the brief flash of something sharper in her expression.

"Professor Whitmore returns to Cairo as well," she continued, nodding his direction. "Which leaves us with dear Clarissa to enjoy the Christmas holidays, if she'll have us." She bowed in Quinn's direction. "And of course, the charming Benedict."

I could stay, to investigate through Christmas. But with all the suspects gone...

"How kind," I managed, though every instinct screamed warnings about accepting hospitality from anyone on my suspect list. "Though I confess I'm not entirely satisfied with the lack of resolution to all of this."

The tension around the table tightened like a violin string approaching its breaking point. My witnesses were about to scatter across three countries, carrying their secrets like private luggage.

"I must agree," Hassan said. "I received a telegram from Cairo this afternoon. The British Embassy has been contacted. Mahmoud Farid's Sunday exposé will claim Egypt cannot protect its own heritage." His voice was tight with barely controlled desperation. "I cannot return to Cairo empty-handed."

I found myself, unexpectedly, feeling genuine sympathy for the inspector. "We both want the truth, Inspector Hassan," I said quietly. "Perhaps that's more important than any artifact."

He looked at me sharply, and for a moment, his armor cracked. "Easy words for someone whose career doesn't hang by a thread, Dr. Bell."

"No," I admitted. "But my credibility as an archaeologist does. Maybe we're not as different as you think."

Hassan studied me for a long moment, something shifting in his expression. "Well," he said slowly, "for an amateur American archaeologist with no respect for proper procedures, you occasionally demonstrate... adequacy."

"High praise indeed, Inspector," I replied, fighting a smile. "And you, for a rigid bureaucrat obsessed with documentation, occasionally show glimpses of actual humanity."

He blinked. Then used his linen napkin to cover what I was certain was the start of a smile.

So, Hassan and I were agreed on this. But my plans for witness interrogation dissolved like sugar in tea when Freddie burst through the dining room doors.

"Begging your pardon, my lady," he gasped, his usual composure scattered. "The kitchen chimney's blocked something fierce—smoke backing up terrible. Cook says we must evacuate immediate-like before someone suffocates or the place goes up in flames."

Lady Blackwood rose with the fluid grace of someone accustomed to domestic crises. "How extraordinary. Winters assured me the flues were cleaned last month."

"Could be debris, my lady, or..." Freddie's voice dropped to a whisper. "Could be something else entirely. You know what they're saying about curses and such."

The evacuation erupted into controlled chaos—servants rushing past with armfuls of silver, guests scattering like startled pigeons to secure their belongings. I watched the dispersal with growing frustration; my carefully planned evening of interrogation dissolving into another interruption.

"How remarkably well-timed," I murmured to Quinn as smoke began drifting from the kitchen corridor.

"Indeed," he replied, his hand guiding my arm as we moved toward the garden doors. The touch sent a spark through me despite everything. Professional betrayal apparently did nothing to diminish physical chemistry.

Which was deeply inconvenient, scientifically fascinating, and absolutely the wrong thing to focus on while potential murderers scattered to unknown locations throughout an estate in crisis.

Quinn left me at the doors, and I found myself swept along in the domestic tsunami.

Field Note: Environmental Conditions Hypothesis: chaos increases inversely to the number of rational people present. Supporting evidence: overwhelming.

Yasmin had assumed command of the evacuation with efficiency, directing traffic flow and ensuring the elderly Professor Montague didn't attempt any heroic furniture rescue.

Richard emerged from his room clutching a leather portfolio and looking as though he'd rather face Egyptian plague locusts than the prospect of a kitchen fire. "Clarissa, surely you should gather your important papers—"

"My 'important papers' consist of pottery sherds and pigment samples," I replied, shouldering past him toward the courtyard. "Hardly worth risking asphyxiation."

Quinn appeared at my elbow with his traveling bag, moving with the fluid economy of someone accustomed to rapid departures. The sight triggered an unwelcome flutter of concern—was he planning to disappear entirely during this distraction?

"Going somewhere?" I asked, attempting casual curiosity.

"Always ready for quick exits," he replied, that maddening half-smile playing at the corners of his mouth. "Occupational hazard of my... various occupations."

The reminder of his duplicitous professional life should have dampened my attraction. Instead, it seemed to intensify the magnetic pull between us.

Apparently, my nervous system had developed a deeply inappropriate appreciation for dangerous men with mysterious agendas.

Lady Blackwood appeared everywhere at once—directing servants toward valuable artifacts, ensuring guest safety, consulting with Winters about ventilation solutions—while maintaining the sort of unruffled elegance that suggested either remarkable composure or extensive practice with domestic emergencies.

"How does one woman manage to be so thoroughly... present during a crisis?" I wondered aloud.

"Experience," Quinn said simply. "Some people thrive in chaos because they understand how to navigate it."

Or create it, I thought but didn't say.

Twenty minutes later, the courtyard had become an impromptu refugee camp decorated with hastily rescued paintings and silver tea services. The smoke had cleared enough to reveal the crisis as more nuisance than catastrophe—a discovery that did nothing to diminish my suspicions about the timing.

Annie found me contemplating the organized chaos. "Miss Clarissa, perhaps now would be a good time to speak with Laila? She's been quite shaken by recent events, and the fresh night air might encourage confidences."

Brilliant woman. I'd been so focused on formal interrogations that I'd overlooked the advantages of informal conversation during emotional vulnerability.

Laila sat on a marble garden bench, still clutching the coffee service she'd rescued from the kitchen—an interesting choice of salvage that immediately caught my professional attention. Her hands trembled slightly as she arranged the cups.

"Laila," I said gently, settling beside her with careful casualness. "What a terrible few days you've had."

Quinn positioned himself under a palm near the garden gate with studied nonchalance, ostensibly admiring Lady Blackwood's roses. The sight of him in protective mode triggered another surge of attraction. Was it our impending departure activating some deeply primitive appreciation center in my brain?

Not the time for that, Bell. Murder investigation first, inappropriate romantic yearning later.

"Oh, Miss Bell," Laila began, her voice carrying the weight of accumulated domestic disasters. "First poor Dr. Thorne, then Mr. Foster, and now chimneys trying to suffocate us all. Cook says it's the curse, for certain."

I made appropriately sympathetic noises and touched the coffee pot. "Tell me about yesterday morning, when Mr. Foster died. You brought him coffee, didn't you?"

"Yes, miss. Mr. Foster rang for coffee early that morning. Said he wasn't feeling well through his door, asked if I might bring something warm."

"How early exactly? And did he say anything else when you brought the tray?"

"Just past dawn, miss. Maybe six-thirty?" Her brow furrowed with the effort. "But I never actually saw him, if you take my meaning. He called out through the door—said he had a terrible sore throat and headache and couldn't bear the light just yet. He sounded very poorly." Her breath caught on this last statement, no doubt from the inevitable comparison to how "poorly" he found himself several hours later.

Quinn's casual rosebush examination had shifted to what I recognized as his listening stance, though he maintained the pretense of horticultural fascination.

"You left the tray outside his door then?" I prompted, noting how Laila's grip tightened imperceptibly on the coffee pot she still held.

"Well, yes, miss. Proper service would've meant entering to arrange everything nicely, but he said to leave it there..." She trailed off, then added with the defensive tone of someone whose standards had been compromised, "I did knock gentle-like when I returned later, thinking the coffee would've gone stone cold, but there was no answer at all."

Excitement flashed clean and bright—the moment when disparate fragments finally clicked into a pattern. "When you returned?"

"Yes, miss. I'd gone to fetch fresh cream, thinking he might want it. Cook always says a proper coffee service includes proper cream, not that tinned nonsense." Laila's domestic pride reasserted itself momentarily before fading back into uncertainty. "But when I came back with the pitcher, maybe ten minutes later, he didn't answer."

"And you encountered other people during these trips?" I asked, though I suspected I already knew the answer.

"Oh yes, miss. Dr. Mujahid was coming down the stairs when I was coming up with the cream. Very kind she was, asked if everything was well. And Professor Montague was in the Library already—had been there since before dawn, I think, because the lamps were lit when I passed earlier."

She paused, accessing memory with the deliberation of someone whose testimony had suddenly become important.

"Mr. Sullivan was pacing about on the terrace, looking quite agitated. Kept checking his pocket watch like he was late for something urgent."

The specimens arranged themselves in my mind. Foster had requested coffee through a closed door—never showing his face, never being seen alive that morning by anyone. The untouched tray outside his room. The ten-minute window while Laila fetched cream.

The only thing establishing his time of death had been Laila's coffee service. But if she never actually saw him... Could someone have impersonated him, to establish the fiction that he was alive and calling for room service? Someone with access to his room and knowledge of his habits?

"Miss Bell?" Laila's voice seemed to come from a great distance. "You've gone quite pale. Are you feeling unwell?"

I realized I'd been staring. The murderer hadn't just killed Foster—they'd stage-managed an elaborate deception to establish false timeline, using poor Laila as an unwitting accomplice in their alibi construction.

From across the courtyard, I caught movement in my peripheral vision—Yasmin approaching with a tray of rescued teacups, her expression neutral but her pace slightly too deliberate. Had she been close enough to overhear our conversation?

Quinn straightened from his rosebush contemplation, something in his posture suggesting heightened alertness. His eyes met mine briefly, and I saw recognition there—he'd heard enough to understand the implications as well.

The morning Foster died, someone had been devising an elaborate performance with multiple moving parts, using the estate's routines and the servants' conscientiousness to create false evidence of life where only death remained.

CHAPTER TWENTY-EIGHT

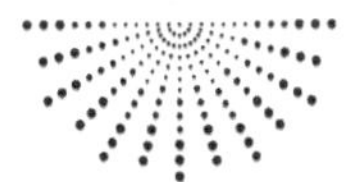

The kitchen fire crisis resolved itself with the same mysterious efficiency that had created it—Winters emerging from the main house with a satisfied expression.

"Debris deliberately wedged in the flue," he announced, brandishing a collection of rags and what appeared to be several estate ledgers. "Someone's been quite creative with our ventilation system."

Lady Blackwood received this news with the serene composure of someone whose domestic catastrophes never truly surprised her. "How extraordinarily malicious. Though I suppose we should be grateful it wasn't actual structural damage."

The return to the main house felt like watching a stage play reset between acts—servants efficiently redistributing rescued valuables while guests emerged from various hiding places clutching their most precious possessions.

Hassan had paced the courtyard throughout the entire emergency, resembling nothing so much as a dragon guarding its hoard, and now seemed about to implode.

"This foolishness has gone on long enough." "Every person in this house will participate in a complete, witnessed inventory," Hassan continued. "Every room, every cabinet, every drawer. If the Sphere exists, we find it. If it never existed, Lady Blackwood's records must document this fiction."

Lady Blackwood's spine stiffened with indignation.

"Never existed! I assure you—"

Hassan waved her off.

Hassan's desperation might just provide exactly what Annie suggested—official documentation and pressure enough to crack whoever's been stage-directing this elaborate performance.

The real investigation was finally beginning.

Hassan's organizational skills, I had to admit, were impressively thorough for a man teetering on the edge of career suicide. Within minutes, he had transformed our motley collection of suspects into something resembling an expedition, complete with witness protocols and documentation requirements.

"Everyone remains present in each room during the search," he declared, producing a leather portfolio with the efficiency of a seasoned bureaucrat. "Lady Blackwood, you will initial a document for every piece we examine. No private consultations, no separate conversations."

Perfect, I thought, catching Quinn's subtle nod of approval.

Lady Blackwood drew herself up with the dignity of someone whose hospitality had been gravely insulted. "Inspector Hassan, I hardly think such extreme measures are necessary. My late husband's collection has been meticulously maintained—"

"Your late husband's collection," Hassan interrupted, "included an artifact that has vanished under circumstances involving two deaths. Extreme measures appear to be exactly what this situation requires."

Richard cleared his throat nervously. "Inspector, surely as an American citizen—"

"Mr. Sullivan," Hassan's voice cut through Richard's objections, "you arrived here claiming romantic intentions toward Dr. Bell. Now you're eager to flee before we've established whether you're involved in artifact theft. Which story should I include in my report?"

I bit back a laugh at Richard's expression—rather like a fish discovering the hook came with consequences.

The first hour proved revelatory in ways I hadn't anticipated. Yasmin, whom I'd initially dismissed as passionate but scattered, ran the room like a proper survey chief: photographing each object before movement, reading off inscriptions for the scribe to transcribe, and cross-referencing old estate labels against prior accession numbers. She handled pieces by their edges, noted condition and prior repairs in a neat hand, and flagged anything with unclear provenance.

"This Middle Kingdom glazed steatite scarab shows telling use-wear," she murmured, examining the base under a hand lens. "The edges are rounded, there's basal polish from repeated sealing, and the perforation is abraded from a suspension cord."

Yes, I see you, Yasmin. You know what you're talking about.

Lady Blackwood's hovering became increasingly pronounced as we worked through the Antiquities Room. Her explanations grew more detailed, more defensive, with frequent glances at her pocket watch. When Quinn suggested examining her private study next, her composure cracked just slightly.

"The Library contains primarily Lord Blackwood's correspondence and research notes," she said quickly. "Hardly relevant to artifact inventory."

Hassan looked up from his documentation. "Nevertheless, thoroughness requires we examine all storage areas. Dr. Bell and Dr. Mujahid, perhaps you could escort Lady Blackwood to the Library while we complete this room."

Brilliant, I thought. Whether Hassan realizes it or not, he's just created the perfect opportunity for detailed observation without the entire group's dynamics clouding the interaction.

Lady Blackwood's reluctance to have the Library searched became increasingly obvious as we approached the oak-paneled sanctuary of her late husband's scholarly pursuits. Her usual confidence had been replaced by something approaching genuine anxiety.

"My husband was quite particular about his filing system," she said, her hands trembling slightly as she unlocked the door. "I'd hate for important documents to be disturbed unnecessarily."

"Eleanor," Yasmin said gently, pausing beside Lord Blackwood's massive desk, "your husband's desk should be examined for completeness, shouldn't it?"

The color drained from Lady Blackwood's face so rapidly I feared she might faint.

"Yes, of course." She rattled among some objects in a top drawer and came up with the key.

A moment later she had the drawer unlocked.

There, nestled in a swath of fabric like a guilty secret finally confessing, sat the Astral Sphere.

Yasmin's face transformed from curiosity to surprise.

Lady Blackwood's expression arranged itself into similar shock.

The artifact was wrapped in period-appropriate linen, positioned with the attention one might give a sleeping infant.

We called the others, who rushed to join us.

Hassan's hands actually trembled as he photographed it *in situ*, his career salvation documented for posterity.

"At last!" he breathed, then turned to Lady Blackwood with renewed authority. "But why was this desk not searched initially?"

Our hostess had recovered her composure with remarkable speed, drawing herself up with wounded dignity.

"Why would I search my husband's desk? He never kept artifacts there."

Especially not an artifact most recently seen in Jasper Thorne's possession. Her explanation felt unsatisfactory, and I couldn't be the only one who felt as though she'd been caught with a smoking gun.

I noted how Quinn's attention had sharpened to laser intensity.

Richard's obvious relief filled the room like cheap cologne. Whitmore nodded and Yasmin watched.

But it was Montague's reaction that caught my attention. The museum curator who should have been most delighted by the discovery of the lost artifact instead stepped backward, frowning.

Curious, I mused, watching our suspects arrange themselves around Hassan's triumphant documentation.

Hassan's relief transformed him into a dynamo, producing forms and protocols with the efficiency of a man whose pension had just been salvaged from disaster. All witnesses signed attestations, official papers were catalogued, and the Astral Sphere was ceremoniously wrapped for transport to Cairo, amidst Lady Blackwood's strenuous objections.

"The artifact must be secured at the government facility overnight," Hassan announced, clutching his leather portfolio like a shield against further diplomatic disasters. "Standard procedure—transport to the local police station in Luxor, then official convoy to Cairo at dawn."

Lady Blackwood's objection arrived wrapped in gossamer. "Inspector, surely one final night in the estate's secure safe would be more appropriate? The sphere belonged to my dear husband, and after such... turbulence... perhaps we might honor his memory with proper ceremony. After all this, to have Dr. Thorne's amazing theories go untested..."

She gestured toward a locked cabinet, its brass fittings gleaming like altar fixtures in the afternoon light.

Hassan wavered, clearly calculating the political ramifications of offending an influential British widow against the safety of following protocol. Not to mention the motivation of stamping out Jasper Thorne's "amazing" theories. I could practically hear the gears grinding in his head.

"Very well," he conceded, though his grip on the portfolio tightened. "But I will personally accompany everyone to Karnak before dawn. The sphere travels under my direct supervision to the Solstice ceremony. And the theft investigation is now closed," he declared. "Dr. Thorne's death, while tragic, is no longer a matter for the Antiquities Department."

How convenient, I thought, watching our assembled suspects begin discussing departure arrangements. The official mystery solved, diplomatic incidents averted, and everyone free to scatter like startled birds.

"So civilized," Lady Blackwood murmured, her smile suggesting she'd expected this outcome all along. "One final night with dear Charles's collection, and then proper scientific recognition at Karnak. Our poor Dr. Thorne would have been so pleased."

The mention of our deceased scholar cast a pall over the gathering. I found myself studying each face—the practiced sympathy, the careful neutrality, the brief flickers of something more complex. After two murders, even genuine grief required authentication.

Quinn's fingers brushed mine as we left the Antiquities Room, sending that familiar jolt racing up my arm. "This is far from over," he murmured, his voice low enough to qualify as intimate conspiracy.

Precisely, I realized, watching Lady Blackwood's renewed confidence.

Freddie and Laila brought a late-evening snack to the Salon for all of us, and within minutes, Richard was already calculating train schedules, Whitmore discussing London connections, and Lady Blackwood graciously accepting condolences on her trying ordeal. Only Yasmin seemed as unsettled as I felt, her dark eyes tracking movements with the same analytical attention she'd brought to our search.

The Astral Sphere was no longer part of the mystery.

Now the question was whether I could solve two murders before the performers took their final bows and disappeared forever—leaving me with nothing but questions.

Well, that, and the increasingly dangerous attraction to a man whose profession involved more deception than I'd initially bargained for.

CHAPTER TWENTY-NINE

The note appeared sometime around ten o'clock.

I was not yet asleep when the gentle tap on my door summoned me, followed by a slip of paper being pushed under it.

By the time I'd wrapped a robe around myself and cracked open the door, the hallway was empty.

The note was written in what I recognized as Freddie's distinctive blend of creative spelling and grammatical optimism:

Miss, got summat important bout the curse an the chimney fire an the stealin. Maybe murder too. Cant say where others might hear. Meet at garden shed midnite. -Freddie

I stared at the paper by candlelight, my exhaustion from Eleanor's social marathon warring with the tantalizing promise of actual information. After an evening that had prevented any meaningful investigation, this felt like discovering water in the desert—possibly life-saving, possibly a mirage designed to lead me further astray.

The sensible course would be to wait until morning, approach Freddie through proper channels, maintain the safety of witnesses and daylight. Unfortunately, sensibility had never been my strongest characteristic, particularly when archaeological curiosity collided with murder investigation urgency.

I was reaching for my shoes when a soft knock interrupted my internal debate.

Quinn's voice carried through the door with that low tone he used when discussing potentially dangerous propositions.

"Clarissa? I saw your light under your door. Everything well?"

I opened the door to find him fully dressed despite the late hour, his hair slightly mussed in a way that suggested he'd been running his fingers through it.

"Freddie's requesting a clandestine meeting," I said, handing him the note. "Claims to have information about the murders, the theft, and today's chimney crisis."

Quinn scanned the paper, his expression shifting through several calculations. "I'm not in favor of your taking late night clandestine meetings alone."

"You think it's a trap?" The same suspicion had occurred to me.

"I think everything since we arrived has been some form of manipulation." He stepped closer in that unconsciously decisive way that rattled every rational objection I could muster.

I steadied a hand against the doorjamb to keep my balance; the rest of the house felt suddenly farther away.

His eyes held mine with an intensity that made clear he was thinking about more than just investigative strategy, and my traitorous nervous system responded with enthusiasm that would have been embarrassing if it weren't so thoroughly reciprocated.

"If we're walking into a trap," I said, proud of how steady my voice remained despite the gravitational pull, "at least we'll be walking into it together."

Something shifted in his expression—surprise, perhaps, or recognition of the trust implied in my words despite everything I'd learned about his professional duplicity. "Together, then. But we go prepared for trouble."

Twenty minutes later, we slipped through the garden gate

like conspirators in one of those sensation novels Annie favored —armed with a small lantern and Quinn's comprehensive lock-picking kit.

The garden felt transformed by darkness, familiar pathways with shadows that suggested threats, which daylight would no doubt reveal as innocent plant life. I attempted to minimize the amount of gravel crunching beneath my practical but acoustically treacherous boots.

"There," I whispered, spotting the shed's angular silhouette against the star-scattered sky. No light showed through its single window, no movement suggested Freddie's presence within.

Despite the uncertainty, or perhaps because of it, the thought drifted across my mind: I didn't have proof that Quinn would protect me. I had no guarantee he wasn't using this investigation for his own purposes. I couldn't verify his sincerity through any scientific method.

And yet, I was choosing to trust him anyway. Making a deliberate choice.

"Freddie?" I called softly as we reached the shed door. Silence answered.

Quinn tested the door handle, finding it unlocked. "Still want to proceed?"

I nodded, though every instinct screamed warnings about proceeding into unknown spaces without proper preparation or backup plans. We entered the shed together, our lantern revealing the expected collection of gardening tools, chemical supplies, and various estate maintenance equipment.

What it didn't reveal was any sign of Freddie or evidence of the promised revelations.

The door's decisive slam behind us carried the finality of a coffin lid closing. The heavy bolt sliding home from outside followed immediately.

"Well," I said, setting down the lantern with composure while internally cataloguing our available options, "this certainly qualifies as a development."

Quinn was already cursing himself and testing the door's

strength, his shoulder applying measured pressure while his hands explored the frame for weaknesses. "We were looking ahead when we should've been watching behind."

"Window?" I suggested, though the single opening appeared both too small for escape and too high for easy access.

"Designed for ventilation, not evacuation."

I examined our surroundings, lifting the lantern to illuminate the shelves full of chemical supplies.

"The cyanide location," Quinn pointed. "Hidden in plain sight."

At which point, the small bulb flickered and died.

So, we were trapped in the murderer's laboratory, surrounded by evidence of methodical preparation, with everyone's dawn departure scheduled in less than five hours.

CHAPTER THIRTY

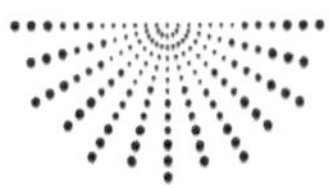

The darkness pressed in around us, absolute and suffocating.

But I felt Quinn's presence beside me, solid and safe in the cramped space, and something in my chest tightened with a feeling I couldn't quite name.

Vulnerability. Pure, unadulterated vulnerability.

Only because we were trapped together, with no way out.

"We'll figure this out," Quinn said quietly, his voice steady in the darkness. "We always do."

Trust is a choice, not a guarantee.

Quinn used his shoulder to the door with the sort of measured aggression that suggested experience with locked barriers, but it might as well have been carved from solid granite for all the give it gave.

I contributed by rattling the handle with desperate optimism.

"Solidly bolted from outside."

I moved to the small window, looking up through glass that revealed nothing but starry darkness. It was barely wide enough for a determined house cat.

"Shouting seems our next logical option." I took a deep breath, then launched into a yell.

Quinn joined his more impressive lung capacity to my efforts, producing a sound that should have awakened half of Luxor. The profound silence that answered suggested we might as well have been hollering into the Valley of the Kings.

"Well," I said, settling onto what appeared to be a reasonably clean crate, "we've made a strategic miscalculation."

Quinn pulled another crate close and joined me.

The cool spangle of light from the desert moon through the window created an oddly intimate atmosphere that made our circumstances feel less like imprisonment and more like a scholarly retreat with distinctly dangerous undertones.

"Five hours until the Karnak departure." I leaned back against the shed wall. "Enough time to reconstruct this entire mess."

"Starting with the most recent revelations." Quinn leaned back beside me, our arms touching. "Laila's testimony about Foster's morning routine."

I forced my mind away from the nearness of Quinn's body and back to the crucial timeline evidence. "Foster requested coffee through his door, claiming illness. When Laila returned with cream ten minutes later, complete silence."

"Which could mean someone else made that initial request. Impersonating him to establish the fiction that he was still alive."

"Right. Someone comfortable with vocal disguise." The answer felt tantalizingly close to revelation. "Someone who understands how servants' routines create opportunities for manipulation..."

The realization struck. "Yasmin," I breathed, the name carrying implications that rearranged everything.

Quinn's attention sharpened. "Her storytelling at Lady Blackwood's contrived ballroom dance event—she switched between three different dialects without missing a conversational beat."

"More than a party trick. She could have killed Foster in the Glasshouse sometime before dawn, then entered his room and called for coffee."

"Which explains her positioning on the stairs when Laila made her cream expedition." Quinn shifted closer, and the movement sent warmth radiating through the narrow space between us. "Perfect alibi construction."

I forced myself to focus on criminal methodology rather than the way candlelight played across Quinn's features. "But if Yasmin murdered Foster, what connects her to Thorne's death? Professional disagreement seems insufficient motive for such elaborate planning."

"Unless we've been approaching this backwards," Quinn suggested, his voice carrying that low intensity that nudged my resolve out of neat alignment. "What if Foster killed Thorne, then Yasmin killed Foster in retaliation?"

The theory crystallized. Maybe we were right all along. "Foster had the technical knowledge, the systematic approach, the suspicious reconnaissance of household routines. He murdered Thorne using the ceremonial cup and cyanide methods he'd researched."

"And somehow manipulated Yasmin into complicity," Quinn added. "Blackmail, coercion, exploiting their past relationship—"

"Then she discovered his betrayal and enacted her own revenge using his methods." I met his eyes in the flickering light, feeling the electric tension that danger and proximity had been building between us all evening. "Two separate murders. Two different killers."

"It fits, but still doesn't really give us a motive for Yasmin to kill Foster. She doesn't strike me as a crime-of-passion sort of woman." Quinn pulled his pocket watch from his waistcoat, the brass catching the moonlight.

"Half past midnight. Four and a half hours until the Karnak departure."

"Yasmin only needs to avoid suspicion until she slips away at the temple ceremony. Dawn prayers, ritual positioning, ceremonial chaos—perfect cover for disappearing into the crowd and catching that noon train to Alexandria. If that's even her plan. Maybe she mentioned it as a decoy."

"And assuming she doesn't feel the need to eliminate additional witnesses."

The implications settled between us. We seemed to possess the solution—two murderers, interconnected crimes, elaborate revenge—but remained powerless. All our deductive brilliance meant precisely nothing if we couldn't act upon it.

"Clarissa, we need to talk about what you've learned about me... about my—"

I held up a hand. "No need. I'm not going to tell anyone, you don't need to worry. Your cover story is safe with me."

"That's not what I meant—"

"Really. Quinn. We don't need to talk about it."

He took the hint.

I knew what he wanted to say. That his feelings were real, he hadn't lied about that, etc.

The safe choice—the rational choice—would be to demand proof. Concrete evidence of his feelings. Verifiable demonstrations of trustworthiness before I risked my heart again. I should wait, observe, require him to earn my trust through months or years of consistent behavior before making any decision.

But sitting here in the darkness, sensing his respectful distance even in this situation... I realized something that terrified me.

I was going to choose to believe him.

Not because I had proof. Not because I could verify his sincerity through any scientific method. Not because trusting him was safe or smart or supported by adequate evidence.

But because the pattern of his actions over time suggested someone who cared more about my wellbeing than his own agenda.

And because, as a wise woman once told me, if I waited for absolute certainty before trusting anyone, I'd spend my entire life alone with my pottery sherds.

The night wore on, our only hope now that we could gain attention of the household in the early morning hours before they left.

Quinn dragged some canvases from the corner, his movements efficient despite the cramped quarters.

"If we're condemned to spend the night among chemical evidence," he said, arranging the fabric into something that might charitably be termed a makeshift bed, "we might as well embrace the experience with appropriate dignity."

"At least our methodology proved effective," I said, proud of how steady my voice remained despite Quinn's magnetism.

"A shame we can't publish our findings," Quinn replied.

"Perhaps something posthumous. Though I suspect our epitaphs might read rather differently: 'Here lie two investigators who solved everything except their own survival.'"

Quinn's laugh rumbled through the close quarters. His eyes met mine in the moonlight, and something shifted in his expression—recognition, perhaps, of how proximity and shared danger had stripped away the professional distance we'd been maintaining.

The night stretched ahead of us, full of possibilities that had nothing to do with murder and everything to do with the gravitational pull between two people who may have run out of reasons to resist.

CHAPTER THIRTY-ONE

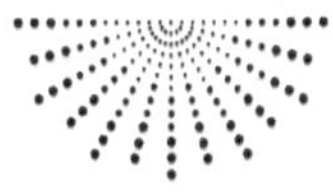

I surfaced from uncomfortable sleep with the gradually dawning awareness that my pillow possessed remarkably firm shoulders and smelled of sandalwood mixed with garden chemicals—a combination that should have been alarming but somehow struck my sleep-addled mind as rather appealing.

Quinn stirred beneath my head, his movement sending ripples through the cramped space between us. The moon had shifted, casting ghostly shadows.

"Nearly five-thirty," he murmured, consulting his pocket watch as if waking up trapped in sheds was merely another weekend activity. "They'll be heading out soon."

"Yasmin is going to disappear forever," I said, struggling upright and immediately missing Quinn's warmth.

The approaching dawn had already lightened our surroundings.

"Quinn, there are more chemicals here than I initially noticed." My training kicked in—always conduct a proper inventory. I scrambled to my feet.

"Your Oxford training didn't cover lock-picking, did it?" Quinn asked, watching me sort through bottles.

"No, but it covered chemical reactions," I replied, lifting a bottle of sodium hydroxide toward the feeble light. "Lye, muriatic acid, various solvents… We've got a treasure trove here."

Quinn's intelligence training also apparently included more than just charming conversation and suspicious antiquities knowledge. "I know what those can do to metal," he said, examining our prison door with renewed interest.

"The hinges," I breathed, following his logic.

"If we can weaken them enough chemically, we might force the door." He moved closer to examine the upper hinge. "It's dangerous—we'll need precise measurements."

I selected the gardening tools we'd need, hyperaware of his proximity as we worked. "Careful proportions," I murmured, calculating ratios while trying not to notice how concentration brought out the determined set of his jaw. "Too much and we risk deadly fumes. Too little and we remain permanently residents of this shed."

I used a shovel to break out the glass of the small window. Some ventilation was better than none.

Quinn applied the solution to the upper hinge pins, then the lower. The acrid smell and gentle sizzle provided the soundtrack to our desperate gamble against time and a killer's head start.

Finally, the door surrendered to Quinn's shoulder-shove, crashing outward in a symphony of splintering wood and tortured metal that probably awakened half the dead buried beneath Karnak.

Quinn steadied me as we stumbled into pre-dawn darkness, both of us gasping from chemical fumes and exhilaration. The estate stretched before us, silent and seemingly abandoned.

"Something's wrong," I said, noting the absence of lamplight from windows that should have been glowing with early morning activity.

We raced toward the main house, our footsteps crunching against gravel, as Freddie emerged from the servants' quarters, fully dressed and looking remarkably alert for someone who should have been deep in pre-dawn slumber.

"Miss!" he exclaimed, genuine surprise coloring his voice. "Thought you'd gone already with the others!"

"Gone? What do you mean gone?"

"Dr. Mujahid came round half-past three. Said you and Mr. Quinn had left early to get some proper viewing at Karnak Temple. The rest scurried out to catch up."

Quinn's hand found my elbow.

"She explained our morning absence," I said, though it wasn't really a question.

"Right informative, she was," Freddie continued. "Said you wanted to watch the ceremony proper-like, with scientific instruments and such. Made perfect sense, considering all your learning."

Yasmin had weaponized our scholarly reputations against us. Who would question two researchers departing early to conduct proper scientific observation?

"And did you slip a message under my door last night, Freddie? Ask me to meet you at midnight in the gardening shed?"

Even in the darkness I could see Freddie's face flush crimson. "Meet you at midnight, Miss? Why would I—"

I shook my head. "Nevermind. I know it wasn't you."

If there had been any doubt that Yasmin had been the one to lock us in the shed, it was gone now.

"How long ago did they depart?"

"Fifteen minutes, maybe twenty," Freddie replied. "Dr. Mujahid seemed right keen to ensure proper timing for the ceremony."

I turned to Quinn. "We have to hurry."

We started across the back of the property. "Freddie, can you get us keys to whatever automobile you have here?"

He slowed to a stop and scratched his head. "No more motorcars here, I fear. They've taken them all."

My voice pitched into panic. "How are we going to get to Karnak?"

"We've got a rather temperamental mare," Freddie offered. "Fast enough, though she's got opinions about riders."

I exchanged glances with Quinn, calculating our diminishing options against the horse's personality. "Opinions?"

"Nothing a firm hand can't manage."

Perhaps another mysterious skill to add to his growing collection.

He raised his eyebrows. "You can ride?"

"Father's education insisted on equestrian training." Though I suspected my lessons in Central Park hadn't prepared me for pursuing murderers across the Egyptian desert at breakneck speed. "I confess this wasn't the practical application I'd envisioned."

Ten minutes later, we were racing through the darkness.

Quinn handled the reins with competent authority while I clung to his waist with what I chose to think of as strategic positioning.

His back was a steady wall beneath my hands; I fitted myself to the line of him for balance and tried to think about speed, not proximity

"There's a constabulary post near Karnak," Quinn shouted over the thunder of hooves and increasing wind. "If we split up, I can alert the authorities while you keep Yasmin from disappearing."

The proposal struck me as optimistic. "You can't seriously be suggesting I confront a double murderer alone?"

"You need to keep her talking until I arrive with backup. Appeal to her cultural principles—she did return the Astral Sphere."

The growing pre-sunrise light revealed the Karnak complex emerging, ancient stones silhouetted against pink sky, with the distant murmur of ceremonial preparations drifting across the desert.

"Fifteen minutes until sunrise, maximum." Quinn's hand briefly covered mine where it rested against his ribs.

If Yasmin planned to run, surely she wouldn't wait long after the awaited moment of the Winter Solstice sunrise.

The constabulary building stood perhaps half a mile from the main ceremony site—close enough for Quinn to return quickly, far enough that I'd be managing a killer's confession entirely through personal charm.

"I'll keep her talking until then." I slid from the mare with less grace than I'd have preferred. My legs wobbled slightly from the hard ride.

He leaned down from the saddle, his eyes intense in the growing light. "Clarissa—"

Whatever warning he intended dropped away, and he simply lifted a hand, a gentle touch against my skin.

"Don't let her leave," he said simply, then spurred the mare toward the distant building.

I stood alone in the strengthening dawn, listening to hoofbeats fade while voices from the temple ceremony grew louder. Somewhere among those ancient stones, Yasmin was enjoying her final performance as grieving colleague and cultural advocate, preparing to slip away with the practiced ease of someone who'd planned every contingency except for two investigators dissolving their way out of chemical imprisonment.

Time to discover whether methodology and desperate improvisation could substitute for actual law enforcement training.

CHAPTER THIRTY-TWO

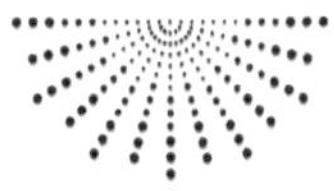

The Karnak Temple complex emerged as if painted in rose gold and shadow, its towering columns already awaiting the first rays of sun.

I spotted our assembled group, clustered near the base of a massive column—Lady Blackwood, Hassan, Yasmin, Richard, Montague, and Whitmore. Even Annie had come along.

"Clarissa!" Lady Blackwood's voice carried across the ancient stones at my approach. "But we thought you were already here."

I felt every eye turn toward me with varying degrees of surprise, curiosity, and—in at least one case—strategic recalculation. Yasmin's expression shifted through several micro-adjustments before settling into confused concern that suggested either genuine bewilderment or impressive acting skills.

"Oh my." Yasmin's voice carried exactly the right note of scholarly confusion. "I must have misunderstood completely when you two explained what you were doing together in the middle of the night."

The explanation possessed the sort of plausible uncertainty that shifted the attention back on me. I manufactured what I hoped resembled embarrassment.

"Quinn will be along momentarily." I scanned the group. "He's securing the horses—you know how particular he can be about proper arrangements."

Lady Blackwood peered toward the eastern horizon. "Not much time now. Mr. Hassan, the Astral Sphere, if you please?"

Hassan begrudgingly pulled the piece from his satchel and handed it to the lady, then hovered nearby with nervous energy.

Was it my imagination, or did the artifact catching early light make its blue pigmentation seem to pulse with inner fire? The sphere's carved surface revealed symbols that had presumably driven Thorne to distraction with their implications.

"Charles would have been so pleased to witness this moment," Eleanor announced, her voice blending grief and satisfaction. "The testing of Dr. Thorne's theories about ancient astronomical knowledge."

Professor Montague stepped forward, consulting a leather journal filled with Thorne's meticulous calculations.

"According to his notes, the sphere must be positioned at precisely seventeen feet above ground level, held at a thirty-seven-degree angle relative to the column's axis, at the exact moment when the sun clears the eastern horizon."

A wooden ladder had already been positioned against the designated column, its angle and height designed to place whoever climbed it at exactly the position specified in Thorne's notes.

A growing crowd of early morning tourists buzzed about. The Winter Solstice was always a noted event, even if they knew nothing of the drama expected to occur at the top of our ladder.

Unfortunately, the crowd also provided excellent cover for anyone planning to slip away unnoticed.

I positioned myself to maintain visual contact with Yasmin while appearing to focus on the scientific demonstration.

Hassan consulted his pocket watch obsessively. "Sunrise occurs in approximately four minutes," he announced, barely controlled panic suggesting he'd prefer conducting official ceremonies with more backup.

Lady Blackwood approached the ladder with determination that would have impressed Napoleon preparing to cross the Alps, arranging her silk morning dress in a way that suggested she'd climbed equipment before.

"This was Charles's vision." She tested the ladder's first rung with her delicate boot. "I should be the one to fulfill it, to honor his memory properly."

Professor Montague's distress materialized instantly into protective alarm. "My dear Eleanor—Lady Blackwood—surely the physical strain would be considerable? The angle required, the precise positioning while maintaining balance..."

The man's romantic attachment had become as obvious as hieroglyphs painted in gold leaf.

"I'm perfectly capable of managing a simple ladder." Though her grip on the wooden rails suggested she found the prospect more challenging than directing servants or managing dinner parties.

"Of course you are," Montague stepped closer. "But perhaps—merely as a practical consideration—someone with longer reach might achieve the required positioning more easily?"

Hassan's anxiety reached new heights as he watched the woman prepare to scale makeshift equipment while clutching a priceless artifact. "The sphere's security must be maintained throughout the procedure!"

No doubt he'd prefer to conduct this entire ceremony from the safety of his Cairo office.

"I could steady the ladder," Yasmin offered. She positioned herself at the base.

I glanced sideways at her. Every gesture appeared helpful, every expression conveyed appropriate scholarly interest, yet my knowledge made even her most innocent actions seem potentially sinister.

How long until Quinn arrived with the cavalry?

Montague's protective instincts ultimately prevailed

through gentle persistence rather than masculine insistence. "Allow me this small honor." He removed his jacket. "Not because you lack capability, but because Charles would have wanted his vision realized safely, with no danger to his dearest treasure—you."

Eleanor finally stepped back with gracious concession, though her expression suggested she found masculine gallantry both touching and mildly exasperating.

"Very well." She transferred the sphere to Montague's steady hands. "But you must position it exactly as specified— seventeen feet, thirty-seven degrees, precisely aligned with the eastern horizon."

Montague began his careful ascent, the ladder creaking softly under his weight while the sphere caught strengthening light like captured starfire.

"Higher—yes, precisely there," Eleanor called from below, consulting Thorne's notes. "Now adjust the angle slightly east- ward—perfect!"

Hassan documented everything with frantic scribbling that suggested either thorough professional diligence or complete nervous breakdown. The growing crowd of observers created a semicircle of anticipation around our theater.

I tracked Yasmin's position with peripheral vision while maintaining the facade of scholarly fascination. She had migrated toward the crowd's edge, her helpful assistant pose beginning to shift toward something more strategically mobile.

Recognition flared like a struck match—confrontation was coming, Quinn or no Quinn.

The sun approached the critical horizon point with cosmic indifference to human schemes. Ancient stones began casting calculated shadows across the temple grounds, their geometry unchanged since pharaohs ruled from Memphis and Thebes.

"Thirty seconds," Hassan announced, his voice cracking slightly under pressure.

Montague strained to maintain exact positioning while holding the sphere at the calculated angle, sweat beginning to bead on his forehead despite the morning coolness. The blue pigmentation seemed to intensify as sunlight struck it more directly.

The assembled crowd fell into anticipatory silence, breath held collectively though probably none of them knew what we waited for.

Honestly, we didn't even know what we waited for. Thorne had been cagey about what would happen next, apparently preferring the drama of a big reveal this morning.

But somewhere among these witnesses stood a double murderer preparing to disappear forever, while overhead, a devoted scholar risked his safety to honor a dead colleague's controversial theories.

The moment crystallized—past and present, knowledge and crime, love and betrayal converging at the exact instant when sunlight would either vindicate or destroy everything Thorne had believed about humanity's forgotten astronomical heritage.

I noticed Yasmin's subtle retreat precisely because I'd been watching for it—three steps back, then four, using the crowd's forward surge as perfect camouflage. Her expression conveyed appropriate scholarly fascination while her feet executed strategic withdrawal.

My heart hammered against my ribs as I calculated angles and timing. Quinn remained conspicuously absent, which meant confronting a double murderer fell squarely onto my shoulders.

CHAPTER THIRTY-THREE

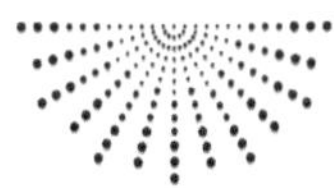

The sun crested the horizon, its rays striking the Astral Sphere at precisely the angle Thorne had calculated with such obsessive dedication. The assembled crowd held its collective breath, waiting for mathematical poetry to emerge from ancient stone and blue pigment.

The silence stretched into profound quiet, like taffy in summer heat.

Not even Yasmin could resist the spectacle. I kept one eye on her and the other on the sphere, unwilling to miss anything.

The sphere remained stubbornly itself, its blue pigmentation catching morning light with all the mystical revelation of a painted tea saucer. No symbols danced across temple columns, no equations pulsed with cosmic rhythm, no forgotten wisdom emerged from centuries of patient concealment.

"Well," Hassan said finally, his voice carrying barely concealed relief.

Lady Blackwood stepped forward the gracious disappointment of a garden party canceled by poor weather. "We honored Jasper's memory properly." It was impossible to miss the satisfaction in her tone. "His dedication to inquiry deserved this respectful attempt."

Montague clung to his ladder perch with determination,

though sweat beading on his forehead suggested the pose had become less sustainable than advertised. "Perhaps I might descend now?" he called down.

"The calculations were quite specific about timing," Hassan declared.

"And Charles would have appreciated our attempt." Eleanor repeated, her voice carrying across the temple grounds with aristocratic authority. "The pursuit of knowledge justifies itself, regardless of specific outcomes."

Montague began his descent. The Astral Sphere remained secure in his grip, its blue pigmentation now appearing rather ordinary in strengthening daylight—valuable certainly, but hardly the key to unlocking humanity's forgotten astronomical heritage.

"The artifact must be secured immediately." Hassan stepped forward, clearly relieved. No unexplained phenomena meant no diplomatic disasters requiring creative explanations to suspicious government officials.

The crowd began its gradual dispersal, early morning tourists drifting toward other sections of the temple complex in search of more reliable entertainment.

Which was precisely when Montague's controlled descent transformed into less controlled catastrophe.

The ladder lurched sideways, as someone in the crowd bumped the base.

"Steady on!" Montague called out. His grip on the Astral Sphere tightened reflexively, though physics and gravity were already negotiating the terms of his surrender.

His foot slipped, sending him tumbling from his elevated position in a graceless pirouette. His ankle twisted beneath him as he landed, producing a yelp.

The Astral Sphere flew from his grasp, spinning through desert air before rolling across ancient stone.

"The sphere!" Hassan shrieked with the vocal range of an opera singer.

The crowd's response resembled nothing so much as a rugby scrum. Multiple hands reached simultaneously for the rolling artifact, creating a tangle of grasping fingers and elbows that would have challenged professional referees to sort out equitably.

"Everyone back!" Lady Blackwood commanded with aristocratic authority, though her voice was thoroughly lost in the chaos.

I forced my way through the surge of bodies. Somewhere in this manufactured pandemonium, a double murderer was preparing to slip away while everyone focused on artifact recovery and injured scholars.

Montague groaned from his position on the ground, clutching his ankle.

Professor Whitmore knelt beside him. "Definitely twisted, possibly sprained," he announced. "He'll need assistance walking."

Hassan's increasingly frantic shouts for order must mean the sphere was still up for grabs.

I spun in place, scanning faces and positions.

My primary suspect had vanished as completely as the sphere itself, while everyone was focused on Montague's descent and the subsequent scramble.

I carved a path through the thinning crowd, focus honed to a point.

Or of Quinn.

I broke away. The temple complex stretched behind me like a limestone maze. Yasmin could have disappeared down any of a dozen pathways. But instinct told me she was rushing toward the exit, not deeper into the complex of ancient courtyards and chapels.

I headed toward the parking area, and its maze of vendor stalls that would provide excellent camouflage for anyone seeking to blend into morning crowds of tourists and merchants.

I caught movement near the temple's entrance—a flash of familiar fabric that might have been Yasmin's morning dress or could have been any women wearing similar colors.

My boots skidded on ancient stone as I rounded a corner,

disturbing a cluster of early morning pilgrims who regarded my undignified haste with disapproval. I offered apologetic smiles while maintaining my pursuit pace.

The eastern pathway led toward the main road where morning transport gathered—donkey carts, the occasional automobile, and most concerning, the railway station only a mile or so away, like a beacon of escape possibilities.

If Yasmin reached a train to Alexandria, she would disappear into the crowd of a major port city, with connections to every corner of the Mediterranean.

CHAPTER THIRTY-FOUR

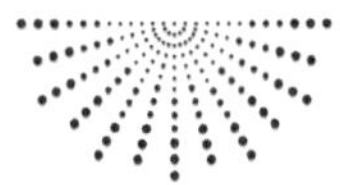

*D*r. Mujahid!"

My voice carried across the temple grounds with more authority than I possessed.

The figure ahead paused at one of the vendor stalls, turning with a perfectly rehearsed innocence.

Yasmin's concerned expression as I approached would have convinced anyone who hadn't recently escaped from her clutches.

"Clarissa! What are you doing away from the ceremony? Did something happen after I left?"

Her performance possessed a flawless authenticity that made my accusations feel absurd. Standing here in morning sunlight, surrounded by perfectly ordinary tourism, the events of the past two days seemed to belong to some overwrought sensation novel.

"I think you know exactly what happened. Just as you knew what would happen when you sent me that forged note from Freddie."

Something shifted in her expression—the briefest flicker of calculation before concern reasserted itself. "I'm afraid I don't understand. What forged note?"

"The one that lured us into your trap. I'm sure you expected to be gone long before we tracked you down."

Her laugh carried exactly the right note of confused academic bewilderment. "Clarissa, you're frightening me. What are you talking about? I've been worried sick since Freddie said you'd left early—"

"The shed where someone took cyanide pellets to use for something more criminal than pest control."

Her hands remained perfectly still, despite the inflammatory accusation. Most people fidgeted when accused of double murder.

"Clarissa, this is deeply concerning." Her voice carried exactly the right mixture of professional worry and personal affection. "Perhaps the stress of recent events has affected your judgment? These wild theories—"

"Not theories. Evidence."

Which was a bit of a bluff. What evidence did we actually have?

The vendor stall provided a strange backdrop for my performance—brass trinkets catching morning light, aromatic spices creating sensory distraction, the comfortable bustle of commercial activity.

"You're suggesting I killed Harrison Foster?" Her voice carried wounded dignity that would have impressed professional actresses. "For what possible reason?"

"What did he put you through, exactly?" I asked, watching for expressions that might reveal underlying truth. "Beyond the failed romance you described?"

"Failed romance. Ha!" The words carried bitter undertones that suggested a more complex history than she'd previously admitted.

"Clarissa!" Lady Blackwood's voice carried relief and barely concealed irritation in equal measures. "We've been searching everywhere. What possessed you to disappear during such crucial moments?"

The group materialized around us. Hassan's face was purple with bureaucratic desperation, while Montague leaned heavily on Whitmore's supportive arm—his ankle clearly requiring more medical attention than temple grounds could provide. Richard bumbled along after them all, and still, no Quinn.

I squared my shoulders and prepared to deliver what I suspected would be either my finest or most catastrophic investigative moment.

The evidence against Yasmin was circumstantial at best. I had no confession, no witnesses to the actual murder, no physical proof she'd been in the Glasshouse when Foster died. What I had was a pattern of behavior, and my own judgment about what made sense.

I couldn't prove Yasmin was guilty. Not beyond a reasonable doubt. Not with the kind of certainty I'd once demanded before making any accusation.

But I could act anyway.

Because waiting for perfect evidence meant Yasmin would disappear on that noon train to Alexandria, and Foster's murderer would never face justice. Because archaeology had taught me that you reconstruct civilizations from fragments, not complete records. Because sometimes you had to make decisions based on incomplete information and trust that the pattern you'd identified was real.

My judgment wasn't infallible. But it was mine.

"Well," I announced, "I'm delighted to report that our morning's entertainment includes not just failed mystical demonstrations, spectacular ladder catastrophes and artifact theft, but also the successful identification of Harrison Foster's murderer."

I paused for effect—and yes, I'll admit it was a bit theatrical.

"Dr. Yasmin Mujahid."

The vendor stalls scattered around Karnak's periphery suddenly felt like an ancient amphitheater, with Yasmin positioned center stage and the rest of us forming an impromptu audience.

The reaction came in waves. Hassan's portfolio nearly

slipped from his grip. Lady Blackwood's fan froze mid-flutter. Richard's mouth opened and closed like a startled fish, which was oddly satisfying given his earlier dismissal of my investigative capabilities.

Yasmin herself remained remarkably still, her dark eyes sweeping across our assembled group with the cool assessment of someone accustomed to navigating dangerous sites. Only the slight tension in her jaw betrayed any reaction.

The morning light caught movement behind me, and Quinn emerged from the direction of the constabulary post, with officers in tow. His eyes met mine briefly.

The trap had closed.

"Dr. Mujahid." Hassan's voice carried the sharp edge of fury finally finding its target. "You will submit to a thorough search. The Astral Sphere has vanished during the chaos, and you were conveniently positioned throughout the ceremony."

My mind catalogued the tactical brilliance of it all: using the failed demonstration as distraction, the crowd's disappointment as cover, the general confusion as the perfect moment for artifact acquisition. Someone had set up this morning's events with considerable skill.

Lady Blackwood stepped forward with diplomatic grace. "Inspector, surely propriety demands that I conduct any physical examination of Dr. Mujahid."

The search yielded nothing more suspicious than a train ticket to Cairo and a leather notebook filled with hieroglyphic translations—disappointingly ordinary for someone I was about to accuse of elaborate murder. Though I supposed truly clever criminals didn't carry signed confessions in their pockets.

"These are serious accusations, Dr. Bell." Yasmin's voice was steady. "I hope you have more than speculation to support them."

"Oh, I do." I pulled my scattered thoughts together. "Let's start with Foster's death, shall we? Specifically, the coffee service that established your alibi so beautifully."

Hassan leaned forward, his earlier fury now channeled into focused attention. "What about the coffee service?"

"Foster requested coffee that morning through his door, claiming illness. The housemaid Laila heard his voice asking for something warm, said he had a terrible sore throat." I paused, watching Yasmin's expression. "But when she returned ten minutes later with cream, there was complete silence. No response at all."

"Perhaps he'd fallen asleep," Richard offered, apparently feeling obligated to contribute despite having no actual understanding of the investigation.

"Or perhaps," I continued, "someone else made that initial request. Someone comfortable with vocal disguise, someone who needed to establish the fiction that Foster was still alive that morning." I turned to Yasmin directly. "Voice mimicry requires both skill and intimate knowledge of speech patterns. You'd observed Foster's mannerisms extensively during your... complicated relationship."

The circle of men shifted closer, their expressions sharpening with the scent of scandal. I could practically see Richard's mental gears turning, reducing complex criminal motivation to simple feminine drama.

Hassan's confusion was almost comical. "What relationship? You said nothing of this!"

"They were lovers." Lady Blackwood's revelation dropped into the morning air. "Years ago, during the Saqqara excavations. Quite the passionate affair, from what I observed."

"You killed Foster in the Glasshouse well before dawn," Quinn said, his voice carrying that professional certainty I found deeply attractive at entirely inappropriate moments. "Then entered his room and called for coffee, making certain Laila saw you on the stairs when she went for cream. Perfect alibi construction."

"You have no proof of any of this." Yasmin's composure remained intact, though her hands had begun to clench.

"Actually, we have several pieces of proof," I said. "Starting with the fact that you locked Quinn and me in the gardening shed all night, then told Freddie we'd gone to Karnak early."

"Freddie will attest to it," Quinn added.

"Freddie isn't here." Yasmin's response came quickly—too quickly.

"No, but I am." Annie's voice carried across the vendor stalls with unexpected fierceness. My supremely capable companion stepped forward, her usual gentle demeanor transformed into something more formidable. "And I remember things too."

I could have kissed her.

"What things, Miss Evanwood?" Hassan demanded.

Annie's face colored slightly. "When I was visiting with Freddie in the pantry off the kitchen—" The blush deepened. "—we saw Dr. Mujahid in the kitchen, hanging about the chimney."

The pieces clicked together. "The chimney fire," I said, watching Yasmin's expression. "You sabotaged it to create a distraction. Everyone evacuating the house, servants rushing about with valuables—perfect opportunity to plant the Astral Sphere in Lord Blackwood's desk."

"In a locked drawer?" Yasmin's objection carried the first hint of desperation. "How would I have accessed—"

"You knew where the key was kept." Lady Blackwood's voice had gone cold. "You asked about Charles's desk specifically days ago, mentioned the locked drawer when discussing his collection. At the time, I thought it was mere scholarly interest."

The accusation hung in the desert air. Yasmin's carefully constructed defenses were beginning to show cracks.

"A woman scorned," Whitmore murmured with the satisfied tone of someone whose theories about female psychology were being confirmed by actual events.

I resisted the urge to kick him. Barely.

Richard appeared particularly energized, no doubt cataloguing this moment for future dinner party anecdotes about the time his ex-fiancée solved a murder driven by feminine hysteria.

Something in Yasmin's expression shifted—the composure I'd admired throughout our acquaintance dissolving into fury that made the morning air practically crackle. Her hands trembled, not with fear but with rage so profound it seemed to rise in waves, like heat from sunbaked stone.

"You think this was about romance?" Her voice cut through their smug pronouncements like a blade through papyrus. "You reduce everything to your pathetic fantasies about hysterical native women."

She took a step backward and lifted her chin.

"Harrison Foster deserved to be killed!"

CHAPTER THIRTY-FIVE

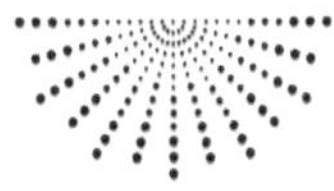

*Y*asmin's declaration echoed off the ancient stones.
The silence that followed threatened to shatter at any moment.

Hassan recovered first, his instincts apparently including protocols for when murder suspects announced their victims deserved death. "Dr. Mujahid, I must warn you that anything you say—"

"Will be used against me?" Yasmin's laugh held no humor. "Inspector Hassan, we both know how this story ends regardless of what I say. The only question is whether the truth gets buried along with Harrison Foster."

I found myself studying her with the same attention I'd bring to a complex artifact. This wasn't the composed scholar I'd observed throughout our investigation, nor was it simple fury at being caught. This was something more dangerous— the rage of someone whose principles had been weaponized against them.

"Then perhaps," I said carefully, "you should explain what really happened. Starting with why you stole and then returned the Astral Sphere."

Yasmin's gaze swept across our assembled group, lingering on Hassan with intensity. "I wanted it returned to Egypt. To

Hassan, to the Antiquities Service, to its rightful home. Foster promised me that was his intention too."

She looked into the distance. "He used my cultural pride against me." The admission seemed to cost Yasmin something. "Convinced me that stealing artifacts from scholars like Thorne was justified if it prevented colonial exploitation. Made me believe we were protecting Egypt's heritage together."

Lady Blackwood's fan stilled. "So, you stole the Astral Sphere *for* him?"

"I thought—" Yasmin's voice cracked slightly. "I thought I was saving it from Thorne's ridiculous theories. Foster convinced me that returning it quietly to Egyptian authorities was the right action, that Thorne's dismissal of our intellectual heritage was the real crime."

So... Foster hadn't been investigating artifact theft—he'd been masterminding it, using Yasmin's legitimate concerns about colonial exploitation as cover for his own mercenary interests.

"But Harrison planned to sell it instead," I said, not quite a question.

"To his mysterious buyer, for enough money to fund a dozen legitimate expeditions." Yasmin's smile held bitter recognition. "He thought I was too naive to realize his real intentions. That my 'sentimental nationalism' would keep me blind to his actual business arrangements."

Richard shifted uncomfortably, no doubt recognizing similar manipulative patterns from his own employer's operations.

The morning heat seemed to intensify, though perhaps that was just the weight of accumulated betrayals becoming visible.

"So, you killed him," I said.

"I confronted him." The distinction appeared important to Yasmin's sense of moral geography. "Demanded he return the sphere to proper authorities. He laughed at me."

She trailed off, but her expression completed the sentence with uncomfortable eloquence. I'd seen that look before—fury and betrayal combining with the terrible recognition that someone you'd trusted had been exploiting your deepest principles.

"Professional disagreement hardly justifies murder," Whitmore said, adjusting his spectacles with disapproval. "Regardless of how offensive his theories or business practices."

"No, it doesn't," I shook my head. "And I still don't see why you had to kill Jasper Thorne to steal the sphere."

"I didn't kill Thorne." Yasmin's response came sharp and immediate. "Harrison did."

The vendor stalls suddenly felt very small. Hassan's portfolio slipped slightly in his grip. Even Quinn's professional composure showed cracks of genuine surprise.

"Foster *did* kill Thorne?" I heard my voice from a distance, my mind racing.

"Harrison asked me to steal the sphere while he created a distraction at dinner." Yasmin's words tumbled out with the momentum of confession long suppressed. "Said it was to prevent Thorne from using it in his ridiculous ceremony, that we'd return it quietly to Hassan afterward. I had no idea his 'distraction' meant murder."

So, I *wasn't* wrong about Foster. Now was probably not the time to point it out.

Lady Blackwood had gone pale beneath her powder. "Charles would have been horrified. He believed in Jasper."

"Your late husband believed in many things, but integrity was not one of them," Yasmin interrupted, her fury finding a new target. "And you're still covering for him. Foster was blackmailing you over Charles's business practices, wasn't he?"

The accusation hung between them like poisoned air. Lady Blackwood's fan resumed its agitated flutter, though she didn't deny the charge. I filed that confirmation away for future investigation—assuming we all survived this morning's entertainment without additional murders.

"The chimney fire," Lady Blackwood said, her voice tight with barely controlled anger. "You could have burned down my entire house. Killed innocent servants—"

"I made certain the fire would be contained," Yasmin shot back. "Unlike Foster, I don't consider collateral damage acceptable for personal gain."

Hassan stepped forward, his fury transforming into something approaching investigative competence. "Explain exactly what Foster did to Dr. Thorne."

Yasmin's shoulders sagged slightly, the rage that had sustained her beginning to drain away. "He crushed the cyanide pellets from Lady Blackwood's Glasshouse supplies and added them to Thorne's ceremonial cup. He wanted everyone to believe in a curse—got the apricot pits from the gardener, planted the threat in Thorne's papers. If people were gullible enough to believe Thorne's astronomical theories, Harrison reasoned they'd accept divine retribution just as easily."

I thought of Foster's careful reconnaissance of the estate, his questions about pest control methods, his extensive examination of Thorne's cup during dinner preparations. Not investigation—preparation.

"But his actions were so obvious," I protested. "Asking servants about the cyanide, handling Thorne's cup where people could see—"

"He told me the servants were too stupid to interfere." Yasmin's voice carried disgust. "Demeaned them constantly, called them furniture with inconvenient opinions. He was inappropriate with Laila, dismissed Freddie as comic relief. His class prejudice made him careless."

Quinn's expression had darkened. "And his supposed evidence against Whitmore?"

"A bluff." Yasmin met Whitmore's eyes directly. "He was going to forge something to give Hassan. Foster was arrogant enough to believe he could implicate anyone, get away with anything. I couldn't let him keep destroying innocent people to protect himself. And when he finally said he'd make certain everyone believed that I had killed Jasper Thorne..."

The morning sun illuminated our strange tribunal with merciless clarity. Around us, the vendor stalls had filled with curious onlookers, early tourists who'd stumbled upon more drama than Karnak's usual historical offerings.

"And Foster's motive for killing Thorne?" Hassan's question carried professional necessity.

"Thorne knew about Harrison's illegal dealings. Had been actively trying to gather proof, hurt his business arrangements." Yasmin's laugh held exhausted bitterness. "It wasn't about theories or artifacts or colonial attitudes—it was about exposure and financial ruin. Harrison killed him to protect his smuggling operations."

I thought of our investigation, how we'd been so focused on academic rivalries and artifact obsessions that we'd missed the simpler explanation. Foster had eliminated a threat to his criminal enterprise, then manipulated everyone—including me—to obscure his guilt.

"You got him to meet you at the Glasshouse," Quinn said, reconstructing the murder. "Before dawn."

"I told him I'd give him the Astral Sphere then." Yasmin's voice had gone flat, reciting facts rather than confessing crimes. "Instead, I dumped water on the cyanide pellets, locked the door behind him, and ran. Used his own method against him."

The simplicity was chilling. No elaborate planning required, just understanding of basic chemistry and a willingness to trap someone in a glass box with deadly fumes. I thought of Foster's final moments—recognition, desperation, inevitable failure.

"And you planned to escape from Karnak," I said. "The noon train to Alexandria."

"Actually, the eight o'clock to Cairo. With everyone focused on the ceremony, no one would notice my absence until it was too late." Yasmin met my eyes directly. "I knew you and Quinn would be found in the shed eventually. I didn't want to hurt you—just delay you long enough to disappear."

"Jolly decent of you." Quinn's dry tone matched my own internal commentary.

Hassan had begun scribbling notes with renewed vigor, apparently determined to document every detail for whatever diplomatic catastrophe would follow. "These are extraordinary claims, Dr. Mujahid. Foster murdered Thorne, blackmailed you into complicity, then threatened to frame you for murder—"

"Unless I gave him the Astral Sphere and stayed silent." Yasmin's shoulders straightened. "I spent my entire career fighting exploitation of Egyptian heritage. I won't spend whatever remains of my life being silent about how Harrison Foster corrupted those very principles for profit."

The confession settled over our assembled group like desert dust—impossible to ignore, coating everything with uncomfortable truth. Foster had been a murderer and manipulator, yes. But Yasmin had still killed him, had still coordinated an elaborate deception, had still endangered innocent people with her chimney fire scheme.

Lady Blackwood broke the heavy silence. "The Astral Sphere. Where is it now?"

"I have no idea. Whatever happened this morning—I was already running." She held her arms away from her body. "Clearly, I do not have it."

Hassan's face cycled through several shades. "Perhaps you handed it off to an accomplice—"

"I've just confessed to murder, Hassan. Why would I deny the theft of Jasper's silly artifact?"

He growled. "You do realize this confession means—"

"Arrest, trial, maybe even execution, given British attitudes toward Egyptian nationals who murder British citizens?" Yasmin's voice carried weary acceptance. "Inspector, I understood the consequences before I sealed Foster in that Glasshouse. The only question was whether those consequences included letting a murderer continue hurting innocent people while profiting from our cultural heritage."

I found myself in the uncomfortable position of understanding her logic while being horrified by her methods. Foster had deserved exposure, arrest, proper justice through legitimate channels. But legitimate channels had failed spectacularly—his class privilege, his connections, his manipulation of investigators like me had all protected him until Yasmin took matters into her own hands.

"This is quite the moral tangle," I murmured to Quinn.

"Justice rarely arrives in tidy packages, Dr. Bell."

The dawn was fully upon us now, Karnak's ancient stones warming under renewed sunlight. Our strange amphitheater of vendor stalls and onlookers had witnessed a confession that would no doubt fuel gossip for years—the British scholar who'd been locked in a shed, the Egyptian archaeologist who'd killed a murderer, the stolen artifact that disappeared at its moment of expected glory.

Hassan straightened his shoulders, apparently reaching some internal decision about protocol. "Dr. Yasmin Mujahid, I am instructing the constables to place you under arrest for the murder of Harrison Foster. You will be detained pending formal investigation and trial."

"Of course." Yasmin's composure had returned, though it carried exhausted resignation rather than defiance. "Though I suspect you'll find that prosecuting me will reveal more about Egyptian artifact smuggling operations than your government would prefer."

The threat landed. Hassan's face suggested he'd just glimpsed the nightmare awaiting him—a trial that would expose not just two murders, but the entire network of illegal antiquities dealing that Foster had represented.

"Well," I said, watching Hassan take charge of a situation that had spiraled far beyond simple law enforcement, "this has been an extraordinarily educational morning."

Richard moved closer, his expression mixing relief and residual shock. "Clarissa, you were magnificent. Though I still think—"

"That I should leave dangerous investigation to men?" I interrupted sweetly. "Yes, I'm sure you do."

Hassan turned to me, and I saw something unexpected in his expression—perhaps a grudging respect?

"Dr. Bell," he said formally, though his tone had lost its

usual edge of condescension. "Your methods are... unorthodox. Theatrical. Frequently irritating."

I braced myself for another lecture on amateur interference.

"However," he continued, visibly struggling with the words, "you identified the real murderer when the rest of us were chasing shadows. You saw patterns where I saw only diplomatic disasters." He paused. "Egypt could use more archaeologists with your particular combination of persistence and... insight."

"Inspector Hassan," I managed, "was that actually a compliment?"

"It was a statement of observable fact," he replied stiffly, though I caught that almost-smile again. "Do not let it inflate your already considerable confidence in your investigative abilities."

I made a mental note to have it engraved on a plaque and mounted in the Cairo Museum of Rare Occurrences.

"Of course not," I agreed solemnly. "Though I'll certainly document it. You've taught me the importance of proper record-keeping."

This time, the twitch at the corner of his mouth was definitely a suppressed smile. "You are still an insufferable optimist with no respect for proper channels, Dr. Bell."

"And you're still a rigid bureaucrat with an unfortunate addiction to unnecessary documentation, Inspector Hassan."

"Then we understand each other perfectly." He straightened his jacket. "When you inevitably stumble into another murder investigation—and knowing your tendencies, Dr. Bell, you will—try to remember that Egyptian authorities prefer to be informed *before* you arrange dramatic confrontations at ancient temples."

"I'll make a note of it," I promised, recognizing this for what it was—as close to friendly regard as Inspector Hassan could express.

Lady Blackwood had recovered enough to begin managing the growing crowd of curious onlookers, her social graces apparently functioning even during murder confessions. Whitmore offered Montague continued support for his injured ankle. The morning's drama was transforming into logistics—how to transport a murder suspect, manage witness statements, prevent diplomatic incidents.

And somewhere in the chaos, Quinn's hand found mine once more. I let our fingers lace and hold there, a mooring line drawing taut.

CHAPTER THIRTY-SIX

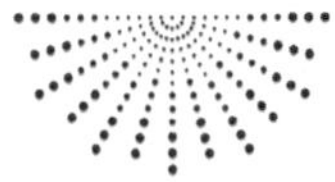

The donkey cart journey back to Lady Blackwood's estate possessed all the ceremonial dignity of a funeral procession, if funeral processions typically featured wounded professors, absent artifacts, and the awkwardness of recent murder confessions.

In the automobile ahead, I knew Montague nursed his twisted ankle while Hassan clutched an empty satchel. His career prospects appeared to be dissolving faster than salt tablets in Nile water.

Quinn rode beside our cart on horseback, his attention divided between scanning the horizon for potential threats and casting sideways glances in my direction.

"Remarkable morning," he commented.

"Quite educational," I agreed.

Lady Blackwood maintained her composure despite hosting what must rank among history's most catastrophic house parties. Two guests murdered, one arrested, priceless artifact stolen, and her precious Winter Solstice celebration transformed into a crime scene that would provide gossip material for seasons to come.

Richard stared ahead with the stiff posture of someone

whose romantic prospects and business schemes had both collapsed spectacularly within forty-eight hours.

We reached the estate and tumbled into the Foyer, as if it were the end of a long day, rather than barely time for breakfast.

After some hastily consumed pastries, Lady Blackwood requested we all converge in the Salon.

The room had hosted more drama than its Egyptian-Christmas décor warranted over the past few days. Now, in the peculiar calm that follows catastrophe, it felt almost anticlimactic—like a theater after the final curtain, still holding the ghost of performance but emptied of actual crisis.

I settled into the chair nearest the window, cataloging the assembled company.

Post-Murder Gathering (Subdued), Notable Characteristics: Collective exhaustion, lingering suspicion, and the distinct aroma of Freddie's overly strong coffee.

Quinn positioned himself near the mantle, ostensibly examining Lady Blackwood's Egyptian artifacts but maintaining tactical awareness of all exits, still.

Richard occupied the settee with the defeated posture of someone whose heroic self-image had sustained irreparable damage. Montague hovered protectively near Lady Blackwood, who'd requested this gathering with uncharacteristic nervousness. Whitmore maintained his usual position of studied detachment, though his sharp eyes tracked every nuance of Eleanor's behavior.

Annie had wisely positioned herself near the door, ready to either summon servants or escape if the conversation deteriorated into further accusations.

"Thank you all for remaining," Eleanor began, her hands twisting the silk of her morning dress in a most un-hostess-like display of anxiety. "I realize we're all exhausted, and several of you have travel arrangements to make. But there's something I must explain. Something I should have been honest about from the beginning."

I exchanged glances with Quinn. His slight nod suggested

he'd anticipated this confession—which meant he'd known more than he'd shared. Again. We would be having words about his tendency toward protective information management. Later.

Eleanor drew a shaky breath, and Montague's hand found her elbow with gentle encouragement. The romantic subplot between them had apparently survived multiple murders and a house full of suspicious guests.

"Charles," she said, the name barely above a whisper, "my late husband, was defrauding his clients for years."

The silence that followed held the weight of revelation—not because the information shocked us (Whitmore had already shared this with me at Karnak), but because Eleanor was finally admitting it publicly.

"He created an elaborate investment scheme," she continued, her voice gaining strength as confession liberated the words she'd been holding. "Respectable British families believed they were funding legitimate archaeological preservation. They thought their money was acquiring important artifacts for eventual donation to museums, for cultural protection during political instability."

"But the artifacts were either grossly overvalued or didn't exist at all," Whitmore supplied quietly. "A sophisticated version of selling shares in fictional excavations."

Eleanor's nod carried the weight of inherited shame. "I discovered everything after Charles died. The ledgers, the correspondence, the documentation of theft disguised as cultural preservation. Dozens of families had 'invested' with him. Respectable families. Families with connections to government ministers, to museum boards, to—"

"To people who would be catastrophically embarrassed if the fraud became public," I finished.

"Precisely." Eleanor's composure cracked slightly. "I've spent the past year trying to manage the situation, maintaining the fiction that Charles died a respected collector rather than an elaborate confidence man."

"And then Harrison Foster discovered your secret," Quinn

said, his voice carrying no judgment—merely the flat assessment of someone stating obvious facts.

Eleanor sniffed. "Foster specialized in locating valuable items for clients with more money than scruples. He found Charles's records, understood exactly what they represented, and saw his chance."

"Blackmail," Richard breathed, looking genuinely shocked. "You poor woman."

"'Protection services,' he called it." Eleanor's bitterness cut through the morning sunlight streaming through the tall windows. "He offered to help me 'manage the situation' in exchange for mutually beneficial arrangements. I paid inflated prices for artifacts he 'located'—some of which I suspect he simply removed from my own storage and resold to me. When he wanted pieces from my collection, I sold them at bargain rates. Every suspicious transaction, every questionable deal—all of it was Foster's extortion. For months, he's been bleeding the estate dry while threatening to expose the scandal that would destroy not just me, but dozens of innocent families who trusted Charles."

So, Eleanor hadn't been hiding guilt over her own crimes, but managing the catastrophic legacy of her husband's.

"You weren't trying to murder anyone," I said slowly. "You were desperately trying to prevent Foster from destroying everyone connected to Charles's scheme."

"I invited him to this gathering because I preferred monitoring his movements," Eleanor admitted. "Keeping him close where I could observe his activities, manage his threats, perhaps find some leverage to end the situation. But murder?" She laughed, the sound brittle with exhaustion. "I'm not that resourceful, Dr. Bell. I'm merely a widow trying to protect people from my late husband's monstrous legacy."

Montague's arm circled her shoulders with protective determination. "Eleanor has been carrying this burden alone. If anyone had understood the impossible position Charles left her in—"

"We might have helped," Whitmore interrupted quietly.

"Or at least refrained from adding to her difficulties with our suspicions."

I felt simultaneously vindicated and ashamed—my investigative instincts had been correct about her hiding something significant, but wrong about what that something was.

"Why didn't you tell us this from the beginning?" I asked.

"And risk the scandal becoming public?" Eleanor's voice carried weary pragmatism. "Foster's death was horrible, but it also freed me from his extortion. Admitting my motive for wanting him dead seemed rather like volunteering for the gallows."

The logic was unfortunately sound, if morally complicated.

Richard cleared his throat, then stood with the abrupt movement of someone who'd reached a decision. "Speaking of public exposure, I should mention I've contacted that journalist fellow. Farid, from *Al-Shura*."

Every head in the salon turned toward him with varying degrees of alarm.

"You did what?" I managed, envisioning my family's reputation becoming front-page entertainment for the Egyptian press.

"While you were all eating breakfast. I gave him the true story." Richard raised his hands. "Don't worry, not all of it. Just that the murders were committed by—well, by someone who wasn't you or your father. That the Bell family had nothing to do with the deaths, that you were investigating rather than perpetrating, and an arrest had been made."

"Richard—"

"Let me finish."

Something in his voice made me pause.

"I was tempted to play the hero, to have him quote me extensively about how I helped solve the case, how I protected you from danger. I wanted to look good in print."

"Naturally," I said dryly.

"But then I realized you wouldn't want that attention." His smile held self-deprecating awareness that suggested actual character growth. "You wouldn't want your name in the newspapers, wouldn't want reporters following you around asking intrusive questions about your involvement in murder investigations. You'd hate the spectacle of it."

I stared at him, genuinely surprised. "So, you..."

"Kept your name out of it entirely," he finished. "Just set the record straight about the family's non-involvement and left the dramatic revelations to others."

The gesture was so unexpectedly considerate that I found myself momentarily speechless—a condition Quinn would no doubt find amusing if he weren't watching this exchange with careful neutrality.

"That was..." I searched for appropriate words. "Actually quite thoughtful, Richard. Discretion suits you."

His face lit up with hope that I recognized immediately as romantic encouragement in the making.

"So, this means—"

"No," I said firmly but without cruelty. "This means you behaved like a decent human being for once, which I appreciate. But it doesn't mean I've reconsidered your marriage proposals or forgotten why I broke our engagement in the first place."

Richard's shoulders slumped, though he managed a rueful smile. "Worth trying."

"Always the optimist," Quinn murmured, just loud enough for me to hear.

"Though I must say," I continued, needing to address the elephant that had been hanging about the Salon since Richard's arrival, "I'm still not certain what to believe about Father's Egyptian acquisitions. Or yours."

Richard's expression grew uncomfortable. "Your father's collection activities are... extensive. But I don't think they're quite as criminal as some have suggested."

"The shipping manifests Quinn discovered suggest otherwise."

"Questionable doesn't always mean illegal," Richard protested weakly. "The regulations are complex, and cultural preservation sometimes requires creative interpretation of—"

"Stop," I interrupted, raising one hand. "I appreciate the attempt at justification, but I'm not ready to parse Father's ethics this morning. The situation is too complicated, and I need distance to think clearly. I'm setting it aside for now."

Quinn's slight nod of approval suggested he understood—some problems were too large to solve in the immediate aftermath of murder and betrayal. Some questions required time, research, and the kind of perspective that only came from stepping away from emotional entanglement.

Besides, I had pyramids to return to. Pottery to analyze. Work that made sense in ways family complications never would.

"If we're finished with confessions and corrections," I said, standing, "I believe I am ready for a break from the drama."

The gathered company seemed to share my sentiment, and Quinn and I soon found ourselves on the terrace, where the desert air carried the scent of heat and dust and the promise of returning to work that didn't involve dead bodies.

"So," Quinn said, leaning against the stone balustrade with studied casualness, "Back to the pyramids?"

"Indeed. Dr. Bradford expects me back at Giza by week's end. Apparently, pottery doesn't sort itself, and someone needs to maintain proper cataloging standards while he's gallivanting around Cairo impressing museum donors."

"Sounds fascinating."

"It's archaeology. Of course it's fascinating." I joined him at the balustrade, maintaining a respectable distance that felt simultaneously proper and disappointing. "What about you? More mysterious antiquities dealing on behalf of the British government?"

"Something like that." His smile held layers of meaning I was still learning to interpret. "Though I expect I'll find myself in the Giza area rather frequently this season. Purely professional interest in the excavations, of course."

"Of course," I echoed, warmth blooming behind my ribs.

The moment stretched between us, filled with possibility and unspoken questions. But before either of us could pursue those dangerous conversational threads, Quinn's expression shifted to something more serious.

"We need to discuss Operation Indigo," he said quietly.

The abrupt return to business felt like cold water after warm tea, but I recognized the necessity. Some investigations didn't end with dramatic confrontations and confessions—they simply continued, threading through years of patient work and careful documentation.

"What we've learned here confirms what I suspected," Quinn continued. "There are two distinct factions within the British government operating in Egypt."

I turned to face him fully, my mind engaging despite my preference for discussing our personal situation instead. "Go on."

"One faction is actively sanctioning—possibly coordinating—the theft and forgery of items containing lapis lazuli. Specifically, items that show evidence of advanced scientific or astronomical knowledge."

"Like the Astral Sphere."

"Precisely. This faction employed Eli Hawke before his death last spring. They're organized, well-funded, and connected to significant power structures. There's a mastermind coordinating everything, someone with enough influence to operate across multiple countries without detection."

"And the other faction?"

"My superiors." Quinn's voice carried the weight of ongoing complexity. "They're trying to expose and dismantle the entire operation. My assignment is to map the networks, identify the key players, and gather enough evidence to force official action."

I processed this information. "So, we're caught between two branches of the same government, each pursuing opposite objectives while maintaining plausible deniability."

"Welcome to intelligence work," Quinn said dryly. "It's considerably messier than archaeology."

"Archaeology is quite messy, actually. We just have better record-keeping."

His laugh was genuine, and I felt absurdly pleased at having earned it.

"The frustrating part," I said, organizing my thoughts aloud, "is that we still haven't identified the mastermind. We never found Hawke's killer. The woman in the violet hat remains a complete mystery. And now another artifact with blue pigmentation has gone missing—and the only person who could tell us where the piece was headed is dead."

"Foster," Quinn confirmed grimly. "Who knew enough to be dangerous but not enough to give us the full picture."

"We're missing something fundamental," I said, frustration bleeding into my voice. "The connection between ancient blue pigments and modern conspiracy. Why these specific artifacts? What knowledge are they trying to hide or obtain?"

"Your father's artifact collection," Quinn said quietly. "The investigation hasn't ended just because we solved the murders. There will be consequences."

I nodded, feeling the weight of that complication settle onto my shoulders. "I know. Father broke the law, probably for years. His reasons don't change that." I sighed. "I love him. I also need to hold him accountable. Both things can be true."

"They can," Quinn agreed. "You're allowed to be angry and sympathetic simultaneously. To understand his motivations while rejecting his choices."

"How can we still have so many questions?"

"Questions we'll answer eventually." Quinn's hand found mine where it rested on the warm stone. "We're getting closer, Clarissa. Each case reveals more of the pattern. Eventually, we'll see the complete picture."

"And in the meantime?"

"In the meantime, we continue investigating. You return to your pyramids, I pursue my leads, and we compare notes whenever possible." His fingers threaded through mine with gentle certainty. "We don't give up. We never give up."

The determination in his voice matched my own stubborn refusal to leave mysteries unsolved. It was one of the things I appreciated most about Quinn—his unwillingness to accept incomplete answers.

Later, I would return to work that made sense. Today, I would simply appreciate having survived another brush with murder, betrayal, and the complicated ethics of artifact preservation.

And perhaps—just perhaps—I would allow myself to hope that Quinn's frequent visits to Giza meant something more than professional collaboration.

But that was a mystery for another day.

CHAPTER THIRTY-SEVEN

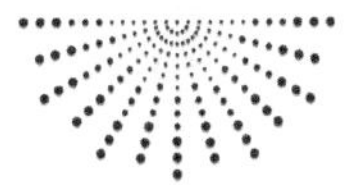

The estate courtyard had transformed into something resembling an evacuation site—luggage scattered, servants scurrying, and guests departing with the politeness of diplomats fleeing an international incident.

Specimen: House Party Conclusion (Egyptian Colonial), 1923, notable for strategic dispersal and lingering awkwardness.

As I passed through the courtyard, Annie and Freddie were bent together over a piece of luggage, bickering cheerfully about packing order. Freddie's protests carried clear across the yard.

"If you insist on wrappin' everythin' like it's the bleedin' Crown Jewels, we'll still be 'ere come Michaelmas."

Annie ignored him, her grin radiant. "Proper packing prevents improper language, Mr. Pike."

He looked at her, utterly defeated—and happier for it.

Hassan supervised the loading of his official carriage, clutching paperwork he claimed would transform two murders and spectacular theft into a face-saving narrative about "recovered cultural patrimony" and "successful diplomatic cooperation." His practiced smile suggested years of experience converting catastrophic failures into administrative victories through creative documentation.

"Most educational visit, Lady Blackwood. The Egyptian Antiquities Department appreciates your... cooperation."

The fact that the Astral Sphere had been stolen again during his watch apparently qualified as minor administrative detail.

Lady Blackwood accepted his departure with the gracious composure of someone who'd survived far worse scandals than two murders and an artifact theft at a holiday gathering. "Do give my regards to Minister Zaghlul. I'm certain we'll all be reading about your successful investigation in the papers."

The pointed reminder that she maintained connections to Egypt's highest political circles sent Hassan into his carriage with more haste than dignity.

Professor Whitmore emerged next, his travel bags already loaded by the efficient Winters. He paused before me, his expression carrying something that might have been regret in a less rigidly controlled man.

"Dr. Bell. I apologize for... the complications my presence created. My methods are sometimes too direct for civilian sensibilities."

I studied him, this man who'd defended empire with such conviction that it looked like fanaticism. But who'd also, in his own rigid way, tried to keep me from investigating too deeply —not to obstruct justice, but to shield me from danger.

"Your intentions were honorable, even if your approach was alarming." I extended my hand. "Safe travels, Professor. And perhaps next time, consider explaining your counterintelligence work before someone mistakes you for a murderer."

His handshake was firm, his slight smile genuine. "Where would be the operational security in that?"

Lady Blackwood saw him off from under the "Sacred Cat Bathroom" portico, her pearls catching the late-afternoon light.

"I do hope," she said serenely, "that Egypt's antiquities will recover from the trauma of our interest."

As his carriage rolled away, Richard approached with a surprisingly subdued demeanor. The past week had stripped away his confident veneer, revealing something more human underneath—still flawed, still self-centered, but at least honest about his limitations.

"Clarissa." He twisted his hat between his hands. "I'm catching the afternoon train to Cairo, then sailing back to New York. Your father will be... disappointed that I failed to convince you."

"Father will adjust," I said, surprised by how easily the words came. "As will you."

"That business with the telegram—" He swallowed hard. "I wasn't lying about loving you. I just... also wanted the artifact. Both things were true."

And there it was. The lesson I'd been learning all week, crystallized in Richard's uncomfortable confession. People weren't equations with single variables. They contained contradictions, held multiple truths simultaneously, made choices for complex reasons that defied neat categorization.

"I know," I said gently. "I even understand why. But understanding your motives doesn't obligate me to trust you with my future."

His shoulders sagged with relief—not at being forgiven, but at being understood without requirement for redemption he couldn't offer.

"I hope Egypt gives you everything you're looking for," he said quietly. "Even if that doesn't include me."

After his carriage departed, I found myself alone in the courtyard, cataloging myself.

Evidence of Character Growth (Personal), Notable Characteristics: Increased comfort with ambiguity, improved boundary-setting, marginally less tendency to trust immediately or distrust absolutely.

"Quite the week." Quinn's voice came from behind me, low and unmistakable.

I turned to find him leaning against the courtyard wall, his traveling bag at his feet, that infuriating half-smile playing at his lips. My heart did something acrobatic and entirely undignified.

"Are you departing as well?" I tried to keep my voice neutral, though I suspected my face betrayed me. "Lady Blackwood is counting on your staying through Christmas."

"That depends." He pushed off the wall, moving closer with that grace that still made my pulse stutter. "On whether *you* want me to."

The question hung between us, weighted with a week of revelations and eight months of correspondence. Quinn, who'd lied about his profession but been honest about his feelings. Who'd asked for trust without offering proof, gambling everything on my willingness to keep his secret.

I could demand guarantees. Insist on complete transparency. Require documented evidence of his trustworthiness before making any emotional commitments. It would be the safe choice, the rational approach.

It would also be impossible.

"You deceived me," I said, and watched something flicker in his eyes—fear, perhaps, or resignation. "About your work, your reasons for being in Egypt, probably half a dozen other things I haven't discovered yet."

"Yes." No excuses, no justifications. Just acknowledgment.

"You had good reasons. Protecting national security, preventing sensitive sites from falling into hostile hands, investigating Operation Indigo."

"Yes."

"Your reasons don't erase the hurt." The words came easier than I'd expected, like lancing a wound. "I'm allowed to be angry even when I understand your motivations."

His throat worked. "You are. And I'm sorry—not for the work I do, but for the position it put you in. For making you question your judgment."

I studied his face, this man who'd become essential to my world in ways I was still discovering. The afternoon sun caught the light in his hair, illuminated the genuine remorse in his eyes.

Trust wasn't about certainty. It was about choice.

And I was choosing to be brave.

"The Giza excavation begins again in next week," I said, watching hope kindle in his expression. "I'm not ready to give up Operation Indigo. But I'll need someone who understands that I won't tolerate being managed or manipulated, and that I reserve the right to be furious when he inevitably keeps secrets for professional reasons."

"That sounds remarkably specific." His smile was breaking free now, brilliant and genuine.

"I'm also establishing boundaries." I held up one finger. "You don't get to make decisions about my safety without consulting me, even if you think you're protecting me."

"Agreed."

"You tell me when you're working on intelligence operations that might affect my research."

"Within the limits of operational security, yes."

"And most importantly—" I stepped closer and my breath adjusted to his. "You earn my trust back through consistent actions over time, not through grand romantic gestures or dramatic sacrifices."

His hands came up to frame my face with devastating gentleness. "I can work with those terms."

"Can you?" I searched his eyes. "Because I'm not offering certainty, Quinn. I'm offering the possibility of trust—with no guarantees, no proof, just my willingness to believe that the pattern of who you've shown yourself to be matters more than the secrets you've kept."

"That's all I've ever wanted. The chance to prove myself, day by day, choice by choice. To show you that I'm worth the risk."

I studied his face, searching for the truth in those copper-flecked eyes.

"I need time, Quinn." The words came out steadier than I felt. "I can't just... leap into trusting you again because you've said the right things."

Something flickered across his face—disappointment, perhaps, though he masked it quickly. "Of course. I understand."

"Do you?" I stepped back, needing distance from his warmth, from the gravitational pull that always seemed to exist between us. "Because I'm not saying no. I'm saying... not yet. Maybe."

His smile was rueful but genuine. "I'll take maybe over no."

"We have Operation Indigo to investigate," I continued, trying to return to safer ground. "We work well together professionally. Let's... start there."

"Professional partners." He nodded slowly. "With the possibility of maybe."

"With the possibility of maybe," I agreed, ignoring the way my heart protested this sensible decision.

And the way it felt so similar to where we left things eight months ago.

I wanted more. Just a little more.

Before I could second-guess myself—before my rational mind could catalog all the reasons this was inadvisable—I stepped forward and kissed him.

Not the desperate, passionate embrace of two people choosing a future together. Not the tender promise of trust rebuilt. This was something else entirely: an acknowledgment of the electricity that refused to dissipate between us, a confession that my body hadn't received the memorandum about professional distance.

Quinn went perfectly still for a heartbeat, then his hands came up to frame my face with aching gentleness. He kissed me back with careful restraint, as if he understood exactly what this was—and what it wasn't.

It was admission without commitment. Desire without decision. A kiss that said *I want you* but not *I trust you*.

When I pulled back, we were both breathing unsteadily.

"That doesn't change anything," I said, hating how my voice shook. "Professional partners."

His eyes had darkened to that dangerous shade that made my knees weak. "And apparently, occasional lapses in professional judgment."

"Don't expect it to happen again." I stepped back, needing distance.

"I wouldn't dream of it." His smile held equal parts heat and resignation. "Though I'll certainly remember it during all those professional meetings we'll be having."

"Quinn—"

"I know, Clarissa." His expression softened. "This doesn't change the terms. I still need to earn your trust. You still need time. But..." He touched his lips briefly, and my stomach fluttered. "Thank you for admitting there's something here worth fighting for."

I turned away before I could do something even more foolish, like kiss him again.

~

Final Field Note: Expedition Satisfactorily Concluded. A series of choices made without certainty. Risks taken despite inadequate data. Trust offered when proof was impossible. Survival, with the bonus of personal growth.

Final-Final Field Note: Next Expedition—pack fewer suspects.

EPILOGUE

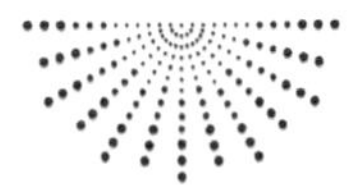

The Graeco-Roman Museum in Alexandria possessed the peculiar quiet of ancient wisdom wrapped in modern bureaucracy.

Professor Nigel Montague adjusted his position behind the curator's desk, his ankle still tender from the unfortunate ladder mishap at Karnak. The afternoon light streaming through tall windows illuminated dust motes dancing above the catalogued artifacts like tiny secrets waiting to be discovered.

His office door bore the brass nameplate reading "Interim Curator"—a temporary appointment that had proven remarkably useful for someone whose actual work required access to Egypt's most significant collections without inconvenient oversight from permanent staff.

The Astral Sphere sat before him on velvet cushioning, its blue pigmentation catching the light with hypnotic intensity.

Not that he'd ever refer to the piece with such a ridiculous name.

But after weeks of quiet maneuvering, elaborate misdirection, and one genuinely twisted ankle, the artifact had finally reached its intended destination. Not Hassan's government facility, not Lady Blackwood's private collection, but here—

where proper research could continue properly, without interference from amateur detectives or bureaucratic complications.

Montague opened his leather journal, pen poised over calculations that would have astounded Dr. Thorne, had that man possessed the intellectual flexibility to see beyond his wild astronomical fantasies. Poor Thorne had been so consumed by imaginary stellar peoples and cosmic alignments that he'd never grasped what he actually held—the key to finding all of the scribe Amenemhat's works, the complete catalog of ancient Egypt's scientific, mathematical, and medical achievements scattered across collections and private holdings throughout three continents.

Montague smiled as he traced the carved symbols with his finger. The disc wasn't a star map. It was an index. A masterwork of compression and encoding that would lead him to knowledge the modern world had lost—practical wisdom worth infinitely more than Thorne's theatrical theories or Foster's greed-fueled schemes.

Foster. Another disappointment in a pattern Montague was beginning to recognize. Like Elias Hawke before him, the man had been competent enough for preliminary work but fatally compromised by his own arrogance. Neither had known who they truly worked for, which was by design—but both had allowed their hubris to make them liabilities.

Foster's blackmail of Eleanor, his obnoxious treatment of servants, his spectacular failure to remain subtle... It had all required correction.

Of course, Foster had no idea that the man who'd hired him to steal the disc was a fellow houseguest. Montague plan was simply to keep an eye on the proceedings without getting his own hands dirty. Instead, he was witness to the fiasco of Yasmin stealing the piece, finding her conscience and returning it, then abandoning that conscience long enough to commit murder. A series of mistakes requiring him to finally hire a thug to knock him off a ladder.

What a nightmare.

Montague's protective feelings toward Eleanor were

entirely genuine, which made manipulating her circumstances all the more effective. She'd served beautifully as unwitting cover for the operation, her desperation to protect Charles's reputation providing perfect camouflage. The widow would recover, eventually. They usually did.

The gentle knock at his office door interrupted his contemplation. "Enter," he called, closing the journal while leaving the artifact prominently displayed, alongside Amenemhat's scribal palette, acquired from Dr. Bell's Giza dig last season.

His assistant appeared with the afternoon's correspondence, her young face bright with academic enthusiasm. "Professor Montague? The winter exhibition preparations?"

"Proceeding beautifully, I trust?"

"Yes, sir. The blue-pigmented collection will draw scholars from across Europe, just as you specified. The invitations have been sent to all the collectors and academics on your list."

Indeed, they would come. The winter season stretched ahead, full of conferences and exhibitions where respected academics would gather to admire artifacts whose true significance they couldn't begin to fathom. Each carefully selected piece another fragment of Amenemhat's scattered legacy, slowly being gathered, catalogued, understood.

Montague gazed through his window toward Alexandria's harbor, where steamships arrived daily from ports across the Mediterranean. Somewhere out there, Dr. Bell was returning to her pyramids, her pottery sherds, her careful documentation. Her talent for criminal investigation had proven... inconvenient. That would require careful management going forward.

Still, she'd never suspect. None of them would. Quinn with his intelligence credentials, Whitmore with his networks —they were all looking for modern conspiracies, political machinations, wartime espionage. They couldn't conceive that someone might be excavating a different kind of treasure entirely.

Montague opened his desk drawer, retrieving notes on three other artifacts that fit Amenemhat's encoding patterns.

One in a private collection in Munich. Another recently acquired by the British Museum. A third rumored to be in a tomb that Howard Carter hadn't yet discovered.

The piece would yield its secrets to patient research and proper methodology. Each symbol cross-referenced and decoded, until the map became clear and Amenemhat's complete works could be reassembled from fragments scattered across millennia.

He hummed a fragment of melody that had been popular during his university days in Vienna, letting the familiar tune settle his thoughts into methodical channels.

Some undertakings required decades of patient development before yielding their most significant discoveries. He'd waited this long. He could wait longer.

The real excavation was just beginning.

1924, Egypt.

Dr. Clarissa Bell has built her reputation on meticulous scholarship and scientific precision. As an American archaeologist specializing in ancient pigments, she's more comfortable with pottery shards than corpses.

But when she's mysteriously invited aboard a luxury Nile steamship to authenticate a collection of rare lapis lazuli artifacts, her peaceful academic life explodes into murder, conspiracy, and international intrigue.

And if that's not enough, there's another complication: Benedict Quinn, the devastatingly charming Brit who needs Clarissa to pose as his fiancée to infiltrate the conspiracy—and who's far too good at making their fake relationship feel dangerously real.

Two Bodies. One Fake Engagement. Secrets That Could Rewrite History.

Order *Amulets and Alibis* today!

EXCLUSIVE FREE SHORT STORY!
Spend Christmas with Clarissa and Quinn...

In the golden sands of Egypt, Christmas is a peculiar affair—palm trees adorned with glass ornaments and gilded gods, kippers served in desert heat, and the distinct possibility that your host's late husband might be haunting the library.

Dr. Clarissa Bell, archaeologist and reluctant detective, finds herself spending Christmas at Lady Eleanor Blackwood's estate, where the recent exposure of Lord Blackwood's financial crimes has left a pall heavier than frankincense. When mysterious happenings begin, Clarissa's scientific mind struggles to find rational explanations.

Is Lord Blackwood's spirit truly seeking redemption, or is someone manipulating events to uncover what he left hidden?

With her trademark wit and scientific precision, Clarissa must solve the case before the estate's secrets claim another victim—and perhaps find something unexpected beneath the Christmas wrappings.

Get your free short story ebook right here:
https://BookHip.com/JHPQRPF

Dear Reader,

Thank you for taking an adventure to ancient Egypt with me! I hope you greatly enjoyed *Palm Trees and Poison!*

You can find lots more about ancient Egypt on my website, along with travel journals of my trips there.

And in case you're curious, here's more than you want to know about me...

I've been writing stories since the time I first picked up a pencil. I still have my first "real" novel—the story I began at the age of eight during a family trip to New York City.

Through my childhood I wrote short stories, plays for my friends to perform (sometimes I had to bribe them), and even started a school newspaper (OK, I was the editor, journalist and photographer since no one took that bribe to join me). Then there were the drama years of junior high, when I filled a blank journal with pages of poetry. {{*sigh.*}}

In my adult years I finally got serious about publishing fiction, and have since authored nearly twenty novels.

When I'm not writing, life is full of other adventures— running a business, spending time with my kids and grandkids, and my favorite pastime: traveling the world. (I speak on cruise ships all over the world! How great is that?)

I started traveling to research my novels and fell in love with experiencing other cultures. It's my greatest hope that you'll feel like you've gotten to travel to the settings of my books, through the sights, sounds, smells, colors, and textures I try to bring back from my travels and weave into my stories.

I'd love to hear your thoughts about *Palm Trees and Poison*, or ideas you have for future books I might write. Get in touch with me at tracy@tracyhigley.com.

Now, onward to another adventure!

(Be sure to join Clarissa's next adventure in Book 3, *Amulets and Alibis*!)

HOW TO HELP THE AUTHOR

I hope you enjoyed *Palm Trees and Poison!*

If you're willing to help, I would really appreciate a review! You can review the book on Amazon, Goodreads, or my website.

More than anything else, reviews help authors spread the word about their books.

It doesn't have to be long or eloquent – just a few lines letting people know how the book made you feel.

Thank so much!

BOOKS BY TRACY HIGLEY

The Clarissa Bell Mysteries

Hieroglyphs and Homicide

Palm Trees and Poison

Amulets and Alibis

The Seven Wonders Novels:

Isle of Shadows

Pyramid of Secrets

Guardian of the Flame

Garden of Madness

So Shines the Night

The Time Travel Journals of Sahara Aldridge:

A Time to Seek

A Time to Weep

A Time to Love

The Books of Babylon:

Chasing Babylon

Fallen from Babel

The Lost Cities Novels:

Petra: City in Stone

Pompeii: City on Fire

The Coming of the King Saga:

The Queen's Handmaid

The Incense Road

Standalone Books and Short Stories:

Nightfall in the Garden of Deep Time

Awakening

The Ark Builder's Wife

Dressed to the Nines

Broken Pieces

Rescued: An Allegory

www.ingramcontent.com/pod-product-compliance
Lightning Source LLC
Chambersburg PA
CBHW031144160726
47991CB00004B/1556